THE WEIGHING OF THE HEART

KAREN HASTIE

FOREWORD

Ancient Egyptians believed that their hearts would be weighed by Anubis against the feather of truth as they entered *Duat*, their afterlife.

Those who had led a virtuous life would be allowed to pass through to paradise, *Aaru*. Those who failed would have their heart consumed by Ammit, and be condemned to remain in the realm of the dead.

1

KILLING

'Blood of the ancient ones,' the man intoned to a bygone god, slowly drawing a curved knife across the heaving chest. A fine, crimson line followed the blade across the ribs and down over a swollen abdomen which parted like a ripe peach as he applied more pressure.

His victim's body arched, straining against the bonds, muffled screams of pain caught in his throat, silenced behind a gag.

'All the evil which was on me has been removed,' he continued, widening the wound and placing his hand inside the warm cavity.

'Detestation of you is in my belly, for I have absorbed the power of Osiris, and I am Anubis.'

The writhing stopped. He felt the life draining away as he deftly removed the man's liver.

Purification. A voice whispered inside his head. Weighing the fatty tissue in one hand, his brother's words reminding him of its function. *The liver is the largest organ in the body, removes toxins, processes nutrients, builds proteins.*

'Always the practical one,' he muttered to himself, placing it carefully into the jar beside him, the effigy of Imsety, son of Horus, carved onto its lid.

Wiping the blade clean on the man's shirt, he stroked the symbols on the handle of the knife with his thumb. Ancient hieroglyphics were carved into bone, ones that formed part of the 'Opening of the Mouth' ritual — powerful spells from another age. A time when the people believed in the afterlife.

Turning to the next of the three jars he smiled, Hapi, the baboon-headed god awaited its sacred offering.

2

DIAMONDS

100, Hatton Garden, London. Saturday 3rd April. 18:54

Detective Inspector Marshall was six minutes from the end of her shift when she got the call from DC Biggs. *So close*, she thought, *I could almost taste that first glass of wine.*

She was beginning to suspect the criminal fraternity were conspiring to ruin any chances of her having a break over the Easter weekend. The meal she'd planned with her mother on Good Friday was ruined by a GBH outside the Lamb Tavern in Leadenhall Market and now today was heading the same way.

It wasn't that Marshall was particularly religious, but her mother was moving back to Bath, and she'd promised to help her pack up the house over the weekend.

The daylight was waning as she walked down Hatton Garden towards a blockade of patrol vans. Passing the shuttered fronts of the jewellery shops, painted blue by the vans' lights, she wondered how much this single London street was worth.

She felt her phone vibrating in her jacket pocket but ignored it — whoever it was, it could wait.

'DI Marshall,' she said, showing her warrant card to the PC standing behind the tape. He made a note of her badge number in his log and waved her through.

The London Diamond Exchange looked more like a sixties office block than a jewellery store. Inside she found DC Biggs waiting patiently with two bewildered businessmen, who Marshall assumed were the owners.

Dark shadows under his eyes told her that Biggs had pulled a double shift.

'Hi boss,' he said, walking over to meet her. 'We're just waiting for the third key holder.'

Behind the two men stood a security door. It was a large, steel plated panel with no obvious sign of a lock.

'Alarms were triggered at eighteen hundred. We're assuming the perps are still trapped inside,' explained Biggs, pointing at the floor. 'The basement's flooded, it's tripped all of the environmental sensors and shorted out some of the override circuits.'

'Flooded?' repeated Marshall, trying not to imagine what it would be like to get stuck in a vault full of water. Ever since she nearly drowned as a child, the fear of being trapped underwater had always haunted her. She took a deep breath and let it out slowly.

Biggs didn't seem to notice and continued. 'We think they came in through the sewers. Fire and Rescue are on their way.'

'And who is the third key holder?'

Flicking through his notes, he found the name. 'There are five apparently. Two are out of the country — we're waiting for Mayerstein. Joseph Mayerstein.'

Her phone buzzed again and this time she pulled it out. The number wasn't one she recognised, but there were three missed calls from it in the last ten minutes.

She held up a hand. 'One sec, just need to get rid of this.'

Walking back out into the street, she tapped the accept button.

'Detective Inspector Philippa Marshall?' said a man's voice before she could speak.

'Yes.'

'This is DCI Sterling, Charing Cross SPIU. This is going to sound a bit random, but do you know a Professor Gresham?'

Marshall felt her heart skip a beat. Everyone dreaded a call that started like this. She always preferred to tell the next-of-kin in person, it was the hardest thing you ever had to do as a copper, but it was important — at least to her.

'Is he okay?'

'Listen, we're dealing with an incident at the British Museum, he's asking for you. Says you'll vouch for him.'

Marshall's initial fear was quickly replaced by annoy-ance. He wasn't dead, or hurt, but had the audacity to assume he could use her as a get out of jail card.

She sighed, watching a large man wearing Jewish cap get out of a dark Mercedes. 'What's he done?'

'Probably best if you come over here.'

The man was obviously Biggs's third key holder. His cheeks were flushed red with anger as he walked past her and straight into the building. 'I'm actually in the middle of an active case myself.'

'He's a suspect. He seemed to think you would want to know.'

For fuck's sake, she managed to stop herself from saying aloud while waving at Biggs.

'Okay, I'll be there in twenty.'

'I've got to go,' Marshall whispered to Biggs, who was watching the security door being raised.

He turned towards her. 'What? Why?'

His eyes reminded her of a lost puppy, and she fought back the urge to tell him what had happened. 'Something personal's come up. I need to sort it out.'

He gestured at the slowly opening door. 'But we're just about to get in!'

Marshall tried to reassure him. 'You can handle it. You've got to wait for the water fairies to show up anyway.'

It was true, he would be fine. Fire and Rescue would be there soon, but still she hated leaving the scene of a crime; as the most senior officer it was tantamount to dereliction of duty.

She was angry at Gresham for putting her in this position. *He's a suspect*, the DCI's words echoed around in her head, *what the fuck has he got himself involved in?*

Men are only good for two things. Anj used to joke. *Taking out the bins and sex — both of which are over in less than five minutes.*

While Biggs tried to stop the three key holders from entering the crime scene, Marshall went out into the street.

Three fire engines were waiting at the end of the street while the cordon was cleared away.

'All we need now is the bloody bomb squad,' joked her boss, DCI Donovan, appearing beside her.

'Guv, something's come up I need to deal with,' she said, praying he wouldn't ask too many questions. 'I need to go.'

The old man frowned. His puffy eyes, even more blood-shot than usual, studying her face.

She held his gaze until the moment passed and he shrugged it off, his expression returning to its usual optimistic mien. Donovan was a legend, one who'd seen it all, nothing was ever going to faze him.

'What have you got so far?' he said, watching the fire-fighters unloading the heavy cutting gear and rolling out hoses.

'Not much, alarms went off at six this afternoon. Biggs reckons they came in through the sewers, flooding the basement. The whole building went into lockdown, and we've been waiting for the key holders to arrive. It's possible that the perps are still down there.'

Donovan sighed. 'SOCOs are not going to be happy with Fireman Sam traipsing all over their crime scene.'

She looked at her watch.

'Go! Leave it with me, but I need to speak to you later about something.'

'Okay, thanks Guv, I'll be back as soon as I can.'

3

GRESHAM

British Museum, London. Saturday 3rd April. 19:20

Walking out of Greville Street, Marshall flagged down a passing black cab. Both ends of Hatton Garden were taped off and a steady stream of people were being shepherded out into the surrounding streets. The police presence was growing, it was quickly becoming a serious incident and she ground her teeth at the thought of being dragged away from it.

The journey to the British Museum would take under ten minutes, less if the traffic was light around Holborn. If she could sort Gresham out without too much fuss, she could be back in under an hour.

She texted Biggs. 'Call me if anything happens.'

There was no response, which was unusual for him. At a minimum she would have expected an instant thumbs-up. They made a good team, over the last two years an unspoken bond had grown between them, to the point where he almost knew what she was thinking. Their minds worked the same way, but he had the advantage of being ten years younger. The 'Boy Scout' was going to go far.

Pulling out onto High Holborn, her thoughts turned to Gresham.

Their relationship hadn't evolved into an official thing. Both were too old to be making grand gestures about love and long-term plans. She'd insisted on keeping it simple and he didn't seem to object. It had only been four months since the Alchemist case, and as far as she was concerned there was nothing wrong with casual, uncomplicated sex.

Except now he'd made it something else. He'd crossed a line.

Relationships with civilians were always inherently difficult: the shifts were anti-social; the stress levels intolerable and the cases confidential. It was why so many officers ended up divorced, too many years dealing with the dark side of humanity tended to make it hard to have normal conversations — let alone relationships.

But there was a golden rule, one they all learned early on; that you never used your position to help family or friends — it was an abuse of privilege. The Department of Professional Standards would throw the book at you, not just ending your career, but potentially putting you away. The thought of jail time was the nightmare that kept certain coppers on the straight and narrow.

Her name and badge number would be entered into the Crime Scene Log. If the DPS were brought in to audit the investigation, they would want to know what she was doing there, especially if it turned out Gresham actually had done something wrong.

She'd never heard of DCI Stirling, but he said he was from SPIU, the Specialist Projects Investigation Unit, a secretive team that mostly dealt with contract killers in organised crime.

Marshall couldn't imagine how Gresham would manage to get himself involved in anything that serious. Although as a Professor of Medieval Studies, he did have some rather dark and macabre interests. The history of torture was one, but it was purely academic, he was nothing more than a spectator, not a player. She could never imagine him hurting anyone, but then again, she'd never seen him angry.

So why was she going over there?

Because he'd asked for her — which was a first. She couldn't remember Gresham ever asking her for anything.

Marshall got out of the cab on Bloomsbury Street and walked on to Great Russell Street. The road was filled with emergency vehicles, their lights strobing across the stucco Victorian facades of the buildings facing the British Museum. A crowd was gathering on the opposite side of the road, holding up their phones to film the firearms officers standing guard at the black iron gates of the museum.

Flashing her ID to one of the officers, Marshall walked through the cordon and into the courtyard.

The spotlit portico of the British Museum shone brightly against the darkening sky and between its columns hung banners declaring the grand opening of the 'Kristiansen Exhibition'.

As a child, this was one of the museums her father would have to drag her away from. He hated it. 'The accumulated trophies of a colonialist empire', he would say, while she marvelled at the posters of ancient treasures. Their adventures to London were always a battle between her love of the grand old imperialist monuments and his socialist morality.

Parked in front of the steps were the unmarked vans of the SOCO team. Marshall spotted the medical examiner's car and wondered if it would be Gates. The fact that an ME was attending confirmed it was a murder. Like crows around roadkill, their presence was always an indicator of death.

She presented her ID to the uniform at the main entrance, who wrote her name in the log before radioing through to the SIO.

A few tense minutes passed.

Marshall knew better than to ask what was going on. This was out of her jurisdiction, even though they collaborated with the Met often, she knew they thought of City police as glorified accountants.

A plain-clothes officer arrived to escort her into the building.

Marshall followed him through the Great Court to the stairs at the far end of the building. Stirling was on level three, the man explained, in the Egyptian gallery.

Following him up the wide, marble stairs, Marshall came to the doors of the gallery. The room beyond was dark, as if the power was out. In the dim glow of the emergency lights, she navigated her way between the glass display cases full of mummies. Passing the desiccated remains of the ancient Egyptians, she could feel the hairs rising on the back of her neck. *Too many horror movies as a teenager*, she thought, trying not to look at them too closely. For some reason it was always the old mummy movies that scared her the most.

Back in those days, her boyfriend, Will, would take her to the Little Theatre at Halloween to watch Boris Karloff, but she'd spend most of the movie with her eyes shut, making out in the back row.

A path of luminescent yellow markers glowed along the floor, a sure sign that forensics had already passed this way.

Approaching room sixty-three, Marshall heard the unmistakable bellow of Doctor Gates.

'Don't touch it man! Were you born stupid?'

He was standing over an open sarcophagus, surrounded by his forensics team all wearing white suits. Bright lights had been set up around the old wooden coffin.

'DCI Stirling is through here,' the officer said, guiding her away from the crime scene and into a side room.

Gresham was sitting on a bench in a blue Tyvek suit while a female paramedic waved a pen light into his eyes.

He smiled weakly when he saw her. A moment of relief briefly crossing his face, before returning to the worried, vulnerable expression that she'd rarely seen. There was none of his usual arrogance, his shoulders sagged, hands clasped together like a condemned man. She wanted to go over to him, but restrained herself, he needed her to be a copper right now, not some emotional support.

'DI Marshall?' a man's voice asked from somewhere behind her.

She turned to find a tall, red-headed man in his forties with a sharp, angular face and fierce blue eyes, ones that looked as if they had seen too much. 'DCI Stirling?'

He nodded and gestured for her to come with him. 'Quick word in private?'

She followed him back into the crime scene.

'What happened?' Marshall asked, watching the SOCOs taking photographs of the inside of the sarcophagus and the floor around it. A pool of blood surrounded the base of the exhibit and four animal-headed jars were placed at each corner.

'Killer removed his major organs,' explained Stirling, folding his arms over his chest as if subliminally holding his own body together. 'Then put them in the jars. Doctor Gates believes the victim was alive, at least for some of it.'

Marshall put her hand to her mouth, grimacing at the odour of rotting meat. It took a moment for the nausea to pass, no matter how many times she experienced the smell of a dead body, the response never quite left you — she had no idea how Gates could do it every day.

'So, what's this got to do with Professor Gresham?'

'He was found unconscious at the scene, but he can't tell us what he was doing here.'

She tried to remember what possible reason Gresham would have for being at the museum. They hadn't seen each other for over a week, but there was a vague recollection of an invitation to a dinner party. *No — an exhibition.*

'Can I speak to him?'

Stirling nodded. 'Once the medic has finished with him. He's not said much, other than asking for you.'

'He's not capable of killing anyone.'

Stirling shrugged, unfolding his arms. 'There was blood on his clothes.'

'Doesn't make him a murderer, there's blood everywhere,' she said, staring at the dark stain on the floor.

The DCI took out his notebook. 'Have you known him long?'

The tone of his voice changed, this was no longer a conversation between professionals, now he was treating her like a witness.

She thought back to the first time she met Gresham at his lecture at King's College. It seemed like years ago, so much had happened in such a short time. 'Five months. He's an academic. He helped me out on my last case.'

'The Alchemist. Yeah, I heard about that one. Tough case,' Stirling said, making notes.

Marshall tried not to react, the memories of that case still gave her nightmares. 'Gresham helped me save the last victim. He's a teacher, not a butcher.'

Stirling nodded in agreement, her answers seeming to satisfy his curiosity. 'He's also not a surgeon, which Gates thinks the killer would have to be.'

'Have you identified the victim?' asked Marshall, trying to reassert her role as detective once more.

Stirling shook his head, putting his notebook back inside his jacket. 'The murderer didn't stop at the organs, he took the hands and head as well. We're hoping that we can get a match on DNA.'

Gates looked up from his work and waved at Marshall, his gloves covered in blood.

Stirling leaned in close and spoke in a low whisper. 'You ever thought about leaving City? Seems a waste of your talent chasing fraud cases.'

Marshall smiled, everyone thought about City Police, that they were just glorified accountants. She was about to mention the jewellery heist in Hatton Garden when the paramedic appeared from the side room.

'He's basically okay,' she said, peeling the latex gloves off. 'Looks like he suffered a mild concussion when he hit the floor. Nothing too serious, but doesn't explain why he went down in the first place. I've given him something for the pain, but he's in shock, so I would advise rest for the next day or so, if he has any dizziness or nausea, take him to A&E.'

Stirling thanked her and they both went back to see him.

'Can we go now?' Gresham asked quietly, his eyes wide like a frightened child.

Marshall nodded, helping him to his feet. 'I assume that's okay?'

Stirling agreed. 'For now, but I will need him to give us a statement in the next day or so.'

4

HOME

Walking out onto Montague Place, Marshall checked her phone for messages. An hour had passed since she left Hatton Garden and she was expecting an update from Biggs.

There was a voicemail.

'Hey. Just to let you know, they didn't find anyone downstairs. The place was cleaned out though, the guv reckons this is going to be one of the biggest heists since the Millennium Dome.'

Searching the traffic for a black cab, she called him back.

Biggs sounded odd when he answered. 'Everything okay?'

She went over to Gresham, who was standing in a daze staring into the distance and grabbed him by the arm. 'Listen, I don't think I'm going to make it back today.'

'That's fine, they've closed it off anyway. The Incident Commander said something about gas, we had to leave. You okay?'

Marshall flagged down a taxi. 'Yes and no, just dealing with some personal stuff.'

She bundled Gresham into the back of the cab and slid in beside him.

'Anything I can do?' asked Biggs.

'Send me your notes. At least I won't look like a total fuckwit at the briefing tomorrow.'

She ended the call and took hold of Gresham's hand, feeling more like a parent than a partner. 'Let's get you home before you do anything else to screw up my career.'

His eyes were wide and unfocused. The painkillers were obviously starting to take effect.

'Thanks for coming to get me Pip,' he whispered leaning in for a kiss. She ignored him, turning her head away and giving the cab driver directions to Gresham's house in Putney.

'Sorry,' Gresham said a few minutes later. 'I shouldn't have called you. I didn't know what else to do.'

'What the hell were you doing up there anyway Michael?' she snapped, her mood worsening as she scrolled back through her emails. There was nothing from DCI Donovan, which was not a good sign.

Gresham rubbed the darkening bruise on the side of his face. His cheek was swelling making it hard for his glasses to sit squarely on his nose. 'It was the opening night of the Kristiansen Collection. I seem to remember inviting you.'

She had a vague recollection of it. 'The Assyrian thing?'

He sighed. 'Martin Kristiansen owns the largest private collection of Mesopotamian artefacts in the world, literally from the dawn of civilisation.'

Noticing that the light on the cab audio was still on, Marshall lowered her voice. 'So how exactly did you end up next to a corpse in a room full of Egyptian mummies?'

He shook his head, running his hands through his hair. 'I've no idea. The event was held on the floor below, in the

Egyptian Sculpture Gallery. The last thing I can remember was drinking with two of my old Oxford professors.'

It was then that Marshall remembered exactly why she hadn't wanted to go; she couldn't face another evening watching him witter on about historical obscurities. Faculty events sounded great until you had to stand and listen to a glorified pissing match between a bunch of academics looking for their next research grant.

Taking a deep breath, she counted backwards from ten as her therapist had taught her. Letting the tension dissipate until she felt the calm, logical side of her mind taking over.

'They're going to want to take a statement from you.'

'I feel dizzy,' he said, licking his lips. 'Do you have anything to drink?'

Gresham's hands shook as she gave him the bottle of water from her bag. His skin was pale and clammy. All signs that he was going into shock, soon it was going to be impossible to get any sensible answers out of him.

'It would be better for both of us if you could try and remember what happened.'

He shrugged, draining the bottle. Rivulets of water running down the side of his face and down his neck.

He's definitely not himself, she thought. *He's lost some of that self-control.*

'Anything? The smallest detail can make all the difference,' Marshall asked.

Crime scenes were all about the little things: a fingerprint on a light switch, a discarded cigarette butt, people never realised quite how much DNA they left behind from just sitting on a chair.

'There's a strange taste in my mouth,' he said, handing back the bottle, 'but other than that nothing.'

· · ·

Gresham's house was an old, converted school on a quiet, leafy street in Putney.

Marshall knew he was rich from the moment she'd met him: his clothes, the car he drove, all classic signs of a man who enjoyed a higher quality of life than she'd ever known.

At first it hadn't bothered her. She wasn't really into stuff, preferring personality over material things. He was clever and reserved, and she found that quite intriguing, even sexy. In many ways, he reminded her of Will, her first love, but without the twisted sense of humour.

The subject of how wealthy he was never really came up. He wasn't overtly extravagant, except with wine. They split the bill whenever they went out, even down to the cab fare, but the first time that Gresham invited her over to his place she began to wonder exactly how rich he really was.

After paying off the taxi she helped him to the door and entered the security code.

Gresham went straight to the kitchen and poured out two large glasses of red wine.

'Should you be drinking? Those painkillers are pretty strong—'

'Helps me think,' he said, before taking a long, slow drink.

'What kind of funny taste?' she asked, accepting a glass from him.

Gresham rolled the wine around in his mouth, savouring the flavour before swallowing.

'Metallic, like after you've had a filling.'

She knew only too well. Her tongue instinctively sweeping over the craters in her back molars. 'Like mercury?'

'I guess so,' he said, walking towards the bedroom. 'I've only had the one. I need a shower.'

'Course you have,' she whispered, sitting down on the leather sofa and taking out her phone. There were five new emails: four from Biggs and one from Donovan.

Biggs had sent her his notes, which were always concise and comprehensive. He was a textbook detective in that sense. Her sergeant used to boast that police work was ninety per cent paperwork, ten percent instinct and one percent luck.

He never was any good at figures.

The Diamond Exchange had been quarantined by Fire and Rescue after they managed to drain the basement and Thames Water had sealed off the sewer. The Incident Commander reported high levels of some kind of gas and various tests were being done on whether it was dangerous.

Marshall was secretly glad she wasn't the one having to wade through a pile of shit that evening.

The owners were sent home to start drawing up an inventory. Biggs's notes included a list of all the main members of the Exchange, which seemed to be a coalition of jewellers rather than one company.

She scanned the rest of the message quickly and jumped to the email from Donovan.

There were just three lines:

DI Marshall, a DCI Stirling from the Met contacted me today regarding a possible secondment. Needless to say I wouldn't be opposed to such a move, but I would have preferred if you had consulted me first rather than disappearing on an active case to attend an interview.

'FUCK!' she shouted, throwing her phone across the room.

The sounds of the shower played out from the bathroom, covering the sounds of her beating her fists against the sofa cushions.

'What kind of arrogant son of a bitch does Stirling think he is?' she said to herself while searching for her phone. She wanted to call Donovan and explain, the formality in his message told her how disappointed he was, *to think that she would do that to him?*

Luckily, the phone was in one piece, but she stopped herself from dialling his number. The guv was old-school, this would need to be done face-to-face.

It took seven attempts and another large glass of wine to compile the response, she kept it formal and short:

I've made no such request, sir. Will explain tomorrow.

Refilling her glass, she noticed that the shower had stopped, and wandering into the bedroom to see if Gresham was feeling any better, she found him comatose on the bed, stark naked. The combination of painkillers and booze had knocked him out completely.

'This day just keeps on giving,' she whispered to herself, pulling the bed covers over him.

5

BRIEFING

Wood Street Police Station, London. Easter Sunday 4th April. 08:00

The briefing had already started by the time Marshall arrived.

DCI Donovan ignored the interruption, his eyes sliding past her as if she wasn't there. She sat down beside Biggs and took the coffee he was offering.

'The alarm shorted out when the water flooded the basement, but there must have been a second team who tripped the secondary circuits on the ground floor. It was a coordinated attack, one that would have taken months of planning.'

He tapped the large touchscreen and a floor plan of the Diamond Exchange and the surrounding streets expanded to fill the display. 'The first team came in through the Leather Lane sewer, which runs parallel to the water main. They tapped into the main and used specialised pipeline drilling equipment to bore through the basement wall, which was over two metres thick.'

Donovan swiped across the screen to a series of photographs from the crime scene. The first showed the inside of the vault with a large, round hole in the wall. The floor was littered with empty drawers and safety deposit boxes.

'Forensics believe it would have taken at least forty-eight hours to cut through. Which means working in shifts, so we need to check the CCTV around the access points for the sewer. Unscheduled maintenance vans and the like. We need to work out where they were operating from.'

'What about the security guards?' asked Biggs.

Donovan shook his head. 'They're still unconscious. Gas was used to knock them out, we're still waiting for them to come round.'

'Haven't they worked out what it was?' asked Marshall.

The DCI paused, his jaw clenching and releasing, as if he were chewing on his words. She was beginning to wonder if he was going to ignore her completely, when he seemed to change his mind. 'Forensics say the gas dissipated too quickly after the security shutters were opened. They didn't get enough of a sample to test.'

'Any idea on how much was taken?' asked Devlin, looking like a man who's lottery numbers were about to come up. Marshall could tell from his enthusiasm there was probably a book running on the value of the haul.

Donovan shook his head. 'We're still waiting on the inventory from the partners.'

He tapped on a thumbnail and a photograph of an overweight man with a dark beard filled the screen. 'This is Benjamin Ramsveld, head of the guild and another of the key holders. He's just flown back from Amsterdam so we need someone to go over and take a statement.' His eyes scanned the room looking for a volunteer, when none was forthcoming he turned to her. 'Marshall, looks like that honour falls to you. Devlin you're on the CCTV and the rest of you start with the background checks on all of the staff. Baxter has the list.'

Marshall knew better than to question his decision. She'd just been demoted in front of the entire team — taking statements was something a DC could do in their sleep.

The briefing over, everyone filtered back to their desks.

'My office,' ordered Donovan as she got to her feet.

Marshall closed the door behind them, knowing that everyone would be listening. The glass walls of his office did little to block out Donovan's bellowing when he was in full flow.

'Sit down,' he said, his tone more restrained than she was expecting.

'Guv —'

He held up a hand to stop her and motioned her to take a seat. 'How long have we known each other Marshall?'

'Five years sir.'

'Five years,' Donovan repeated, sitting behind his desk and folding his arms across his large stomach. 'And in all that time have I ever struck you as a man that held a grudge?'

She was confused, struggling to see where this conversation was headed. 'No Guv, you've always been straight with me.'

He nodded taking out a plastic canister of pills from his drawer and struggling with the child-proof cap. 'These days I try to maintain a simple, uncomplicated life. One that doesn't involve politics or arse-licking. Thankfully, most of my complications ended when my second wife left me for that wanker in the Flying Squad. The quack said it's not good for my heart. So you might ask why I get so agitated when some DCI from the Met comes sniffing around after one of my best detectives.'

Marshall took the compliment without a flicker of emotion — this wasn't leading to a promotion.

'I didn't ask him to do that,' she said through gritted teeth.

Donovan finally managed to open the cap and popped one of the pills under his tongue. 'So what was the disappearing act about yesterday?'

She told him about the call, and Gresham. He sat quietly sucking on the tablet and listened as she described the scene at the museum.

'I heard it was pretty gruesome,' he said, rolling up his sleeves. 'Sounds like your boyfriend was in the wrong place at the wrong time.'

'He's not my boyfriend,' she corrected him.

'Sorry, what's the politically correct term for it these days? Partner? Significant Other?'

'He's just a friend.'

Donovan laughed and the tension between them eased slightly. 'If you say so, I can't think of many people you would leave an active investigation to go and bail out.'

Marshall smiled, the old man was right, of course. There was something about Gresham that made her care. Somehow he'd got under her skin, but she couldn't put her finger on what it was exactly and that in itself was very frustrating.

'So you're not thinking of leaving us for the Met then?' Donovan asked directly.

She shook her head. 'No sir.'

He shrugged. 'Well, don't be so quick to dismiss it. Stirling is a good copper, and his team have a hell of a caseload. You'd get to work on some seriously big cases.'

It was her turn to laugh. 'Sounds like you want me to go.'

'I'm just saying, don't burn your bridges.'

6

HATTON GARDEN

100 Hatton Garden, London. Easter Sunday 4ᵗʰ April. 11:00

I t was a twenty minute walk from Wood Street to Hatton Garden and Marshall needed the time to clear her head.

Passing St. Barts Hospital and into Smithfield, she marvelled at how much the place had changed; the old warehouses and market buildings were being renovated into hipster coffee shops, bars and serviced offices, reminding her that London was permanently in a state of flux — it was one of the things she loved about living here, nothing ever stayed the same.

Stirling's transfer request had knocked her sideways. Marshall always assumed she'd stay in City. They were a good team, so good that when her ex-boyfriend, James, took a job at the National Crime Agency in Manchester, she chose to stay behind. There were many other reasons, of course, but the CID at Wood Street was a big part of her life and she wasn't willing to give that up.

Except, ever since the Alchemist, she was beginning to

find her other cases a little boring. The killer, Fabell, may have been insane, but he was right about the fact that he'd changed her. After the dust settled and the media frenzy and book deals dried up, she'd tried to get back to normal, but it wasn't easy.

Stirling's offer was a shock, but there was something intriguing about moving to the Met and working on a dedicated Murder Squad, even more so than diamond heists.

Hatton Garden was still closed. Uniformed officers stood stony-faced behind the blue tape keeping back the crowds of camera crews and true crime bloggers desperately trying to get a story.

The press parted as she flashed her warrant card, ducking under the tape to the relative safety beyond the cordon, ignoring the questions being hurled at her from the crowd.

Walking along the empty street towards the Diamond Exchange, Marshall noted the CCTV cameras on many of the shuttered shop fronts. It had been London's jewellery quarter since the nineteenth century. The surrounding streets were home to over three hundred related businesses, including workshops, studios and vaults all dedicated to the production of precious stones. As such, it was one of the most heavily monitored streets in the City, although sitting outside the borders of the financial district, it still remained under the protection of the City Police.

The offices of the Exchange were quiet now. Forensics had left their usual hallmarks of dark smudges on door frames and discarded evidence bags.

She nodded to the PC on the door and showed her ID for the log. He informed her that Benjamin Ramsveld was working on the second floor and to take the stairs, as the lift had been out of commission since the raid.

Marshall thanked him and headed for the stairs. In stark contrast to the post-modern exterior, the wood panelling and dark carpets of the interior made it feel more like a Masonic Lodge.

Climbing the stairs, the gilt-framed portraits of long-dead presidents of the Exchange watched her with cold, hard eyes. Each one looking more stern than their successor, with company names that she associated with the mining industry: De Beers, Alrosa and Rio Tinto.

Marshall knew a little about the jewellery business, mostly thanks to what James had told her. He worked in organised crime before moving to the NCA and used to complain that gems were one of the hardest markets to regulate, that gangs converted cash into jewels because they were easier to move. It was a shady world, with a chequered history and inexorably linked to crime from the moment the raw gems were dug out of the ground — at least in some countries.

The second floor was a suite of sumptuous offices set off a long corridor, each with a brass plaque displaying the trader's name.

Benjamin Ramsveld was waiting for her, his arms folded over his blue pin-stripe suit.

'Detective Inspector Marshall?'

She nodded and produced her warrant card for the third time in ten minutes. 'Mr Ramsveld?'

'*Ramsvelt*,' he corrected her, 'the "d" is pronounced as a "t"'

While his accent was a strong South African Afrikaans,

his appearance was more of a stereotypical Jewish businessman: orthodox ringlets hung down either side of his bushy
beard and his balding head was partially hidden beneath a
dark blue kippah.

'Please come in,' he added, waving her into his office.

It was a small room, with wooden cabinets of tiny drawers
lining one wall and a large flat screen TV on the other. An
antique mahogany desk sat in the centre, its green leather
top stacked high with box files on which was balancing a
laptop.

'Sorry for the mess,' he said, gesturing at the desk. 'I'm
still trying to unravel my predecessor's indexing system.'

Marshall took out her notebook. 'Your predecessor?'

'My father,' said Ramsveld, bowing his head. 'Peace be
upon him. Died six months ago and I am still struggling to
understand his system.' He tapped his temple with his index
finger. 'I think most of it was in his head.'

She made a note.

'So, where were you between Friday the second of April
and Saturday the third?'

The man looked slightly offended, but shrugged it off
quickly, his face resuming a more reflective expression. 'In
Amsterdam, as I told your colleague. I have a workshop over
there. It's mostly for grading and polishing.'

'Can anyone confirm that?'

His frown brought both of his bushy eyebrows together
until they were nearly one.

He doesn't like his integrity being questioned, Marshall
made a mental note. *Or is he hiding something?*

'I'm sure UK border control will have a record of my
leaving and entering the country. Otherwise you can call

Jacob, the manager, he will be able to provide you with my alibi.' Ramsveld produced a business card from a pocket inside his jacket and handed it to her. The details of the Amsterdam office were embossed on one side in silver type. The London address was on the other side in gold.

She slipped the card into the front of her notebook and changed her approach slightly. 'Has there been any unusual activity recently? Issues with the alarm system, unscheduled maintenance?'

Ramsveld relaxed a little, pausing for a second to think and then shook his head. 'Not that I'm aware of, but there will be a log somewhere.' He opened a drawer and rifled through a set of folders, before handing her a book with the letterhead of the alarm company emblazoned on the front.

'Banham,' said Marshall, opening the log.

'Papa always insisted they were the best.'

They're certainly one of the oldest, thought Marshall taking down the details of the last maintenance visit.

'How's the inventory going?' she asked, handing back the book.

Ramsveld shrugged, raising his hands. 'As well as can be expected. They knew what they were doing, they left the smaller stones and focused on the paragons, the most flaw-less ones.'

'And approximately how valuable were those?'

He winced. 'My stock alone was worth in excess of three hundred million, but there was one particular stone that I was holding for a client. A red diamond, a singular stone that was particularly valuable, not just because of its quality, but its provenance.'

'Who was the client?'

Ramsveld paused as if considering whether to protect

the anonymity of his client. 'One of my father's oldest clients. A Saudi businessman.'

'Can you tell me his name?'

He shook his head. 'He's a very important man.'

He's scared, thought Marshall, watching the man's hands tremble.

'He entrusted me with a very rare stone. One that he believes belonged to a Sumerian queen. He will be a very unhappy man when he discovers it has been stolen.'

'How much was that diamond worth?'

'We had a buyer who was willing to pay eight million pounds.'

She gasped. 'For one gem?'

Ramsveld nodded, wringing his hands. 'Our name will be ruined. My life will be in danger.'

'We can protect you,' she tried to assure him. 'But it would help us if you gave us his name.'

The jeweller muttered something in Afrikaans that she couldn't quite catch. 'I have already lost everything, there is little more that he can take from me, except perhaps my life. His name is Ahmed Hussain Al-Shammari.'

Marshall wrote down the name.

'Who else knew this diamond was being kept here?'

Ramsveld scratched his beard. 'No one, apart from myself, Al-Shammari, and the other key holders. And of course my father, but he is beyond your reach. Zikhrono livrakha'.

7

MOVING HOUSE

Chiswick, London. Easter Sunday 4th April. 17:00

Her parents' house felt like an empty shell.

Not that it was ever really Marshall's home, her mother and father moved into it seventeen years before from Bath. Now, it was as if some exorcist had drained the personality from the place. All the familiar knick-knacks and photographs were gone, carefully wrapped and put away in one of the many packing cases that were stacked all over the house.

It was sad to see their entire life reduced to a collection of nondescript cardboard boxes.

Except her father's study.

Ever since he died, her mother said she'd found it too painful to go in there, so she'd asked Marshall to come over at the weekend to help with the final arrangements, but Marshall knew it was really to go through his things because someone had to decide what to keep and what to throw away.

His study was exactly as she remembered, in the box room at the top of the stairs. Her father insisted it was too small for a bedroom, but a perfect little office for hiding away from her mother.

He'd lectured in architecture for most of his life and his study was a shrine to everything he loved about his job. Shelves of books on his favourite architects: Norman Foster, Richard Rogers and Le Corbusier, lined one wall, while images of buildings adorned another.

Marshall sat in his chair, itself a classic design, and closed her eyes. It was like stepping back in time. The room smelled of him, a lingering mixture of old books, papers and leather, stimulating childhood memories, not of this room, but one like it back in Bath. Same books, same photographs. Her sitting on his lap as he helped her to draw something for her mother.

He was a good teacher; kind and patient, and an accomplished artist. He preferred the term 'draughtsman', but her father had a natural, fluid style with a pencil that her mother always said was wasted on buildings.

'Draw me a horse,' Marshall would beg him. 'With wings.'

'Pegasus,' he would say, his deep voice resonating through her back as they drew. He told her the story of Perseus killing Medusa using the reflection on his shield and how the winged horse had been born from her severed neck. It was a gory story for a seven-year-old, but she loved it.

She loved everything he did.

He left a gaping hole in her life, one that she tried hard to ignore, filling her days with other complications to keep the grief at bay. There were only two men she could ever say she truly loved, and both of them were dead.

Opening her eyes before the tears came, she tried to focus on the task at hand.

His desk was covered in unopened mail, mostly from the Royal Institute of British Architects and other affiliations. She shuffled them into a pile and began to work through the drawers.

An hour later, Marshall had cleared out the desk, sorting the contents into two piles. Most of the old bank statements and university correspondence could be burned, but there were a few mementos he'd squirrelled away in a drawer and forgotten about. Photographs of them on holiday when she was nine or ten, badly painted clay tokens she had made at a pottery class at school, even an old tin containing one of her baby teeth.

She would keep them with the other photos he'd left her.

Turning back to the post, Marshall began to open each one, his letter opener slicing satisfyingly through them like a knife through butter.

Subscription renewals and meeting minutes were quickly assigned to the burn pile, but one letter caught her eye.

The address was handwritten and the postmark was Bath. The envelope was square and purple, all the hallmarks of a card.

A birthday card.

Inside there was a simple message.

'Happy Birthday Dad, all my love, Martha x.'

Marshall read the line twice, then checked the address on the envelope once more, it was definitely addressed to him. Whoever this Martha was, she clearly didn't know that he was gone, but more importantly why had she called him Dad?

'Shall we order a takeaway?' her mother called up the stairs.

Marshall panicked, quickly stashing the card back inside the envelope and into her keeper pile.

'Yes Mum, coming.'

8

GUARDS

Wood Street Police Station, London. Easter Monday 5th April. 08:00

Biggs was acting like an excited puppy when Marshall walked into the office. There was a small Easter egg sitting on her desk, a present from Donovan for those who had to work over the holiday weekend. She wondered if Biggs had eaten his already.

'What?' she said, unable to bear the suspense.

'One of Ramsveld's security guards woke up,' he said, jumping to his feet and grabbing his jacket. 'The Guv wants us to go down to London Bridge and get a statement.'

Still taking statements, she thought to herself.

She made them stop to grab a coffee on their way down to London Bridge Hospital. It was her second of the day, but Marshall made them add an extra shot.

'Rough night?' asked Biggs.

'Couldn't sleep,' she admitted, adding two sachets of sugar to the latte.

Gresham called her on Sunday night, sounding as if he'd slept right through the day. She wasn't in the mood for a deep and meaningful conversation, and told him that she was staying at her mum's to help with the packing, which was a convenient truth. The birthday card was playing on her mind and combined with the uncomfortable sofa bed, made for a fitful night's sleep.

The next morning, she couldn't bring herself to ask her mother about the birthday card. Somehow it didn't seem appropriate over breakfast, so she decided to do some more digging: if her father had skeletons, she wanted to know who they were and where they were buried before involving her mother.

'So, where did you get to on Saturday? If you don't mind me asking,' said Biggs as they walked over the bridge.

Biggs was one of those friends that she could always tell to back off, but she owed him some kind of explanation.

'Professor Gresham got caught up in a murder at the British Museum. I had to go over and bail him out.'

'Actually in the museum?'

She nodded, sipping the coffee and relishing the caffeine as it kicked in. 'Amongst the mummies. Somebody carved up a corpse in one of the sarcophagi. He was found at the scene.'

'Did he see who did it?'

'No, he can't remember anything. Some kind of temporary amnesia.'

'Fuck, that's insane. Who's the SIO?'

'Some arrogant DCI,' Marshall replied, trying to sound disinterested. 'Stirling I think he said his name was.'

Biggs scoffed. 'Daniel Stirling? You're kidding right?'

'You know him?'

He walked ahead and turned to face her. 'Dan Stirling runs the most elite fucking team in the Met. The Special Projects Investigation Unit. That means your Professor probably walked in on a hit. The SPIU don't get involved in any old murder.'

She tried to play it down. Biggs was acting like she'd met some kind of rock star. 'He's an asshole.'

Who tried to poach me, she thought, wondering if Biggs would be so enthusiastic if he knew about the transfer request.

'Anyway. Gresham will be fine. The entire floor was covered by CCTV, I'm sure they'll have the killer on tape.'

London Bridge Hospital. Easter Monday 5th April. 1100

Two firearms officers guarded the entrance to the isolation ward. Their body armour and MP5 submachine guns looking entirely out of place in the clinical surroundings, and were obviously making the nursing staff nervous.

Biggs flashed his warrant card and the guards moved aside to let them through. Another officer was sitting in the room while the medics attended to their patient.

'His SATs are still dangerously low,' the consultant warned, walking towards them. 'There may be permanent damage to his lungs.'

The patient was olive-skinned with dark hair and haunting eyes, ones that studied Marshall intensely as she came to stand beside his bed.

'Haval Barzani?' asked Biggs, taking out his notebook.

The man nodded, removing the oxygen mask from his mouth. 'Yes.' He answered in a strong Middle Eastern accent.

'Five minutes max,' the consultant warned as he left. 'And make sure he keeps that on.'

Biggs nodded and then continued. 'Mr Barzani, can you remember anything about the raid?'

The man shook his head and coughed, a hollow wheeze that sounded like someone who smoked four packs a day.

A nurse replaced the mask and Barzani inhaled deeply. After a few breaths the coughing subsided and he relaxed, pulling down the mask once more.

'I remember the smell of the gas, then men, then nothing.'

Biggs wrote into his notebook.

'Can you describe the men who attacked you?' asked Marshall.

Barzani's red-rimmed eyes widened as they landed on her.

'They wore masks, how do you say?' He raised his hand to his face, bunching it into a fist by the side of his mouth.

'Respirators? Like a gas mask?' Biggs suggested.

He nodded.

'How many of them?'

Barzani uncurled his fist, holding up three fingers. Marshall noticed that the little finger was missing.

'Three?' asked Biggs, unsure of the missing digit.

'Three,' he confirmed, breathlessly.

Biggs made another note and closed the book.

Panting, Barzani grabbed Marshall's hand. 'I'm from Kurdistan, from Halabaj. I was there when they dropped the bombs, they smelled of apples. Same with this gas. I held my breath and ran for the door. I don't think Valadmir was so lucky.' He pointed to the glass wall that separated the two rooms.

Valadmir Dachenko was the other security guard. He

was found close to the shuttered vault door, while Barzani collapsed out on the street. Marshall could see Dachenko in the next room, surrounded by life support systems and covered in tubes.

'Poisonous gas?' said Biggs, making quick notes.

'Killed my village.'

He coughed again and struggled to catch his breath.

The nurse returned and checked his saturation levels, replacing the oxygen mask and increasing the air flow.

'I think you should leave now,' she said in a tone that made it clear she wasn't prepared to negotiate.

Marshall took a long deep breath when they got outside. Something about the crackling sound in the man's chest made her remember the time she'd nearly drowned.

'You okay?' asked Biggs, coming to join her.

She nodded.

'I've got a copy of his tox screen. Not sure what half of it means, but I'm guessing there should be some trace of whatever gas they used.'

'Chemical weapon,' Marshall corrected him. 'They used a chemical weapon.'

Biggs's face paled slightly. 'And we were standing right in front of it.'

'Donovan's going to go mental,' Marshall said, taking out her phone. This was definitely one conversation she wasn't looking forward to. It was going to make things more complicated and Donovan hated complicated.

9

HOPE

Marshall poured herself another glass of wine and pulled the envelope from the stack of papers she'd brought back from her mother's house.

Happy Birthday Dad, all my love, Martha x

'Who the fuck are you Martha?'

Laying back on the sofa, she studied the writing on the back of the envelope. The lettering was round and open, formed in a similar way to her own. There was a hand-writing expert in the forensics team, who she'd used on more than one fraud case. They would be able to tell her all manner of psychological traits just based on the slant of the letter 'L' but it wouldn't bring her any closer to knowing who the sender was.

The postmark was dated three days before his birthday last year, and it was clearly marked as Bath, but that wasn't going to help her find the sender.

On the front of the card was an illustration of the De La

Warr Pavilion in Bexhill, one of the first modernist buildings in Britain and one of her father's favourites. There was no mistaking it was for him.

She felt an icy knot form in her stomach. The chilling realisation that this might be real, that somewhere out there was a sister she'd never known. It was something she'd dreamed of throughout most of her childhood. A baby sister was all she talked about when she was six, it must have driven her parents crazy — whether there was a medical problem or something else, her parents never had another child.

Taking a large sip of the wine, she pushed the thought to the back of her mind. There was no way she could see her father having an affair. Whoever this woman was, Marshall needed to find her.

'Who the f— '

She was interrupted by the door buzzer.

It was Gresham. Who, no matter how many times she reminded him of the entry code, he still managed to forget it.

The professor came through the door like a man possessed.

'He's done it before Pip!' he ranted, waving sheets of paper in her face, obviously something he'd printed from the internet.

'Who has?' she asked, following him through into the kitchen.

Gresham handed her the printouts and opened the fridge. She tried to ignore the face he pulled when he read the label on the wine from the corner shop.

'The murderer, I found another case where the victim had their organs removed.' He pulled out the cork with his teeth and poured himself a large glass, which he proceeded to drink in one go. Marshall had never seen him quite so animated. It was a distinct change from his normal reserved self, and she quite liked it.

'Do you have anything to eat?' he added, rifling through the cupboards. 'I haven't had much of an appetite in the last couple of days.'

'There's some peanuts above the bread bin,' she said, assuming he wouldn't be interested in yesterday's left-over curry.

The header on the first page read 'True Crimes Investigated', it was one of those morbid blog sites that had been spun off the back of a TV show, playing on the public's fascination with unsolved murders.

Below the headline was a photograph of a woman in her mid-forties with long, dark hair standing outside a school. The caption read: 'Alexandra Hope taught English at St. Martins, Bermondsey.'

Having found the nuts, Gresham emptied the remainder of the wine into his glass and ate loudly while waiting for her to finish the article.

It wasn't a long piece, and there was little in the way of detail, the official term for this kind of content was 'click-bait'. A page just long enough for it to appear in search results and get impressions for the adverts surrounding it. As far as Marshall could ascertain, the woman's body was discovered in a disused London garage in 2018. The same four major organs were removed and placed in four containers around her corpse. The investigating officer, DCI Catherine Dobson, was quoted as saying she believed it to be a botched organ-harvesting by a Ukrainian syndicate, but nothing was ever proved — according to the blog.

'It's remarkably similar to the one at the museum, don't you think?' Gresham said, when she put the last page down.

He was right, that she couldn't deny. The similarity between the murders was too close to be coincidental, although she had to wonder what kind of search terms he'd used to find it.

'Why put them in jars?' Marshall asked, then regretting it immediately. His eyes lit up, and she knew that look, she was about to get a lecture.

'Well—'

'Hold that thought,' she said, taking another bottle from the fridge and fishing the corkscrew from the kitchen drawer.

Marshall went back to the sofa and made herself comfortable.

Grabbing a handful of peanuts, he walked into the centre of the room.

'The Egyptians used to take the preparation of the dead very seriously,' he began, putting the nuts and his glass down on the coffee table before brushing the crumbs off his hands on his jacket.

'In fact it was a key part of their belief system. The preservation of the body was critical if the deceased was to be accepted into the afterlife. The mummification process had many stages; beginning with the removal of the brain, pulled out through the nose with a metal hook,' he took the corkscrew from the table and pretended to ram it into a nostril. 'Which was subsequently thrown away. Then the four major organs: the liver, lungs, stomach and intestines were removed and placed into canopic jars, to be buried alongside the body, which was cleaned with wine and coated with oils before natron salt was used to dehydrate the remains.'

Marshall winced at the thought of a corkscrew reaching into her brain. 'What about the heart? Surely that's the most important organ?'

'Indeed it is!' said Gresham, his eyes twinkling with boyish excitement, which for some reason made her smile. She wasn't sure if it was the effects of the wine or his slightly eccentric behaviour, but she was beginning to remember why she liked him.

'The heart remained within the body so that it could be weighed against the feather of Maat, the god of truth. If it was found wanting they were consumed by the crocodile-headed Ammit, the soul-eater.'

Gnashing his teeth, he collapsed into a chair and picked up his wine. 'I think this cheap crap has gone straight to my head.'

Ignoring his dislike of her favourite brand, Marshall picked up her laptop from the table. 'So why do you think the killer is trying to mummify his victims?'

Gresham shrugged and picked up the printouts. 'I'm no psychologist, but he's acting out a ceremony that hasn't been seen in two thousand years. I'd say he was a deeply disturbed individual with an unhealthy obsession with ancient Egypt.'

'You're sure it's a man?'

He considered the question, taking off his glasses and putting one of its arms into his mouth. In another time he would definitely have smoked a pipe.

'The victim must have weighed over a hundred and forty kilos. I doubt a woman would have been able to lift an obese, paralysed man into that sarcophagus.'

She had to admit, he made a good point.

'Disturbed individual with an obsession with Egypt,' she repeated. 'I think I met a few of those at the last faculty dinner.'

He smiled. 'They're odd, but not dangerous, or fit. This man would be very strong. All I'm trying to say is that I think he's done it before. Surely it'll be in the police database?'

Logging into HOLMES, Marshall typed in the name of the victim. 'So, you think he's a serial killer?'

He picked up his wine and came to sit beside her. 'Well, that depends, how many cases of disembowelment have there been?'

She frowned, clicking on the search icon. 'I don't think there's even an option for that in the search criteria.'

As they waited for the screen to refresh she turned towards him. He was sitting close enough for her to catch the scent of his cologne. He smelled good, the kind of good that made it hard to concentrate. His eyes were dark and staring directly into hers. She had to try very hard not to kiss him, but then she remembered she was still supposed to be angry with him.

'Have you remembered anything more?' she said, turning back to her laptop, ignoring the warm sensation spreading across her chest.

He shook his head. 'I arrived at the museum around five. Had a drink with the host, and then mingled with some of the faculty. Watched the presentation and then went for a wander, the rest is a blank until I woke up amongst the dead.'

'I'm sure they'll have it all on CCTV.'

Assuming that the power failure hadn't affected the cameras.

He looked slightly relieved. 'Yes, they will won't they.'

Her laptop pinged as HOLMES finished its search and

the case notes of Alexandra Hope appeared on screen. Marshall scrolled through them quickly, finding it slightly awkward that he was watching over her shoulder — strictly speaking they were breaking more than one law.

'It's still open,' she said, tapping on the relevant part of the screen, 'and it looks as if DCI Dobson retired after this case.' She drilled down into the forensics report. Images of the crime scene appeared in a gruesome slideshow. 'The head and fingers were left intact, which is why they were able to identify her, so not quite the same MO, but you're right, it's an unusual way to end someone's life.'

He raised his glass and put on a fake Victorian accent. 'I leave the rest to you Watson. Personally I don't know how you can look at that every day.' Pointing at the gruesome images.

'You get used to it,' Marshall said, trying not to laugh. 'Well, kind of. The first time is always the worst. Nothing can prepare you for that.' Shutting the laptop, she placed it back on the table.

'So will you tell DCI Stirling about it?' he asked, dropping the accent.

She shook her head. 'It's his investigation. I'm sure he's got a team working on it already.'

Officially Marshall should report it, but she didn't want to give Stirling another reason to start up a conversation, especially after the unprompted transfer request. She wasn't sure what she would say to him after what Donovan had said.

Gresham looked disappointed. 'But, it could be important.'

'It is,' she said, taking his hand and squeezing it gently. 'But, I've got my own case to focus on. Have you heard about the heist in Hatton Garden?'

He looked at her blankly, and she remembered that he didn't have a TV, nor did he read the news. Unless it happened six hundred years ago — he wasn't interested.

'A gang broke into a diamond repository on Saturday. They estimate the haul was well over three hundred million.'

He frowned. 'In diamonds? That's quite a lot of stones.'

Surprised, she let go of his hand. It wasn't the response she'd been expecting.

'One of them was worth eight million on its own, a red diamond belonging to an old Sumerian queen.'

His eyes lit up once more, as she knew they would.

'Not Queen Pu-abi of Ur?'

She shrugged. 'I guess so. All we know is that it belonged to a Saudi businessman, we're trying to track him down.'

'Good luck with that, gems are not the easiest things to trace.'

'How do you know so much about diamonds?'

Gresham's expression changed, his eyes hardening, as if she'd asked a question he wasn't comfortable answering. 'My brother is a sightholder for De Beers.'

That was when she was sure he must be still suffering from the after effects of the medication, it was the first time he'd mentioned his family.

She finished her drink, and realising there was no more wine in the house said: 'Let's go out and get something to eat and you can tell me all about it.'

10

CURRY

The Ruby, Ferry Street, Docklands. 5th April. 20:30

'So your brother's a diamond merchant?' asked Marshall as they sat in the local curry house. She was enjoying how uncomfortable he looked amongst the velvet flock wallpaper and the gilt-edged images of Vishnu.

Gresham grimaced as he picked up a laminated menu. 'Sightholders are awarded contracts from De Beers. David buys rough diamonds from their mines in the Northern Transvaal, manufactures and sells them to the USA. It's our family business, my great grandfather started it before the First World War.'

That explains the money, Marshall thought.

'In South Africa?'

He nodded. 'We have a factory outside of Cape Town.'

'Do you have any other family?'

Gresham was studying the menu. 'No,' he replied without looking up. 'We're all that's left. I haven't spoken to him in years. Are you sure there isn't somewhere else you'd rather eat?'

'It's good food, and quick. And you said you were starving. Try the Lamb Kurbaani, or the Chicken Chattinad, they're good.'

'I thought you were vegetarian?'

She smiled. 'Sorry to break it to you, but you're not the first carnivore I've brought here.'

The waiter came over with the wine and took their order.

'So, you don't sound very South African.'

'I'm not. My mother and father broke up when I was twelve. She brought me to the UK and put me into a boarding school. David was eighteen, so he decided to stay with my father.'

Marshall held up a hand. 'Please don't tell me it was Eton.'

He nodded. 'Only the best for the Greshams.'

She smiled, imagining what her father would say if she'd brought him home. 'Elitist wanker,' sprang to mind.

'That explains a lot.'

Gresham glared at her. 'It wasn't my decision. You think I enjoyed being pulled out of my home and sent half way around the world to some posh boys' school in the middle of Berkshire?'

The waiter returned with a hostess trolley carrying steaming bowls of food.

'Sorry, I kind of assumed that it was every rich boy's wet dream.'

Distracted by the smell of the food, Gresham seemed to relax. 'It was a good school. Probably the best place for me, especially after my mother died, but that's one period of history I'm not keen on reviving. Let's just stay in the present for now.'

'Fine by me,' she said, picking up her fork and scooping

up one of the vegetable dishes. 'Now try the tarka daal, the chef adds a pinch of Peruvian chilli that knock your socks off.'

He dutifully opened his mouth and took the daal from her.

His eyes lit up as the spices hit his tongue. 'Wow. That's amazing.'

'See how you shouldn't judge a curry house by its decor?'

'Nor its wine list?' said Gresham pointing at the wine.

She smiled. 'Well, I didn't say it was perfect.'

'I have to go in and make a statement on Wednesday,' Gresham said as they walked arm-in-arm back to her flat. It was beginning to rain and they huddled under the golf umbrella the curry house had lent them.

'You'll be fine,' Marshall tried to assure him, she could tell he was worrying about it. 'Do you want me to come with you?'

'No,' he said, gripping her arm a little tighter. 'I'll be fine, and you have work.'

'I don't mind.'

She stopped and turned into him. 'I'm sorry about the other day. Sometimes the job can stress me out. And getting a call saying you were involved in a murder is possibly the worst news I could get.'

He put his arm around her, pulling her close with his free hand.

'I didn't want him to call you, but I couldn't think of anyone else, my head was all over the place. I know how important your work is.'

'It's okay Michael,' she whispered, leaning closer. 'Now shut up and kiss me.'

11

SHABTI

Paddington Station NCP, London. Monday, 5th April. 23:00

The voice of ambulance control crackled into life through the speaker.

'Alpha-Charlie-Two-Zero, what is your current status?'

Suddenly he was back in the desert.

The constant chatter of the comms buzzing in his ear. The gritty mixture of sweat and sand chafing against his neck. The smell of the bodies beside him in the personnel carrier as it followed the civilians and another Spartan APV through the bombed-out streets of Tikrit at high speed.

They were twenty miles out from the base in hostile territory.

'Contact ahead,' came the warning from the lead vehicle. 'Switching route to Charlie Delta.'

His driver took a hard left onto a road leading out towards the river Tigris, but it was too late, a plume of flame burst out from below the first armoured vehicle, flicking it end-over-end like a toy.

The suicide bomber driving the bus swerved around the burning wreck and detonated seconds later, sending the civilian truck into the air and into the path of his vehicle.

Those who live today will die tomorrow, those who die tomorrow will be born again; Those who live Ma'at will never die, he could still hear the words his brother spoke to him the morning he'd woken in the field hospital.

They'd learned the proverb so many years before, when they were children. When their father taught them the words from the Book of the Dead, taught them the concept of Ma'at; of balance, truth and order.

Now, looking down at the ruined body in the back of the ambulance, he wondered how the old gods would judge his actions, how would they weigh his heart?

Offering a prayer to Osiris, he lifted the liver from the paramedic's chest and placed it into a plastic container.

His brother's voice whispered inside his head: *Remember, this is no longer a man, but a vessel, a Shabti, a servant of the dead.*

Like my men, he thought of all those that died that day in Tikrit, their bodies torn apart like discarded toys.

Taking great care to remove the organs in the sacred way, he tried to recreate his brother's art. But still he was not as delicate, not as refined, he was nothing more than a clumsy butcher compared to the mastery of the skilful Saadah.

The *Shabti's* heart was no long beating, his eyes staring blankly into his own, his face contorted by the agony of a slow death.

I have become Anubis, he thought, pressing the blade to the throat, feeling the skin part under its edge, *god of death*.

The radio sprang to life once more. 'Michael are you okay? Please respond over.'

Reaching inside the man's abdomen, his hands searched for the internal scars until his fingers touched the hard edges beneath the tissue.

'You hid it well my brother,' he whispered.

12

KNIGHTSBRIDGE

Wood Street Police Station, London. Tuesday 6th April. 09:00

Marshall struggled to focus on the crime scene report from Hatton Garden. Her hangover was taking longer than usual to clear and she was finding it increasingly difficult to concentrate on the finer details of the drilling equipment the crew left behind.

None of this was helped by the lack of sleep, but she wasn't complaining about that. If there was one thing Gresham did very well it was drunk sex.

Biggs slammed down the lid on his laptop. 'Bollocks.'

'What's up?' she asked, pretending to be concerned, but actually just relieved to have an excuse to stop reading.

'Ramsveld's client, Al-Shammari, is off limits. MI6 has flagged him as a person of interest.' He added air quotes to emphasise the phrase. 'And now I will be too.'

They both knew that even just trying to access his file would set alarm bells off inside Vauxhall Cross — commonly known as spook central.

'Do you think I should tell the Guv?' he asked, looking as if it was the last thing he wanted to do.

Picking up her coffee, Marshall leaned back in her chair. 'To expect a visit from the secret service? No I'd keep that one to yourself if I were you. Is his record totally redacted?'

Biggs thought twice before reopening his laptop. 'I guess the damage is already done.'

Scrolling through the records, he paused at a piece of clear text. 'So from what I can see, he's got diplomatic immunity under the Saudi embassy. Lives in Knightsbridge, and has a few minors for parking, usual crap.'

Marshall grabbed her jacket from the back of her chair and stood up. 'I'm bored of reading about power tools. Fancy a visit to Hyde Park?'

Biggs nodded eagerly, getting up from his chair.

'Marshall!' barked Donovan, coming out of his office waving her latest report in the air. He was an old-school kind of copper, preferring everything to be printed out.

'Yes, Guv?'

Her desk was one of the closest to his door, it was meant to make it easier for them to talk without disturbing the rest of the team, except Donovan's voice could be heard on the floor above if he was angry.

'You think they used some kind of chemical weapon?'

'That's what Barzani said. He was at Halabaj when they dropped a combination of VX, mustard gas and sarin on the local population. He told us it was the same smell — like sweet apples. It probably saved his life.'

'You realise I have to flag this with SO15?'

'Sorry sir,' she replied, wondering if this was the time to mention MI6, and get all of the bad news out of the way in one go, then decided against it.

Donovan rubbed his hand through his thinning grey

hair and sighed. 'Never should have taken this one,' he mumbled to himself. 'Nothing but grief where diamonds are concerned.'

He walked back into his office and slammed the door.

Knightsbridge, London. 1100

'Why is it called Knightsbridge?' Biggs said as they walked out of the tube station. Traffic was always bad around the West End so it was quicker to use the Underground than take a car.

'I mean, was there even a bridge?' he continued, looking both ways along the street.

'I read somewhere it costs forty-three grand a square metre to live around here,' she said, looking into the window of Harvey Nichols. 'Not in your average copper's price range.'

Biggs laughed. 'Not the honest ones at least.'

They crossed over to the Mandarin Hotel, taking the Serpentine Walk towards Hyde Park.

Michael's got one of those, Marshall thought, walking past the Rolex store. The windows were filled with gleaming chronometers, ones that Biggs was eyeing up like a kid in a sweetshop. She imagined that this was the kind of area where Gresham might spend his Saturdays, browsing through Harvey Nichols and Harrods, looking at watches that cost more than a month's salary — somewhere she'd never dreamed of going.

She wondered how many diamonds it would take to buy one. The night before, Gresham had changed the subject pretty quickly when it came to his family, and she'd had the sense not to push it, but it was the first time he'd opened up about his past. It wasn't much, but it was something, and explained a little of why he was such a closed book, a rich, lonely boy left to grow up in one institution after another.

Marshall couldn't remember ever feeling poor when she was younger. There had been times when money was tight: her father taking on extra tuition at weekends, more than one holiday spent at her grandmother's house in Wales and slicing a Mars bar into sections for dessert.

She still preferred a Mars in slices, not that she could afford the calories these days.

The entrance to the apartments of One Hyde Park was a large glass atrium filled with exotic plants, and it reminded her of the Palm House of Kew Gardens.

They both showed their warrant cards to the concierge, a middle-aged South Asian man with a neatly trimmed moustache and an annoyingly unquenchable air of entitlement. His golden name badge read: 'Amit'

'How may I help you today?' Amit asked, standing up from behind his desk.

'We would like to speak with Ahmed Hussain Al-Shammari,' Biggs replied, checking his notebook. 'Apartment twenty-four.'

'The penthouse suite,' the concierge said proudly. 'With a fine view of the park.'

'We're not here to buy one,' Marshall growled. 'Can you just tell him we're here.'

Amit's head seemed to wobble slightly at her sharp tone, but nothing seemed to affect his permanent smile.

'I'm afraid I cannot,' he said through bright white teeth.

'Company policy does not allow me to reveal the identity of our residents.'

Marshall was confused. 'He's in apartment twenty-four.'

'I did not say that. I merely pointed out it has a wonderful view.'

'And is Mr Al-Shammari currently enjoying that view?' asked Biggs, trying a different tack.

Amit shrugged. 'That I couldn't say.'

Marshall folded her arms. 'Do you want us to come back with a search warrant?'

The concierge shook his head and replied as tactfully as he could: 'Some of our residents enjoy certain privileges, ones that require a level of diplomacy, shall we say.'

Biggs was about to say something when Marshall pulled out her business card and handed it to Amit. 'Fine. Would you be so kind as to give the current resident of apartment twenty-four my card and ask him to call me.'

Nodding, the concierge took the card and placed it into his pocket.

'I will, as soon as he returns.'

'He's not here?'

Amit's eyes narrowed a little. 'That particular apartment has been empty since Saturday.'

Marshall thanked him and they left.

'Where next?' asked Biggs.

She looked out towards Hyde Park. The cloudless sky was blue and cherry blossoms covered the trees, signalling that spring had finally arrived.

'Want to grab an early lunch? My shout?'

He checked his watch, it was quarter to twelve. 'Well, if you're buying.'

13

SERPENTINE

Serpentine, Hyde Park, London. Tuesday 6th April. 12:00

'So you've no idea who she is?' Biggs asked, turning the birthday card over.

'Not a clue.'

The waitress arrived with a tray of steaming coffees and rolls.

'Were there any others?'

Marshall shook her head, taking a bite out of her tuna melt and fighting to stop the cheese hitting her chin.

'Classy,' said Biggs, cutting his in half with a knife. 'I thought you'd gone veggie?'

'I am, mostly. I just have a thing about tuna and cheese.'

Biggs grimaced. 'Sounds like a terrible combination. Anyway, so did you ask your mum about her?'

'Are you kidding? She still lays a plate for him at dinner. This would kill her.'

'You honestly think he's got another daughter?' He opened up one half of the sausage baguette and added mustard from a sachet.

Marshall considered talking to Gresham about the card last night when he started talking about his brother, but somehow it didn't feel right. She didn't want to admit to anyone, let alone herself, that her dad might have been unfaithful, let alone contemplate the idea that there might be a half-sister.

'I want to know for sure, before I tell her. It could just be some psycho. The last thing she needs now is to find out he was shagging someone else.'

'Good plan,' agreed Biggs.

'Except we've got nothing to go on apart from a post-mark,' she said, taking the envelope back and running her thumb over the first-class stamp. 'We could try getting DNA from the back of the stamp,' she wondered aloud.

'Do you think she'd be in the database?'

Marshall shrugged. 'Worth a try though.'

He nodded. 'Also, Martha's not that popular a name. I'm guessing if you check the registry for Bath there won't be that many in the last thirty years.'

Marshall spooned three heaped teaspoons of sugar into her coffee. 'It would be less than that, my parents moved up to London seventeen years ago.'

He smiled. 'There you go — halved the workload already!' Then took a large bite out of his baguette.

Sipping her latte slowly, she searched for the right way to ask the question, then decided to go for the direct route. 'Can you do it for me? I'm not sure I can face it.'

'Sure no problem,' Biggs said, wiping his mouth with a napkin. 'Leave it with me.'

He took the envelope and put it carefully into his coat pocket.

· · ·

Her hangover finally clearing, Marshall relaxed back into the chair.

Letting the sun warm her face, she watched the passers-by walking alongside the Serpentine, wondering who they were and where they came from.

'What do you think Al-Shammari did to end up on an MI6 watchlist?'

Biggs shrugged, finishing a mouth full of baguette. 'Probably linked to terrorism. Saudi's supposed to be the largest funder of fundamentalist groups. Bin Laden was brought up in Saudi Arabia.'

Her phone started ringing, it was DCI Donovan. Marshall mouthed his name to Biggs and got up, walking out of the café and into the relative quiet of the park.

'Marshall where are you? Sounds like you're in the country?'

'Knightsbridge, following up on the owner of the stolen red diamond.'

'Okay, good. Listen, Devlin thinks he's found something on the CCTV, an empty shop at the southern end of Leather Lane. He says the builders were coming in and out at all times of day and night. Can you meet him over there? Preferably before he destroys any evidence.'

Babysitting Devlin, thought Marshall, *still not quite off the hook then*. The Detective Sergeant wasn't a great one for subtlety, his style of policing was straight out of the Sweeney.

'Okay. I'll be there in twenty minutes.'

'Duty calls?' asked Biggs, waving the bill when she returned to the table.

She nodded, grabbing her jacket from the back of the chair. 'Devlin thinks he's found their base of operations.'

Biggs laughed and waved her away. 'Don't worry, you go. I'll get this, but the next one is going to involve beers.'

She was already running for the high street.

14

SEWER

Leather Lane, London. Tuesday 6th April. 13:10

By the time Marshall arrived at Leather Lane it was already cordoned off. A group of harassed-looking market traders were being slowly evacuated ahead of a line of uniforms, their complaints echoing down the street sounded like an angry mob.

The lane ran parallel to Hatton Garden, with stalls lining both sides of the road. One side was lined with cafés and restaurants, the other comprised of the rear entrances to the various diamond shops and offices.

A team of SOCOs were busy erecting a white tent around the entrance to the shop, while armed officers in black combat gear were standing guard.

Marshall spotted DS Devlin talking to a senior officer from SO15, by the look on his face, it was not going well.

He seemed relieved to see her when she walked up to them.

'DI Marshall,' Devlin said as a way of introduction. 'This is Commander Warren, he's heading up Counter Terrorism.'

Warren nodded.

'When can we go in sir?' asked Marshall, guessing the reason for Devlin's frustration.

He glared at her, clearly this wasn't the first time he'd been asked. 'Soon as we have the all clear from the tech team,' he said sternly.

She knew the commander was just following protocol. The alleged use of chemical weapons meant that Counter Terrorism and their biohazard team would have to make a sweep of the building before anyone could set foot inside.

Marshall thanked him and turned back to Devlin.

'What did you find on the CCTV?' she asked, ignoring the look of satisfaction on his face, Devlin was obviously enjoying the fact that she'd failed to get any more information from Warren than he had.

He took out his notebook and flipped to the relevant page. She caught sight of his handwriting, it was child-like and mostly in capitals. 'Three groups of men working in twelve hour shifts since last Thursday. Two came out on the Saturday, but one never showed up again.'

'How many in each group?'

'Three or four. All wearing hard hats and masks, kept their heads down. Cameras are too high for any chance of getting facial recognition.'

She looked around the street at the camera positions, sighting two within thirty feet of their position.

'Can you track them back?'

Devlin shook his head. 'MetCC is still trying. They were clever. Came in separately. Each team member taking a different route every time. They knew what they were doing.'

Marshall walked over to the other side of the street. There was a small newsagent wedged between a narrow space in two office buildings. The window advertised everything from Western Union to iPhone repairs.

Sitting below one of the lottery ticket displays was a small webcam, pointing directly towards the door of the empty shop.

'Someone was running their own surveillance by the look of it.'

Devlin squinted through the window and into the darkened shop. 'I'll get right onto it.'

Commander Warren gave the all-clear forty minutes later. The biohazard team came marching out of the tent in full hazmat suits like something out of a sci-fi movie. Marshall knew what to expect, she'd been on the training, they all had since the Novichok incident in Salisbury, but there was still something unsettling about the sight of those luminous yellow suits and gas masks on the streets of London.

'You're not going to wait for SOCO?' she asked as he stepped through the doorway.

Devlin winked at her. 'Thought I heard someone call out.'

From the ruined interior, it was unclear what the shop used to be. Cables and pipes hung from the ceiling like the innards of a gutted fish, and the floor was mostly joists. Someone had nailed a path of boards across them to a set of stairs that descended into the basement.

'Building's been empty for two years,' said Devlin hanging back in the doorway and consulting his notes. 'The owners are some overseas investment firm.'

'Based in Saudi?'

'Yeah,' said Devlin, sounding a little surprised. 'How did you know?'

'Just a hunch,' she said, stepping carefully onto the makeshift floor. The flimsy boards groaned and looking down between the wooden rafters, Marshall could see that the lights of the so-called builders were still in place arranged around a large hole in the basement floor.

The stairs were only in marginally better condition, old and worn. She made her way down to the lower floor with Devlin in tow.

It smelled of damp, like a cave. The old plastered walls were covered in black mould, and the floor an uneven brick paving that looked as if it were straight out of a Dickens novel. Drilling equipment and discarded food packaging lay scattered around the hole which had a tripod suspended over it supporting a winch.

Devlin walked around to the opposite side of the hole, being unusually careful where he stepped.

Using the torch from his phone, he peered down into the void. 'Smells like shit,' he said, his nose wrinkling .

Marshall assumed it would. This was how they breached the sewers and got into the water main. She had no intention of going down there, she was more interested in the rubbish they'd left behind. This wouldn't be the first time someone got caught from a half-finished sandwich.

Putting on a pair of latex gloves, she began to rifle through the empty cartons. It was mostly junk food, empty packets of fries and hamburger cartons, like a teenager's house party. She took out an evidence bag and dropped the remnants of someone's filet-of-fish into it.

There was a whirring noise and she turned to find Devlin with the control device for the winch.

'What are you doing?'

'There's something down there.'

The metal line went taught, the gears grinding as the machine struggled to bring its burden back to the surface.

Marshall tilted one of the lamps and watched as the slowly spinning package rose towards the surface.

'What the fuck is that?' asked Devlin, squinting into the dark hole.

'Who the fuck is that?' she corrected him as the torso came into the light.

15

PARAMEDIC

Paddington Station Car Park, London. Wednesday, 7th April. 06:00

Stepping down from the back of the ambulance, Doctor Gates pulled off his latex gloves and took a crumpled packet of Marlboro Reds from his inside pocket. Fumbling like a drunk who just pulled an all-night session, he offered one to DCI Stirling.

Stirling hadn't smoked in three years, but took one eagerly.

Neither spoke for a minute, letting the smoke fill their lungs and banish the smell from their nostrils.

Gates stared into the back of the ambulance, it was a mess, the sides covered in the victim's blood.

'No head, but there's an ID,' he said, wiping the laminated badge on the sleeve of his blue Tyvek suit.

Stirling took it and studied the details. 'Michael Avery, Paramedic,' he read aloud.

'Organ donor too,' added Gates, handing Stirling the man's wallet. 'Not that there's much left to donate.'

The detective took another drag from the cigarette and tried not to cough, the medical examiner was renown for his grim sense of humour.

'You think it's the same MO as the museum?'

Gates nodded, his chin receding into his flabby jowls. 'No doubt about it, same incisions, same organs extracted. I'll know more when I get him back to the lab.'

Stirling looked around the car park. It was a standard NCP design, a sixties pre-fab bunker with dark corners filled with rubbish and damp, oil-stained concrete.

There were a few cars badly parked in bays beneath flickering neon lights, most likely stolen or abandoned. The car park was used by drug gangs and crack addicts and was widely known for its dodgy CCTV coverage amongst the homeless and desperate.

The ambulance sat at the furthest end of sub-level three, as far from the camera as possible. The manager called it a 'blind spot', which meant this was planned. There weren't many NCPs that had the clearance for the height of a Fiat Ducato, making it pretty clear that this was a premeditated murder.

He gave the ID and the wallet back to Gates who slipped them into an evidence bag.

'Why bring him here?' Gates wondered to himself, closing the bag and writing on the label with a Sharpie.

'His controller said he responded to a call in Westbourne Green, a heart attack. The number was a pay-as-you-go.'

'Don't they usually work in pairs?' added Gates.

Stirling nodded. 'They found his partner in an alley on the Hallfield Estate. She's been taken to St. Mary's.'

Gates finished his cigarette and ground it into the floor

with the heel of his shoe. 'Then this wasn't random, no one goes to this much effort over a random.'

16

COYS

'Gary Collins,' Donovan announced, tapping on the large touchscreen display. A mugshot of a broken-nosed, bald man in his late forties expanded to fill the screen. Looking every part the career criminal, Collins had spent a significant part of his life behind bars — he had the dead-eyed stare of a man who'd sold his soul.

'Twelve counts of armed robbery, four for GBH and numerous aggravated assaults. He's been out on probation since last November, one of a group of four arrested over the Heathrow raid in 2010. His body was found yesterday hanging from the winch in the basement of thirty-five Leather Lane.'

Donovan swiped his hand over the screen and the mugshot was replaced by a corpse whose head, hands and feet were missing.

'Luckily for us, Gary has some rather unique tattoos.' The image zoomed to a close-up of the upper chest where the insignia of Tottenham Hotspur had been inked over his heart. Below it was written 'C.O.Y.S. 2008', on the other pectoral was a very badly drawn portrait of Jonathan Woodgate.

'Collins was a known member of the Tottenham Massive, and thanks to his illustrious career on the terraces, gives us a pretty definite fix on one of the crew.'

The display changed again, this time to what seemed to be an older version of Collins. 'Most of his known affiliates are still inside at the moment, including his brother Terry, who's serving a ten-year sentence in Pentonville for possession of a firearm. Marshall, I want you to go down and find out what he knows. According to the records, the Collins brothers were inseparable, there's no way Terry wouldn't know what Gary was up to.'

Marshall nodded.

'Biggs, how are we getting on with the inventory?'

Biggs stood up and opened his notebook. 'Ramsveld is estimating it to be around three hundred and fifty million pounds.'

Two members of the team cheered. Punching the air as if they'd won the lottery. Donovan gave them a long hard stare, and they quickly sat down.

'Any update on the gas that was used?'

It was Baxter's turn to get to his feet, clearing his throat as if he were about to give a wedding speech.

'Your Kurdish guard was correct when he likened it to the smell of sweet apples. The chemical traces that forensics have managed to extract from the canisters in the shop contained chloroacetophenone and cyanide, a deadly form of tear gas that damages the eyes and lungs. He's lucky to be alive.'

Baxter ambled over to the white board and wrote the names of the two compounds on the white board. 'The use of these has been banned since the First World War.'

'Unless you're Saddam Hussein,' said Marshall.

17

PENTONVILLE

HM Pentonville Prison, Islington, London. Wednesday, 7th April. 13:00

The bleak outer walls of the Victorian prison dominated the streets around it, reminding Marshall of something from a Dickens novel. It was raining hard, dark clouds gathering above the white portico of the main gate, making it easy to imagine what it would have been like to get locked up in 1842.

Passing through security ahead of the visitors, she wondered how many of the inmates were men she'd help put away. Pentonville held category B and remand prisoners, not murderers or sex offenders, but who still posed a threat to the public.

City Police dealt mostly with fraud, money laundering and financial crime, so it was unlikely that she had. Which was lucky for them, the 'Ville' had a bad reputation; staff shortages and ageing plumbing led to a litany of problems: gang affiliations, drugs and issues with weapons meant prisoners were spending less than two hours a day outside of their cells.

On the other side of security the Duty Governor waited impatiently, while Marshall went through the body scanner. She was a short, squat woman in her late fifties, wearing an ill-fitting two piece brown suit.

'DI Marshall,' she said, squinting at a list on her iPad.

Marshall nodded. 'This is DC Biggs, we're here to interview Terry Collins. Has he been told about his brother?'

The Governor looked up from the tablet, her expression grim. 'He didn't take it well. We've had to put him into segregation, the doctor has prescribed him Haldol.'

Terry Collins was the elder brother, arrested during a bank raid in Dalston three years ago and currently serving ten years for possession of a firearm with intent.

Marshall read through his case file on the tube, the man was a serial offender. Starting his career at the age of fourteen, he'd been in and out of jail for most of his adult life. Gary had dutifully followed in his older brother's footsteps, along with a sister who was currently on remand for handling stolen goods. The entire family were bent.

'Follow me,' the Governor instructed, leading the way down a whitewashed corridor and into the main prison.

Segregation was part of E Wing, one of the four main wings that met in the centre of the prison.

They were joined by two other prison officers, who went ahead to unlock the gates.

Terry was being held in a large holding cell, sitting behind a table with another officer standing beside him. He was docile, Marshall thought, even a little bit stoned. The man looked haggard, his skin grey and sagging on a face that was obviously related to Gary.

'Terry,' began the Governor, 'this is DI Marshall and DC Biggs, they're investigating your brother's murder, do you still feel up to talking to them?'

His heavy eyes narrowed until they were two tiny dark slits. 'Yeah,' he said in the hoarse voice of a heavy smoker. 'I'll talk to them.'

Marshall expected some kind of slur; they were Pigs, Fuzz, Ekkies and a hundred other slang terms for the enemy, but Collins didn't seem to care about a confrontation, all the fight had been knocked out of him. Haldol was an antipsychotic drug, which according to some reports, many prisons used to pacify the inmates on a regular basis.

The Governor motioned for them to sit down on the other side of the table, which they duly did.

Terry ignored them, unwrapping a tobacco pouch and rolling a cigarette. Marshall noticed the yellow nicotine stains on his fingers, and the blue swallow tattoos on his hands.

'I'm sorry to hear about your brother Terry. Had you spoken to him lately?' she asked.

He took his time answering, lighting the cigarette and blowing out a stream of blue smoke into her face. 'Not since Christmas.'

She ignored the smoke and continued. 'And what did he say?'

Marshall knew Gary had served time with his brother, but was released the year before.

'That he'd got a job with a foreign crew. Cracking ice.'

Ice was another name for diamonds. Gary's record showed he had a predilection for jewellery jobs, he was well known as a peterman, a safe-cracker.

'A foreign crew? Not from London?' asked Biggs, taking out his notebook.

Terry laughed, his breath wheezing in his chest like a hollow reed. 'Not from these shores. Towel-heads or some such. Terry was bragging that he was gonna teach them how to do it proper.'

'Did he give you any names?' Biggs continued.

Collins sneered, taking another long drag on his cigarette. 'Mufasa, Rafiki and Pumbaa. How the fuck should I know?'

'Did he say where he met them?' interrupted Marshall.

The old lag shrugged. 'On the internet, some dark website for nonces or something. They sent him a phone, special encrypted kind of shit, ex-military.'

Marshall knew organised crime were using modified phones, there were a number of companies selling encrypted handsets, most were using Soviet encryption hardware. 'Russian?'

Terry shook his head. 'Nah, more like Middle-East.'

'Where's he been staying since he got out?'

He sighed, stubbing the cigarette out in the ash tray. 'At mum's place. Stonebridge Road.'

His eyes seemed to clear, and for a moment Marshall saw something close to an emotion in them, it was grief. 'They told me they cut his fucking head off.'

She nodded.

'Fuckers.'

'We'll get them Terry,' she assured them.

He sucked air in through his broken, tar-stained teeth. 'You do that. And when you bang them up, make sure you send them my way.'

His knuckles went white as he bunched his fists on the table.

. . .

Walking out into the car park, the storm had cleared, but Marshall couldn't shake the sense of doom that hung over the place.

She checked her messages, finding there was a text from Gresham, reminding her about his interview with Stirling's team that afternoon.

Marshall quickly texted Gresham back. *I'm on my way.*

'You think the phone will still be at the mum's house?' asked Biggs, looking around for a taxi.

'It's worth a shot. Operational Eternal shut down Encro-Chat last year, so whatever they're using these days it makes sense that it would be ex-military.'

Biggs didn't look convinced. 'Doesn't sound like it will make it any easier to trace.'

A black cab pulled up to the kerb.

She shrugged, opening the door. 'Frazer likes a challenge. You go and visit the mother. I'll meet you back at the station.'

'Where are you going?' he asked, his voice failing to hide the confusion.

'I forgot, Gresham's got to make a statement. I'll be back in a couple of hours.'

Before Biggs could respond, Marshall slammed the cab door and was gone.

18

COLLINS HOUSE

Stonebridge Road, Tottenham. Wednesday, 7th April. 17:00

Biggs walked up the front path to the Collins's house, carefully avoiding a broken washing machine and a burned out microwave lying on their sides in the overgrown grass. He noted there were recent repairs to the front door: the woodwork around the new lock had yet to be painted and a glass panel had been replaced with plywood. It was obvious that someone had kicked it in.

Above the door, an English flag flapped limply from a bedroom window.

He knocked, secretly hoping that there would be no reply.

'What the fuck d'you want?' shouted an old lady through a slightly open front window.

He held up his warrant card to the net curtains. 'DC Biggs, I've come to ask you about Gary.'

'He's dead!' the woman replied. 'What more is there to say?'

Somewhere inside a dog began to bark.

Biggs stepped back into the front garden, wondering if it wouldn't be safer to conduct the interview through the window.

Moving the yellowing curtain aside, the woman stared myopically at him through a pair of thick-lensed glasses. She appeared to be well into her eighties, lines on her face were stretched taught over the bones of her skull. There were dark hollows under her eyes and her jaw moved as though she had very few teeth.

'Mrs Collins?'

She hissed, or laughed, Biggs couldn't tell.

'Wait 'til my Terry finds out. He'll string 'em up by their bollocks, fucking cunts!'

Trying not to react, Biggs reminded himself that this was the mother of three hardened criminals whose father used to hang out with the Krays. They had a different kind of justice, they looked after their own.

'We spoke to Terry this morning,' he said, putting away his warrant. 'I need to see Gary's room, we're looking for his phone.'

The woman shook her head, letting the nicotine-stained nets fall back across the window. 'Gary's dead,' she croaked. 'My little boy's dead. He don't need no phone.'

Biggs smelled cigarette smoke, heard her rattling cough.

'Terry said Gary was staying here after he got out. I just need five minutes to look through his things. The phone might help us catch whoever killed him.'

'Terry said that?' There was doubt in her voice.

'He said that you would know where he kept it,' Biggs lied, hoping that her confusion was a mild form of dementia.

There was a long silence and then the front door opened.

Mrs Collins was hardly five-feet tall, her steel-grey hair pulled back in a tight bun giving her an extra few inches of height. She was wearing a long knitted cardigan over a floral apron.

'I've locked her in the kitchen,' she said as Biggs stared over her shoulder into the hall. Something large and vicious was barking and scratching at the door at the end of the hall.

The old woman studied him closely, her eyes magnified by the glasses. 'You're a bit young for a detective.'

'Biggs, my name is Biggs.'

'Biggs! I had a cat called Biggs once, used to bring home the fattest pigeons,' she cackled, showing off the last of her broken teeth.

The room looked as if it had been decorated by a teenager. Posters of Tottenham Hotspur and Formula 1 racing cars were pinned over the old wallpaper, some of which would have fallen down without it.

'Gary wasn't home much,' his mother explained, going over to the wardrobe. 'When he was, it was only for a few days, but —' With unusual amount of strength for her size, she pushed an old wardrobe to one side, exposing a hole in the wall where a fireplace would once have been. 'I could always hear the scrape on the boards when he came back.'

Inside the old iron grate, someone had stashed a dark brown satchel, Gary's initials were carved into the leather flap.

She handed it to him. 'He used to call it his secret treasure when he was a kid.'

Biggs opened the satchel. Inside was a large roll of twenty pound notes, two bags of what he guessed was cocaine and a black phone.

'Thanks Mrs Collins,' he said, carefully slipping the phone into an evidence bag.

'Fuck off.'

19

INTERVIEW

Charing Cross Police Station. Wednesday, 7th April. 16:00

Professor Gresham was waiting for her outside the station. He looked terrible, as if he hadn't slept since she'd last seen him. Part of her wanted to wrap her arms around him, but this was work and she needed to keep it professional — especially in front of Stirling.

'Thanks for coming,' he said meekly.

'It's fine Michael,' she reassured him. 'It's just a formality.'

They walked into the station and Gresham gave his name at the front desk.

Marshall showed her warrant card and they were both shown through to an interview room.

There were two chairs on each side of the table. A female officer stood as they entered the room and introduced herself as Detective Sergeant Novak.

Gresham sat down opposite her.

'You're here in what capacity?' she asked Marshall, in a slightly Eastern European accent.

'Professor Gresham asked me to accompany him. We worked together on my last case.'

The woman nodded, although Marshall thought she caught a look of doubt in her eye, and opened her file.

'Professor Gresham, can you tell me why you were at the museum on the night of Saturday the third of April?'

'I was invited,' he began quietly, 'the Kristiansen Foundation made a generous donation to the History Department at King's. His collection houses some of the earliest recorded artefacts of civilisation.'

The detective made a note on the file. Marshall knew it would mean nothing, she used the same technique in her interviews, it made the interviewee feel like they were being listened to.

'And you came alone?'

He glanced at her out of the corner of his eye. 'Yes. Although there were a number of colleagues attending. They will vouch for me.'

She nodded. 'They have. They say you left the party at six-thirty.'

Gresham looked a little confused. 'Yes, around then.'

'Why?'

He sighed, sitting forward in his chair. 'I went up to see the Dendra Zodiac. It was on loan from the Louvre.'

'CCTV shows you entering the Egyptian Gallery at six-forty-five then the power went out. Can you remember what happened next?'

The professor rubbed his hands through his hair. 'It was dark. There was a strange smell. I used the torch on my phone and saw someone in a mask. Then I must have passed out.'

The detective looked up from her files. 'A mask?'

Gresham nodded. 'Of an Egyptian god. All of the catering staff were wearing them that night. It was the Jackal — Anubis.'

She wrote it down.

Marshall bit her tongue. It was the first time Gresham had mentioned a mask.

'And can you describe the strange smell?' Novak continued.

He shook his head. 'Not easily, it was sickly sweet, like game.'

'Like meat?'

'Well-hung meat,' he corrected her.

The smell of a dead body, thought Marshall.

'And you don't remember anything else?'

Gresham paused, his head bowing slightly as he tried to recall any other details. Marshall wondered if he'd forgotten about the taste — the clear sign that he'd been drugged.

He closed his eyes, his tongue wetting his dry lips. 'When I came around, there was a taste, a metallic taste in my mouth.'

The DS nodded. 'The paramedic said you were showing signs of drug use.'

Gresham opened his eyes. 'What kind?'

Novak shrugged. 'We're still waiting for the tox report.'

'Do you know who was murdered?' asked Marshall unable to stop herself.

'That's not something I can disclose at the moment.'

They don't know, Marshall realised, struggling to keep her mouth shut. *She should be asking about what he saw before he went to see the mummies. Did he see anything strange?*

It was hard to be a spectator in someone else's interview.

'Thank you for coming in,' the officer said closing the file and standing up. 'We just need to take a DNA swab and then you're free to go.'

'What happens now?' Gresham asked as they walked out into Agar Street.

'Why didn't you mention the mask before?' she replied, ignoring his question.

He looked confused. 'I only just remembered it.'

'Is there anything else?'

The professor shook his head. 'I could do with a drink.'

Marshall checked her phone. There were several messages, one from Biggs telling her he'd found the phone.

'Sorry, I've got to go.'

Gresham nodded. 'Duty calls.'

20

BYTECODE

Wood Street Police Station. Wednesday, 7th April. 17:00

Biggs squinted at the thousands of lines of code scrolling over Frazer's screen trying to ignore the slightly stale unwashed smell emanating from the Head of Cybercrime's t-shirt. The guy was a brilliant software engineer, but not so great on personal hygiene.

'So this is the byte code?' he asked, having taken a programming course in his last year at university, he was reasonably sure that was what they were looking at.

Frazer nodded wisely. 'I've Jailbroken the phone, so we can get to the Java source code. Only problem now is that the files are encrypted five ways from Sunday.' He picked up the phone case, which he'd taken apart to get to the motherboard. 'This is military grade hardware, black ops shit. Whoever sold it to them wiped the OS and installed some modded version of EncroChat. Which thanks to Operation Eternal we now have all the keys for.'

Biggs knew that the Met had broken a major phone network that used modified smartphones to encrypt communications between members of organised crime gangs. Over a hundred and seventy arrests were made and thirteen million pounds recovered, as well as Class A drugs and firearms.

Tapping on the keyboard of another PC, three screens flickered to life. Each one was running a separate program that generated hundreds of random codes per second. It looked like something out of 'The Matrix'.

'Just got to let these beauties work their magic until we get something that resembles the English language.'

Biggs took the case from him. 'Any idea which country this came from?'

Frazer sucked air through his teeth. 'At first I thought it was Russian. The FSB love this kind of shit, but the board's got a US Snapdragon 810 processor, which can't be exported to the motherland. So my guess is it's either ex-CIA, Mossad or maybe imported from South Africa.

'So basically it's untraceable.'

'Yup.'

'So what do you think we can get from this?'

Sitting back down in his chair, Frazer ran his hand through his shoulder length greasy hair and sighed. 'If we're lucky an offline cache of the messages, maybe a name. People tend to be less paranoid when they think they're using a piece of military tech. They get sloppy. Worst case is that I can get the sites they were using and maybe some account handles or IPs.'

Biggs watched the man's fingers blur across the keyboard as he began to write a new routine. 'Now if you wouldn't mind fucking off, I've got a long night ahead of me.'

· · ·

Marshall appeared as Biggs got back to his desk. She was carrying a brown bag, the delicious aroma of cheeseburgers hitting his nose the moment she opened it.

'Payback for yesterday,' she said, taking out a large packet of fries for herself before handing it to him. She didn't need to say any more, he knew it was a round about way of thanking him for helping out with her sister.

'How's it going with the Collins's phone?'

Biggs shrugged off his jacket and hung it on the back of his chair. Sitting down he began to unwrap the burger. 'Frazer reckons it will take all night.'

She smiled. 'He always says that. Was the mother helpful?'

He laughed, nearly choking on his food. 'You're kidding, right! She could've been the Krays' grandmother.'

Marshall grabbed a couple of ketchups and went back to her own desk.

There was a long list of unopened emails in her mailbox and she scrolled down to the bottom and started with the oldest.

It took ten minutes before she got to the email from Biggs. It was short and to the point:

Doctor Martha Jones, born 1990. Mother: Melissa Jones, Bath.

She glanced up from her screen, Biggs was busy on a call.

Beneath the text was a LinkedIn URL, her cursor hovered over it, Marshall wasn't sure she was ready for this. All the time the mysterious Martha had been a signature at the bottom of a birthday card it hadn't felt real. Now she was about to see her photograph, read about her career. It would become something she would have to deal with, or at least stop pretending that her father wasn't the saint she'd always believed him to be.

She took a deep breath and opened the link.

Doctor Martha Jones. Currently clinical research fellow in Neuroscience at University College London Hospital.

The photograph beside her bio was like looking into a mirror. There was no mistaking that Martha could be her sister, apart from the hair colour, they were almost twins.

There was a short list of positions she'd held at other hospitals, and under education, the Royal High School and Bath University.

The Royal was a private school, one that all her friends from her comprehensive used to take the piss out of. It was where all the entitled, posh kids went. The ones whose parents owned holiday cottages in Wales and flats in Mayfair.

Her career read like the life Marshall was planning to have before Will died, it was like reading about another version of herself.

Biggs finished his call and leaned over the desk.

'Did you hear there's been another murder like the one at the British Museum?' he said, breaking her reverie.

Her eyes snapped away from the laptop. 'Another one?'

Biggs nodded. 'Yeah, in a car park next to Paddington Station. A paramedic apparently. Had all of his organs removed in the back of his own ambulance.'

Closing her laptop, she grabbed her jacket and got up from her desk. 'I need a drink, you coming?'

Biggs eyed the rest of her fries. 'I'm supposed to be going to the gym.'

'Help yourself,' she said, dropping them on his desk.

21

MI6

Island Gardens, Docklands. Thursday 8th April. 06:00

The next morning started with a run.

Marshall woke early, put on her running gear and found her headphones. Taking her usual route alongside the Thames and down into the Greenwich tunnel.

The sun was rising over the trees as she made her way past the Maritime Museum and up into Greenwich Park.

The air was cold and fresh, and the dew on the grass seeped into her shoes. She didn't care, she needed to run to clear her mind. The discovery of a potential sister was clouding her judgement, making it hard to focus on the job.

And she needed the focus.

The last few months had been hard. She still hadn't dealt with the death of her father, not really. It was easier to let other things keep her busy. Staying in the comfortable pattern of the daily grind had kept the dark thoughts at bay — and when they didn't there were always distractions like wine and Gresham.

But now there was Martha, and a past that she never imagined her father could have had.

Wood Green Police Station. 0800

Sitting in his office with his arms crossed, Donovan looked as if he was about to have a heart attack. His cheeks were flushed and one of the veins in his neck was pulsing rapidly beneath his collar. On the opposite side of his desk sat a man in a three-piece suit.

Spook, thought Marshall, closing the door behind her. *Secret Intelligence Service.*

'DI Marshall,' announced Donovan, obviously relieved to have someone else join the meeting. 'This is Section Chief Reed, he seems to think we've been sticking our nose where it's not wanted.'

The man got to his feet. He was in his fifties with dark, hawk-like eyes and a stunning smile. His skin was light brown, potentially of Middle-Eastern descent.

'Pleased to meet you,' Reed greeted her with a firm handshake. 'Malcolm Reed.'

His accent was straight out of a public school, but the way he held himself spoke of the Army — *Sandhurst*, she thought, *and I doubt that's your real name.*

'I assume you're here to discuss Al-Shammari?' she said, releasing his grip.

Reed nodded and sat back down in his chair, casually crossing one leg over the other. 'We've been monitoring him for a while. We believe he's involved in the funding of an Islamic fundamentalist group known as "The Brotherhood" based here in the UK. The question is, what on earth were you doing at his apartment?'

Donovan cleared his throat, but Marshall stepped in before he could answer.

'There was a robbery, a jewellery heist in Hatton Garden. His was one of the more expensive items that was taken.'

The spook frowned. 'What kind of item?'

Marshall hid her surprise at the question, she always assumed MI6 knew everything. 'A red diamond. The jeweller estimated it's worth eight million pounds. He said it once belonged to some Sumerian queen.'

Reed nodded sagely. 'It wouldn't surprise me. Al-Shammari's been trafficking artefacts out of the Middle-East ever since the beginning of the Iraq war.'

'He's smuggling gems?' asked Donovan.

'One of the simplest forms of untraceable currency,' replied Reed. 'An emerald mined by a warlord in northern Afghanistan would be sold to a drug baron who then sells it to a trader in Peshawar who smuggles it into Colombia, where it is mixed with Colombian emeralds and enters the global market. Someone in Canada buying an emerald pendant from a jeweller would never know the gemstone was used to buy weapons for a warlord's militia or launder money for an Afghan drug lord.'

'And you think he's working for ISIS?' Donovan continued. Marshall could see his mind working: if the heist could be linked to a terrorist group, SO15 would jump in and turn the entire case into a circus. The gas they'd used was evidence enough, *but then why would they steal a diamond from a man who was already funding them?*

Reed uncrossed his legs and leaned forward. 'There are active cells in the UK right now. Al-Shammari has been very careful to cover his tracks so far, but this development may be the breakthrough we've been waiting for.'

'We can share what we know so far,' offered Marshall, 'but it isn't much.'

The section chief got to his feet and adjusted his jacket. 'No, thank you. In fact, I would appreciate it if you stopped pursuing him altogether. Leave him to us.'

With that he left.

Donovan raised a wiry eyebrow. 'Well, that's a first. I've never been told to back off by a spook before. Did you find anything at Al-Shammari's place?'

Marshall raised her finger to her lips, watching Reed leave the floor and then went to close the door.

'He's not there, the concierge wasn't that co-operative, but I reckon he hasn't seen him for a while.'

He scratched his grey, three-day-old beard. 'Do you think he was involved in the heist?'

She frowned, her lips twisting into a sneer. 'Not sure. It would seem weird to steal your own gem. Unless this is some kind of insurance scam.'

Donovan shook his head and sighed. 'SO15 is going to have a field day with this.'

Marshall shrugged. 'Not necessarily, I've got nothing solid to go on yet. I take it you're going to formally tell me to steer clear of Al-Shammari?'

Her boss smiled, they'd worked together long enough to know each other's ways. 'Officially, yes. Off the record, do whatever it takes. This is still our case, even if we've got MI6 and Counter Terrorism trying to muscle in on it.'

'Yes Guv.'

22

GATES

Westminster Morgue, London. Thursday 8th April. 15:00

Doctor Gates was in his usual jolly mood when Marshall entered the lab. His headphones clamped on either side of an unruly mane of hair, humming along to some random seventies prog rock while he removed various parts of a corpse's internal organs and placed them onto silver trays.

'Marshall,' he growled, looking up from the body over his spectacles. 'Wondered when you would make an appearance.'

She handed him a coffee, which he sniffed appreciatively and placed beside Collins's liver without a second thought.

'Have they recovered the head yet?' he asked, pulling off his headphones and letting them rest around his neck.

She walked around the other side of the table to face him. 'No, they've got a team searching the sewers, but it's probably in the Thames by now.'

Gates grimaced. 'Eels can do terrible damage to a body.'

Marshall shuddered at the thought of hundreds of black snakes devouring the man's face and changed the subject. 'What did they use on him?'

The pathologist held up the stump of an arm, showing a cleanly sliced section through it. 'By the serrations on the ulna and radius, I would say it was an angle grinder, it's actually a very efficient amputation tool. Would have been through it in seconds.'

'And is that what killed him?'

He chuckled to himself and laid the arm back down on the table. 'No, that's the ironic thing, he actually died of a heart attack, which was rather unfortunate in the middle of a job.' Gates picked up one of the man's lungs. 'Looking at the state of his lungs and liver, I would say he was a sixty-a-day man, with a penchant for whisky chasers with breakfast.'

No one had considered the fact that Collins might have died of natural causes, leaving the rest of the crew with a body to dispose of. What was more interesting to Marshall was how they did it.

'Don't you think it's a bit too similar to the victim at the museum?' she asked, trying to imagine the chaos his sudden death would have caused. The rest of his crew had seconds to decide what to do with the body.

Gates waggled his head from side-to-side. 'Similar amputation, although not the same weapon. The victim at the museum was cut between the joints, with a sharp knife, not a power tool. And his organs were removed,' he added, dropping the lung back onto a metal tray.

'I heard they've found another victim in Paddington?'

He picked up his coffee, his whiskers collecting foam as he slurped it loudly.

'News travels fast,' he said, nodding towards a body

sitting on the next mortuary table. It was covered with a cloth.

Marshall put down her coffee and covered her nose with her hand before lifting the sheet. She'd lost more than one lunch to the smell of a corpse.

The headless body was in its fifties, fine grey hair covered the chest. The pallid skin showing signs of lividity on the backs of the arms.

'Do you know who he was?' she asked, looking at the Y-shaped incision across the torso.

'A paramedic. Stirling told me he was responding to a call near Westbourne Green.'

Stirling, Marshall thought, *we're long overdue a conversation about that transfer request.*

If Gresham was right about Alexandra Hope's murder in 2018, this would make three victims with the same MO. She knew she should report it to the DCI, but he would take it as a sign she was interested in working with him, which she was trying to convince herself she wasn't — not when moving to the Met meant leaving Donovan and the team in the middle of a case.

'How many times have you seen victims with hands, head and feet removed?' Marshall asked.

Gates frowned, putting down his coffee and scratching his beard. 'Other than these two? Not in a long while. Generally they're either whole or in pieces, mostly for easy storage. Removing the main sources of identification is a very specific form of maiming.'

Marshall replaced the sheet and came back to Collins's headless torso. His tattoos now distorted by the incisions

Gates was making into his chest. 'They didn't know about these,' she said pointing at them.

'No, he was fully clothed, and they were probably rushing. Obliterating his identity was their only way to keep the rest of them safe.'

'Seems too much of a coincidence, don't you think?' she said quietly to herself. 'Three beheadings in one week.'

'Hmm?' said Gates, nonchalantly picking up a bone saw and running his finger along the man's sternum.

Marshall shook her head. 'Nothing. I'll see you later.'

23

THE CALL

Thursday 8th April. 17:00

'DI Marshall,' DCI Stirling's voice sounded harsher down the phone. 'How can I help you?'

'You went behind my back,' she began, slightly confused by the fact that he recognised her number. 'Donovan thinks I instigated the transfer request.'

He laughed. 'I simply saw an opportunity. One that I think would benefit both of us.'

Arrogant twat, she thought, biting her lip to stop herself saying it out loud. 'You should have asked me first.'

'And what would you have said? It's easier to beg for forgiveness than permission.'

There was no doubt she would have been interested, but that wasn't the point. He was a maverick DCI looking to recruit talent. Marshall knew his Charing Cross team were notorious for their high-profile cases, there was no other squad in London that came close to their arrest record.

'That's not the point. I need to know I can trust you.'

'Do you? Isn't it more about your ego? Admit it, you're

wasted at City, a big fish in a small pond. I know you've thought about it. Once you've had a case like the Alchemist, you can't go back. It's like heroin, you need that thrill. Tell me you don't think about it every night, in the dark.'

So what if I do, you weren't there. You didn't see what I saw.

'I'm not looking for some kind of glory. I just want to do a good job,' she snapped, trying to work out why she was having to justify herself to him.

'As do we all. So why are you calling me?'

She took a deep, calming breath, letting the anger drain away.

'I've found something. Another murder that matches the MO of your latest victims, but it's from 2018.'

The line went silent. Marshall could hear the cogs grinding as he processed the information.

'You're sure?'

'Victim was left in pretty much the same state. I think he's done it before.'

'Send me the details and I'll take a look. And Marshall, if you're right, then it really is time for you to jump ship.'

She ended the call and opened her emails. Scrolling down until she found the article that Gresham had forwarded to her, she pasted it into a new message to Stirling. There was a slight pang of guilt at the fact she was taking the credit for his find.

This was a perfect opportunity to tell Stirling to back off. To state categorically that she wasn't interested in his offer — just send over the information and walk away, but part of her couldn't deny she was far more interested in the murders than the diamond robbery.

He was wrong, it wasn't like heroin, it didn't give her a high. Her mind loved the intricacies of a homicide, like a jigsaw puzzle with no picture. She could feel she was using more of her mental capacity, triggering parts that would otherwise lie dormant.

Not only was it more challenging, it made her feel like she was actually making a difference.

Her thumb hovered over the send key, re-reading the message, it was brief and non-committal.

Please find attached details of Alexandra Hope case from 2018. SIO was Catherine Dobson, case number 89200-102.

She sent it.

24

DINNER

The Athenaeum, London. Thursday, 8th April. 19:20

'He said what?' Gresham said, half-choking on his wine.

They were seated in the Morning Room of his private club in Pall Mall, its golden walls shimmering in the candle-light and casting shadows over the gilt-framed portraits of its famous, if long-dead members.

The room was filled with the great and good of London society. Actors and authors sat in deep conversations beside politicians and scientists. Marshall recognised some of them, others Gresham had to remind her of their names — she'd never felt more out of place.

'He said I was a big fish in a small pond. That a case like the Alchemist was addictive, like heroin.' She rubbed her arm instinctively, feeling the ridges of the newly healed scars beneath the fabric of her sleeve. There weren't many nights when she didn't dream of the cuts he'd made into her skin. The doctor said they would fade eventually. If they didn't, she was thinking about getting a tattoo.

Gresham shrugged, putting down his glass. 'I suppose a traumatic event like that would change your perspective.'

It wasn't the reaction Marshall was expecting. Stirling was being an arrogant twat and she was looking for some kind of emotional support, not a cool academic response.

'Doesn't it bother you that he's trying to poach me?'

The professor narrowed his eyes. 'He's a senior police officer who recognises your talent. Why would it bother me? Surely the Met has more to offer you than City?'

For a second, Marshall was lost for words. She couldn't explain how wrong it was, nor did she feel that she should have to. She felt an overpowering sense of loyalty to her team, even if Donovan thought it was a good move for her, she couldn't imagine leaving them, especially in the middle of a case.

But it was more than that, there was something about Stirling that made her feel uneasy, his self-assurance was unsettling, she felt threatened by it, as if he would judge her and find her wanting.

She'd done some digging on him and found he had quite a reputation, not just for closing cases, but the turnover of staff on his team was higher than most other squads. Some officers left the force after a stint on his crew.

I'm a good detective. She repeated to herself. *It's just imposter syndrome.*

'You wouldn't understand,' she said, avoiding the deeper reasons. Gresham wasn't a copper, he didn't know what leaving your team was like. People she'd worked with for the last five years, day in day out, ones whom she trusted with her life. They were more than friends, they were family.

It suddenly struck her, that she'd never met any of his friends, just a few associates from the faculty.

He smiled, a knowing glint in his eyes. 'Because I'm not

one of you? I don't think we're that different. My work involves as much deductive reasoning as yours. What did he think of my work on Alexandra Hope?'

It was her turn to choke on her wine. 'He's following it up, but that's not the point. You can't seriously compare your sheltered life of academia with mine. Just because you rode shotgun on one case, doesn't make you Sherlock Holmes. You've no idea what it's like.' She held up a finger to silence his protest. 'The hardest part of your day is marking essays, mine is asking a mother to identify the body of her son. I work crazy hours, you clock off at four — and then swan around in places like this!'

She waved her hand around the room, suddenly noticing that the other members were staring at them. Marshall stood up. 'I don't even know why I agreed to come here. This isn't me. I don't do posh. I'd rather be in some grimy old pub on Watling Street. Do you realise you ordered a bottle of wine that cost more than my shoes?'

Gresham stared at her blankly.

She left before he had a chance to answer.

25

MOTHER

Chiswick, London. Friday, 9th April. 09:20

Her mother was waiting for Marshall on the driveway with her coat and suitcases, like a child being evacuated during the war.

Marshall was late, the pool car she'd reserved had a flat tyre and the duty sergeant took a painfully long time pulling strings to find her a replacement.

'Sorry mum,' she said, getting out of the car. 'I had some problems with the car. You should've waited indoors.'

Her mother shrugged, looking back at her old house. 'Nothing left in there to sit on,' she said, 'and too many memories.'

She was moving back to be nearer her sister, who owned a farm on the outskirts of Midsomer Norton near Bath.

The removal guys were busy loading up the last of the boxes, which would be shipped down over the weekend, ready for her mother to move in the following Monday. Marshall was taking her down to her sister's house on Sunday. It meant she would be staying at her flat on Saturday, which was all the motivation Marshall needed to clear out the spare room and unpack the last of her things.

Her mother was a very house proud woman, something that Marshall had never quite understood, nor really felt the need to emulate. Now she was coming to stay, she wanted to show her that she could look after herself.

Marshall gave her a hug and grabbed a suitcase in each hand. 'Why don't you get in the car and I'll go and sort out the keys and stuff.'

Her mother nodded, clearly relieved to have her daughter take over. 'There's an envelope on the shelf for their beer money.'

With her bags deposited in the boot, Marshall left her mother in the passenger seat and went into the house.

There were two bunches of keys hanging on hooks by the coat stand. She took her own set out to hang beside them and noticed that her father's set still had the small medallion attached to the ring. She bought it for him one summer in New Quay. It was silver, with a Welsh Dragon embossed on one side.

Holding it between her fingers, she could feel the years of wear it had taken, sitting in his pocket with the keys. There was something comforting about knowing he'd carried it with him all that time.

Hot tears welled up in her eyes as she slipped it from the keyring and put it on her own.

Marshall found the beer money in a large brown envelope on the shelf above the fireplace. It was stuffed with ten pound notes, *that's going to buy a hell of a lot of beer* she thought handing over to one of the removal team. It was bribery of the oldest kind, but it was worth it to ensure that her stuff was treated with care.

Standing at the front door, she looked back down the hall. The house was never her home, but over the last seventeen years she'd come to think of it as theirs. It was where her father spent his last days and Marshall always assumed they'd been happy here, but since finding the birthday card she wasn't so sure.

Their reasons for moving up from Bath were supposed to be nearer to her, or so they told her at the time.

What if there was another reason? she asked herself, *what if it was because of something dad did?*

Walking back out to the car, she rubbed the dragon disc with her thumb. He called it his lucky charm when she gave it to him, and it seemed to be, he'd never lost it once in all those years. Marshall wished she could use it now — to go back in time and ask him.

Somehow Marshall needed to get through the next few days without telling her about Martha, and it wasn't going to be easy. Her mother had an innate sense for when her daughter was hiding something.

26

BATH

Midsomer Norton. Sunday, 11th April. 12:30

The drive down to Bath on the Sunday was like a game of twenty questions, mostly about Gresham. Her mum was intrigued by the professor, wanting to know more about his family, and the usual kind of motherly concerns about his psychological profile. She never held the political leanings of Marshall's father, who would have given his daughter the third degree about his wealth, she just wanted to make sure he wasn't a serial killer.

Her questions made Marshall think about what she was actually doing with him and the answers didn't come easy, if at all. Which made her more uncomfortable than discussing her sex life with her mum.

After an hour she gave up and an awkward silence descended as she stared out of the window, occasionally making random comments about other people's driving.

Marshall knew she was thinking about her dad, that somehow it felt like she was leaving him behind.

.   .   .

Her mum's sister was older and had lost her husband a few years before. They owned a farm near Midsomer Norton, and her mother had bought a small bungalow nearby. Marshall's Uncle George had dealt with the sale of the old house, and her aunt had found the property for her sister. It was all pretty painless, until they were pulling into the long drive up to her aunt's house, and Marshall realised how much she was going to miss having her mum around.

'I'm only down the M4,' she joked when she first told her daughter about her plans.

'It's a two hour drive mum, and you don't like motorways.'

'I'll get the coach.'

She'd tried to talk her out of it, but there was no changing her mind.

After her dad died, Marshall spent most weekends with her mother, taking care of her shopping and bills had become a regular part of her routine.

Her aunt was waiting on the porch when they pulled up. She was a white-haired, rounder version of her sister, with a personality that would light up the dullest day.

She insisted that Marshall stay for dinner and drive back on Monday. Marshall reluctantly agreed, she was already feeling bad about not being able to take the time off to help her unpack.

After she deposited her mum's suitcases in the spare room, she made her excuses and went to visit Will's grave.

The gravestone sat in a far corner of Haycombe Cemetery on the outskirts of Bath. It was seventeen years since the funeral and this was the first time she'd been back to see him.

Not that he was really there, but it was something that she'd promised herself to do the next time she came back to Bath.

Will was her first and possibly only true love. A clever, witty guy with a passion for life that she'd never really experienced since.

He'd been killed in a fight outside a bar in Bath. His parents never forgave her for it. Will had been protecting her from a drunk who was trying to rape her, and it had escalated badly.

Freshly cut flowers sat in a vase in front of the marble slab, a symbol of his parent's devotion to their son.

He would have hated it, Marshall thought, *the way they've wasted their lives grieving over him.*

The inscription was even worse, straight out of a funeral directors list of banal epitaphs. 'Beloved William, a beautiful soul taken before his time.'

She nearly laughed wondering what he would have chosen. 'Damn it's dark down here...'

There were still times when she wondered what it would be like if he hadn't died. Whether they would still be friends. What would he think of her life? Of her choices of men.

'You'd tell me to dump him wouldn't you?' she asked the grey slab.

You deserve to be happy, he'd told her once, and she was, blissfully happy then, wrapped in his arms.

'I think you set the bar too high Will,' she whispered,

kneeling down beside the grave. There were tears on her cheeks.

'Did I mention I might have a sister?' she added, wiping them away and laying a rose on the ground in front of the stone. 'I've no idea what dad was up to but .'

27

SO15

Wood Street Police Station. Monday, 12th April. 08:00

The Monday morning briefing was a welcome relief after a weekend spent in the company of her mother and her indomitable aunt.

The mood in the office was grim, Donovan walked out of his office like a condemned man. Marshall had driven back from Bath early that morning. She'd switched her phone off after Gresham started persistently texting her and hadn't had a chance to catch up on her emails, but it was clear from his expression that something was very wrong.

'So,' Donovan began with a deep sigh, 'the Super is putting together a joint task force with SO15. We've been asked to provide support, share everything we have so far.'

There was a collective groan from the room — everyone knew that Counter Terrorism didn't like playing second fiddle. Once they joined an investigation they expected to lead it.

'I know, I know,' he continued, waving his hands to quiet them down. 'We're going to have to suck it up. This is going to turn into a shit show and we're going to be dragged along. Just make sure everything's filed tight and tidy. I don't want them thinking we can't run our own case.' Donovan's steely glare caught Marshall's eye. 'A word in my office, DI Marshall.'

She followed him like a scolded child.

He motioned her towards an empty chair and sat down heavily in his own. 'Tell me you've got some good news on Collins's phone.'

Marshall wished she had better news, she could see how desperately he needed something. 'Sorry Guv, we've got nothing. Frazer's still working on it. To be honest I don't think he's been home.'

'I know the feeling,' he said, rubbing his hand over the stubble on his chin. He looked and smelled like he hadn't been home for days. The bags under his eyes carrying more weight than usual.

The old man crossed his arms over his chest and leaned back in his chair. 'I've been thinking about that offer Stirling made you.'

'I haven't,' she lied.

He tilted his head and frowned. 'You may want to rethink that. I've just heard that the SO15 lead on this is going to be Commander Davidson.'

That was a name Marshall hadn't heard in a long time.

Alex Davidson was a bastard. They'd worked together four years ago on the London Bridge attack. His nickname was 'Teflon', because nothing ever stuck to him. When the internal investigation found inconsistencies in their reports, he tried to throw her under the bus. She'd nearly lost her job because of him.

'I can handle Davidson,' she said through gritted teeth.

Donovan took a bottle of pills out of a drawer. 'I'm sure you could,' he said, wrestling with the child-proof cap. 'But I think this is one battle you don't need to fight.'

'Is that an order?'

He popped two pills into his mouth and washed them down with the dregs of a cold coffee. 'Marshall I've known you long enough to realise I can't make you do anything you don't want to do. So, treat this as advice from an old bugger who has been there. You're a good copper, Christ probably the best I've seen in years, but you don't ingratiate yourself with the top brass. They're so tied up in politics and risk management they just see you as a liability. Davidson has golden bollocks, untouchable, you won't win if you have to go up against him again.'

She crossed her arms, feeling the anger rising. 'So you're kicking me out?'

He shook his head. 'It's a secondment, a temporary transfer until this one blows over. DCI Stirling is a good man, even if he's a bit of a maverick, you can learn a lot from him.'

Marshall bit her lip. She couldn't deny that she was dreading the idea of working with Davidson again, and usually wouldn't think twice about avoiding it, but Stirling was going to be a hard man to impress, and if she screwed this up, it might have long-lasting repercussions on her career.

'Do I have a choice?'

Donovan paused, his wiry eyebrows arching as he pondered her options. 'Well, I suppose you could take some leave. God knows you've earned it after that last case.'

Marshall shook her head, that was the last thing she

wanted. The job was the only thing keeping her sane. 'No Guv, I'll do it.'

Opening another of his desk drawers, the DCI pulled out a form and slid it across the desk. Marshall saw that he'd already filled it out. 'Good, sign here.'

Picking up a pen, she laughed, a little surprised by his tenacity.

'When do I start?'

'Friday, Baxter will organise a drink for Wednesday night to make it official. I know the gang will want to give you a decent send off.'

Marshall cringed at the thought of having to explain her reasons for the transfer to the entire team. They all had highly-tuned bullshit detectors, and a sudden transfer to the Met smelled bad no matter how you pitched it.

'It's okay, I'll tell them you've been requested,' he assured her, seeing the concern in her eyes. 'Not your decision.'

For some reason, Donovan had always been able to read her — since day one. He was without doubt the best boss she'd ever had. She was going to miss him most of all.

'You okay?' she asked, nodding to the pills.

He grunted. 'Blood pressure, the doc wants me to lose a stone or preferably two and quit the booze.'

'Sounds like good advice,' she teased, knowing that he would do neither.

He laughed, dropping the pills back into his drawer. 'If I ever need your medical opinion DI Marshall, I'll ask for it. Until then, kindly fuck off.'

'Yes boss.'

28

TUESDAY

Wood Street Police Station. Tuesday, 13th April. 08:30

After the conversation with Donovan, Marshall spent the rest of Monday writing up her notes, filing reports and generally tying up loose ends.

Biggs was off that day, so it wasn't until Tuesday that she got the chance to speak to him personally, but thanks to the office grapevine, he'd already heard the news.

'You're leaving us then?' he said, handing her a cup of coffee and looking like someone had run over his dog.

'It's not like it's forever,' she replied, trying to make light of it while dumping a pile of reports on his desk. 'Going away present.'

He tried to smile, but failed.

She picked up her coffee. 'Do you want me to take you through it?'

Biggs's eyes lit up. 'I was hoping you were going to say that.'

. . .

They went over to the large whiteboard that Baxter had set up. He'd pinned up a large map of Hatton Garden with post-it notes on all the key sites. Surrounding the map were grainy CCTV photographs of the men DS Devlin spotted, all wearing hard hats or hoods, red lines connecting them to different locations.

Beneath it were the crime scene photos from the vault and the abandoned shop.

'So what do we know so far?' Marshall asked, sitting on one of the desks and folding her arms.

Biggs stared at the board while scratching the back of his head.

'We know there were at least two crews, of between four or five men. One of which was Gary Collins, who we think was recruited in a chat room.'

'Who had a military-grade encrypted phone.'

'Did you get anywhere with the drilling equipment?'

She pulled out a file and handed it to him. 'It was all specialist, but not that hard to get hold of — especially second hand. The serial numbers were unreadable and forensics couldn't find anything useful.'

'What about the food?'

'The filet o' fish? They found DNA, but there's no match on the database.'

Biggs shrugged. 'So our only lead on the crew is Collins's phone.'

Marshall nodded. 'If Frazer can hack into it, you should get at least some of his contacts. If not the leader.'

'If he can hack into it,' Biggs said, rolling up his sleeves.

'He will,' she reassured him.

Turning his attention to the photographs of the vault, Biggs continued. 'So what bothers me, is why spend days secretly breaking through a two-metre thick wall if you're going to trip all of the alarms when you flood the basement, and then send a second team in to take out the security guards with some kind of chemical weapon. Doesn't make sense.'

'I think they panicked when Collins had the heart attack. The second team was only there if things went wrong. If everything had gone to plan we wouldn't have known about it until after the bank holiday weekend and they would be long gone.'

'Bit extreme though, going in with poisonous gas?'

'Collins's brother said they were a foreign crew — towel-heads as he put it. Maybe look into recent visa applications and foreign nationals travelling from Iraq, Syria and the Middle East. Whoever wanted these stones was willing to use some nasty characters.'

Biggs scribbled down a note.

'How are the security guards by the way?'

'One died, the other, Barzani is still critical but they think he may pull through.'

So it's murder now, she thought. Although the maiming of Collins's corpse was a terrible thing to do to a body, it wasn't officially a killing. That would please Davidson no end, having at least one fatality made it so much easier to sanction lethal force.

'And obviously we're not looking into Al-Shammari.'

Biggs smirked. 'No, of course not.'

Donovan wandered out of his office and came over to join them.

'Handing over?' he asked, folding his arms and leaning against the desk next to Marshall.

'Yes, Guv,' replied Marshall. 'Just want to make sure I've covered everything.'

His mouth tightened into a thin white line. 'You heard about the security guard, Dachenko?'

She nodded. 'So it's a murder case now.'

The colour rose in his cheeks. 'It's a fucking mess is what it is.'

29

THE SEND OFF

Hawksmoor, Basinghall Street, Guildhall. Wednesday, 14th April. 18:30

The private dining room at the Hawksmoor was packed with the team when Marshall arrived. Its narrow, wood-panelled room looked more like it belonged on the Titanic.

'Hey boss,' said Biggs, handing her a drink after the waiter had taken her coat.

'This is a bit fancy,' she replied, taking in the surroundings.

'Apparently Baxter knows the manager and got the place for half price.'

She spied Donovan holding court at the other end of the room, *telling stories of his early days no doubt*. Marshall had heard them all, as had most of the team, but to the newer members he was something of a living legend. *Who I am kidding? We all still love his stories.*

.   .   .

The long table was already cluttered with empty glasses and the volume of chatter told her they'd been at it for a couple of hours already.

She'd taken her time getting there, mainly because it was the last place she wanted to be. This was her team and leaving them felt like abandonment. There were pitifully few others in her life that she considered to be friends. Apart from her best mate Anj, virtually everyone else was connected to work somehow.

When she left Bath to join the force, she'd walked out on her old life. Will's death had broken her. The grief was hard enough to bear, but the hostility from his parents, who blamed her publicly, turned everyone against her — all of their friends walked away, everyone except Anj.

I wish you were here now honey, you'd know what to do, what to say.

'Ah there you are!' bellowed Donovan, making his way through the crowd. 'The woman of the hour!'

Marshall raised her glass, and the DCI tapped his whisky tumbler against it. His face was flushed, the veins in his nose turning purple.

'Ladies and gentleman, a little bit of hush,' he shouted over their heads, waiting for them all to turn towards him. ' Before we all get so drunk we can't remember why we came. It falls to me to say a few words about DI Marshall.'

'I can think of a few,' joked Devlin.

Donovan scowled at him, waiting for their laughter to fade before continuing. 'I've had the pleasure of working with her for over five years now. And it's fair to say we've had some interesting times together, good and bad.'

He turned towards her, and she felt the colour rising in her cheeks as she became the centre of attention.

'In my book there are only two kinds of coppers: Thief-takers and penpushers. You either care about catching the bad guys or your laddering up your case win ratios. The force has enough of the latter, but real coppers, like Marshall are hard to find. Whatever the job throws at her, and Christ knows it tried its level best recently, she takes it on the chin — no complaints, no exceptions. You lot will have your own personal stories about working with her, but I will never forget her first day.'

He took a long sip of whisky and put his hand on her shoulder.

'She was straight out of uniform, ten years as a bobby and suddenly she's dropped into one of the worst years for terrorist attacks since 2005. First Manchester, then Westminster and on the third of June, 2017 — London Bridge. What a mad fucking day that was, and she was one of the first on the scene.'

Marshall's memory of that day was still something of a blur. Three terrorists drove a van into pedestrians on London Bridge, then crashed into the central reservation and went on a killing spree around Borough Market. Eleven people died that day, as well as countless injuries. She'd arrived just after they hit the Boro Bistro Pub, and helped get over a hundred members of the public into the Thameside Inn before going back to witness the three men get shot by firearms officers.

Which is where her version of events differed to that of Commander Davidson.

The men were wearing fake bomb vests, water bottles gaffer-taped under their jackets. Protocol dictated that they should be shot before they had the chance to detonate, but a civilian was caught in the crossfire, and questions were raised about whether all necessary precautions were taken.

.   .   .

Donovan raised his glass and the others followed suit.

'To DI Marshall, don't get too comfortable over there, the City needs coppers like you.'

Everyone repeated the toast.

'Speech!' Baxter called out from the back and others took up the call, banging their glasses on the table.

This was the moment Marshall had been dreading.

The room quietened as she waved to them to stop.

'Thanks Guv, I don't think there's anyone who deserves to be called a thieftaker more than you.'

Everyone clapped, nodding in agreement.

'I fucking hate leaving you guys. I couldn't have asked for a better team to work with, apart from maybe Devlin.' Everybody laughed. 'But you're all treating this like some kind of wake, it's not like I'm leaving for good. It's just a secondment. I'll be back here before you know it. So can we stop crying into our beers and get on with some serious drinking?'

They all seemed to agree with that sentiment.

It was late when Marshall got back from the pub, but she was too wired to go to sleep.

Taking a bottle of wine from the fridge, she sat down on the sofa and poured herself a large glass.

It had been a good night, even if Devlin had made a pass at her. Donovan's speech had reminded her how far she'd come in the last five years and as the team had slowly drifted away over the course of the evening it had ended with her, Biggs and the DCI drinking whisky and listening to him talk about the Nilsen case.

Listening to him tell it, she knew she'd made the right decision, no one cared about how many fraud cases she solved, and even the diamond robbery would sink slowly into obscurity, but the Alchemist was already the stuff of legend within the force. She was proud of the fact that she'd been the one to solve it, bringing down one of the most corrupt peers in UK politics.

Lord Pullman was serving ten years for his part in the murder of Elizabeth Fabell, a man who thought money could solve everything.

She knew that Stirling's team would give her more opportunity to prove what she was capable of, assuming she didn't screw it up.

Taking a drink, she opened her laptop — it was time to deal with the other problem in her life.

She'd got Martha's email address from the UCLH website and had been toying with the idea of sending her a message for the last few days.

Dear Martha, she started typing a new email.

My name is Philippa Marshall. It seems you may have known my father. I'm terribly sorry to have to inform you that he died six months ago after suffering a series of strokes brought on by a tumour.

Who the fuck are you?

And why are you sending my dad birthday cards?

Yours sincerely,

His daughter

Marshall giggled, reading it out aloud as she sipped her wine.

Deleting the first attempt, she started again.

Martha,

My name is Philippa Marshall, we appear to have the same dad. Who knew?

Well, obviously you did, because you sent him a birthday card to our address.

Would be good to hear your side of the story sometime.

Fancy a drink?

Pip.

She held down the delete key, watching the words disappear in chunks.

Taking a deep breath, she closed her eyes and tried to focus her drunken thoughts. *What do I say to a sister I never knew I had?*

Hi,

I wish I known you when I was younger, you and I could have played together.

Except you went to a posh school and I didn't, and now you're a doctor and I'm a copper.

Did my dad have an affair with your mum? Well, obviously he did, but why?

Why?

That's all I want to know. It's like a part of my life's just got rewritten and I don't know how to deal with it. The past is supposed to be fixed isn't it? How am I supposed to remember him now?

Sometimes I think I should just forget about it and move on.

But, you're still there, a living reminder of my father's unfaithfulness.

Not that it's your fault of course, nor is it mine.

So why do I feel so bad about it?

Why do I hate you?

Marshall stopped typing and wiped the tears from her cheeks. She closed the laptop and picked up her glass, draining the last of the wine from it.

Her phone lit up, it was a text from Biggs.

'Don't drink any more, and definitely don't message anyone.'

There were a series of emojis at the end, illustrating the dangers of drunk texting.

She laughed picking up the bottle walking back to the fridge. 'Going to miss you buddy.'

30

ANJ

'Hey stranger you okay?' Anj's voice sounded remarkably clear considering she was on the other side of the world.

'Yeah,' replied Marshall, pushing herself up in the bed. It was early, at least it felt like morning from the amount of daylight that was filtering through the half-closed curtains.

'Sorry, I've only just got your message. Sounds like you're having a hard time?'

Her head was pounding. Putting the phone on speaker, she reached for a glass of water and a packet of ibuprofen.

'It's been a weird couple of weeks.'

'So, you've got a new job?'

'Kind of, it's only temporary, they want me to help out on a case.'

'But it's the Met right? And they asked for you specifically — that's got to be good?'

Anj always saw the positive side of any situation, and although the hangover was pretty intense, Marshall could remember most of the evening, especially Donovan's speech. It still gave her a warm glow inside when she thought about it.

Thieftaker.

'Yeah, it's great. Just wish I didn't feel like I was leaving my team in the lurch.'

Anj laughed. 'They're big boys, I think they'll be fine. Now tell me about the case.'

When Stirling heard that she'd accepted the transfer, he immediately emailed Marshall the crime scene report on the British Museum. It was a horrific murder, but her best friend loved anything CSI and made her go over the gruesome details more than once.

'Sounds like a fucking psycho,' she concluded. 'With a god complex.'

'Gresham thinks he found another victim, back in 2018.'

'And how is the lovely professor? Still got that twinkle?'

If there was one thing she could rely on with Anj, it was her obsession with other people's sex lives. Marshall had a theory that it was because she spent so long hopping from one country to the next that she never had time for a serious relationship of her own.

'We're having a break,' she said, trying to avoid the subject. 'I need to focus on the new job.'

'Really? I thought he sounded like a keeper.'

'There's something else.'

'Someone else — God you're a dark horse aren't you?'

Marshall sighed. 'No, not like that. I think I've got a sister.'

The line went quiet for a few seconds, which was unusual for Anj. She generally spoke first and engaged her brain afterwards.

'A sister?'

Marshall told her about the birthday card, and what Biggs found on the internet. Sending Anj the link to Martha's bio in the chat.

'Fuck, she looks exactly like you.'

'Dad had some pretty dominant genes I guess.'

'He had an affair?' asked Anj, unable to hide the doubt in her voice. 'When?'

'Before I was born. When he was working at the University.'

'Damn! Do you think your mum knows?'

'I don't know, and I can't ask her.'

'No, that would be weird. What are you going to do?'

That was a good question, she vaguely remembered trying to write an email to Martha the night before, but there was nothing in her sent items.

'I'm going to meet her. See what she has to say.'

Anj went quiet. 'I've got to go, but look I don't think he would have cheated on your mum, he wasn't that kind of bloke.'

Marshall took some comfort from that, Anj was a very good judge of character, especially when it came to men.

She put the phone down and got out of bed, the drugs were already kicking in as she walked into the bathroom.

31

SCD-99-01

Charing Cross Police Station. Friday, 16th April. 08:00

C haring Cross had once been a hospital and from the outside, Marshall thought it had some of the Victorian charm of Wood Street, but once she got inside it was a very different experience.

The station was a hive of activity, PCSOs were milling about by the front desk, waiting for the shift change. She tapped in using the PIN number Stirling had sent her and made her way to the fourth floor.

The Special Projects Investigation Unit were a department of thirty hand-picked detectives. They generally focused on gang-related, contract killings, drugs and firearms cases. Under DCI Stirling's command, his team had never lost a case; it was an impressive track record considering the types of underworld criminals they were up against.

Their location was not widely known to the public, and there were no obvious signs on the door as she pushed it open, just the rather oblique designation. 'SCD-99-01'.

The office was empty, but she could hear someone talking and followed the sound until she came to the door signposted 'Briefing Room'.

'DI Marshall,' Stirling's loud voice announced as she entered the room, every head turning towards her. 'Sorry, I should have mentioned that briefings begin at seven-thirty sharp.'

Great start, thought Marshall, smiling awkwardly and sitting down in the nearest empty chair.

'Everyone, this is Detective Inspector Philippa Marshall, she's joining us from City. Most of you will remember her from the Alchemist case last December. I hope you'll all make her welcome. Marshall, we were just discussing the Hope case,' he continued, tapping on the digital display, 'do you want to give us an overview of what you've found?'

'Sure,' she said getting to her feet. *Drop me in the deep end.*

Although the team was mostly men, Marshall noted there were more women than at City. Regardless of gender, they all wore hard, unforgiving expressions, this wasn't the kind of crew that gave second chances to nervous newbies. *So much for the warm welcome,* she thought.

The screen displayed the files that Gresham had uncovered online, and Marshall felt a little guilty presenting his work after their last conversation, but she didn't let it show.

Remember you found the Alchemist, she reminded herself, *and saved Samantha Pullman.* It was the biggest case in the City for years and the media went to town on it. They would have all read about how she solved the ritualistic murders and put a peer of the realm behind bars, although she couldn't tell if they were impressed from their impassive faces.

Marshall took a deep breath and walked over to the screen.

'Alexandra Hope was a primary school teacher who was found in a disused garage in Deptford, in 2018. The SIO at the time believed it was a botched organ-harvesting by a Ukrainian syndicate.' She zoomed in on some of the crime scene photographs. It showed Alexandra's body laid out on cardboard on the garage floor. Her clothes torn away, exposing the terrible damage to her chest and abdomen.

'As you can see the wounding is very similar to that of the recent victims.'

'Any idea why they chose her?' asked one of the female officers, she recognised her as the one who'd interviewed Gresham.

Marshall shook her head. 'DCI Dobson concluded that it was a random killing, wrong place, wrong time.'

The woman's eyes tightened slightly, as if unsatisfied by her answer.

'I'm going to speak to the SIO this weekend,' Marshall added.

There was a subtle nod of approval.

'Right, good,' said Stirling, clapping his hands. 'DS Novak, you're babysitting DI Marshall, bring her up to speed on the investigation and sort her out a desk.'

The woman nodded and got up from her desk. 'Yes boss.'

Stirling turned back to Marshall while the room rapidly emptied. 'Good to have you on board, I assume you're happy to start by looking into the Hope case?'

'Yes, sir.'

His eyes studied her intensely for a moment. 'Excellent, we're a tight team, but we've got a few more resources than you're used to at City. Don't be afraid to ask, we tend to get what we need.'

DS Novak waited with arms crossed until he finished and then stepped forward.

'Come with me,' she said with the hint of a smile. 'I'll show you around.'

Once DS Novak had shown Marshall where the toilets and the canteen were located, she left her with the office manager, a female equivalent of Baxter in every way. The woman took her through a mind-numbing hour of station regulations that seemed like it was never going to end.

The office was sub-divided into five small desk units, each enclave staffed with suited thirty-somethings studiously scrolling through screens of data. Marshall felt as if she were standing in the middle of one of Gresham's study sessions, there was no banter, it was like sitting in a library.

She sat down at a desk beside Novak, who was halfway through a bacon roll.

Marshall's stomach growled, reminding her that she'd been too nervous to contemplate breakfast earlier and was now beginning to regret the double-shot latte she'd grabbed on the way in. There was a breakfast bar in her bag, but it would have to wait.

'So tell me about Hope,' said Novak, putting down her roll and wiping her mouth with the back of her hand. Her tone was professional, but her brown eyes were kind. The DS was in her late twenties with dark black hair pulled back in a tight pony-tail, high cheek bones and a sharp nose, part of her Polish heritage Marshall guessed.

Marshall took out her laptop. It was an older model than Novak's and the boot up took forever.

'Like I said in the briefing. She was a teacher, at St. Martins Primary School in Bermondsey. The last known sighting of her was on June 12th, 2018.'

'So how did you find her?' asked Novak bluntly.

It was the obvious question, one that she would have asked herself had the situation been reversed. Marshall hesitated, conscious of the fact that it wasn't her discovery. These first few days were all about creating a good impression, and Novak was bound to be asked what the new girl was like by the others. The last thing Marshall needed was everyone finding out it wasn't her idea.

'The case I was working over at City had a death with a similar MO. Doctor Gates told me about your victims and I did some digging.'

It was half true, which made it a slightly less painful lie to tell.

Novak seemed impressed. The harsh line of her mouth twisting slightly upwards.

'I like Gates. He's a bit dziki — crazy.'

Marshall smiled. 'Eccentric, but in a good way,' she agreed, wondering what Gates would make of them bonding over him.

'So where do you want to start?' asked Novak as Marshall's laptop finally sprang to life.

'Can you give me an update on the case so far?' she said, logging into the network.

Novak gave her the short version: The victim at the museum was still unidentified, although CCTV did show that one of the caterers had left the party twenty minutes before the murder. The staff were all wearing Egyptian masks as part of the event. Which would explain why Gresham had seen Anubis. All of the guests were questioned as well as the waiters, but everyone was accounted for, except for the professor.

'Your boyfriend was in the wrong place at the wrong time.'

'He's not my boyfriend. So this waiter that disappeared, did any of the others give you a description of him?'

Novak pulled out her notebook. 'Medium height, medium build. Brown eyes, blue eyes, clean-shaven, beard, mid-thirties, mid-forties — usual kind of useless shit. They're zero-contract workers, they don't ask too many questions and do their best to fade into the background. Most of them never worked for the company before, they were all hired through a temp agency.'

Marshall opened the case file and scrolled down the crime scene report.

'Says the power went off at seven. Do we know why?'

Novak nodded. 'They found devices attached to the switchgear in the basement. Cut through the cables for that particular room.'

'So it was planned.'

She raised her eyebrows. 'Oh yes. The tech team says it was a custom build. They've not seen anything like it. It took out the cameras and the lights at exactly 6:50.'

Marshall opened one of the photographs of the victim and zoomed in. The body of the man was covered in blood, as were the inner walls of the sarcophagus.

'Seems a lot of trouble to go to kill a man.'

'Depends what he did.'

That was an interesting way of looking at it, thought Marshall, remembering that in this team most of the victims were usually not innocent themselves.

She clicked through the photos until she came to the severed neck. 'Have they found the head?'

Novak shrugged. 'No, nor the hands. It's going to make it pretty tricky to find out who he was.'

'Not like the paramedic?' asked Marshall, moving to the second case file.

'No, Michael Avery was found in the back of an ambulance in a multi-storey in Paddington. No head, but left his wallet. Stirling is handling that one. The body was a complete mess apparently.'

Novak took another bite of her bacon roll, totally unfazed by the gruesome images.

'I know, I've seen him,' Marshall agreed, suddenly not feeling very hungry. 'Have they managed to get anything from CCTV?'

'They're checking, but it's not looking hopeful. The systems are old and not well maintained.'

'Maybe we should go and take a look.'

The DS frowned. 'The boss put us on the Hope case, he's not going to like us going off piste.'

Marshall came around to Novak and lowered her voice. 'I'm seeing the SIO on Sunday, and waiting for Hope's parents to confirm a date next week. There's not much more I can do other than read her case notes and I've been through them ten times already.'

Her phone pinged, it was an email.

'It's from Gates. I sent him the details from Hope's autopsy, he says to drop by when I have time.'

Novak smiled, throwing the rest of her roll in the bin and grabbing her coat. 'Sounds like we have a plan.'

32

GATES

Westminster Morgue, London. Friday, 16th April. 15:00

The pathologist was nowhere to be seen when Marshall and Novak entered his office. It made a refreshing change from the mortuary, although by the size of the stack of unopened mail on his desk, the man spent very little time in here. In fact, the room hardly looked as if it was used at all. There was little in the way of personal effects: a coat stand in one corner had two old raincoats and a broken umbrella. Two chairs held cardboard boxes filled with what looked like expenses claims.

'Coming!' Gates's voice echoed down the corridor outside.

'Dziki,' Novak said with a half-smile, sipping her coffee.

He arrived at the door balancing a plate of biscuits on his briefcase like a tray. Marshall hardly recognised him, he looked too smart, wearing a dark blue, pinstripe three-piece suit. Even his hair and beard were combed into a reasonable semblance of neatness.

'Been in court,' he explained, setting down the plate on the only empty space on the desk. 'The Cromwell Road case. Nasty business. Help yourself by the way.'

They both nodded. The Cromwell Road case was on the front page of all the papers. A father of three murdered by his next-door neighbour after an argument over a shared driveway. The neighbour tried to put the police off the scent by accusing another man, who'd killed himself in custody. It was a truly tragic case involving three kids under ten.

'You said to drop by?' Marshall reminded him, handing him his usual coffee.

'Yes, I thought you'd like to hear what I found on the Hope case,' he continued, looking quizzically at Novak. 'Are you two working on this now?'

'I've been transferred,' explained Marshall. 'To Charing Cross.'

Gates grunted approvingly, he picked up a bourbon cream and waved it at her. 'So Donovan let you go play in the big league, did he?'

'Kind of. It's just a secondment. So, what did you find?' Marshall asked before he asked any more uncomfortable questions.

He took off his jacket and hung it on the coat stand. She could see he'd been sweating profusely through his shirt as he shifted the boxes of expenses from the chairs.

'Sorry, don't get many visitors.' He said, sitting down and putting on his reading glasses.

'The pathologist who performed the autopsy was Jack Makepiece, who was a good friend of mine, died last year of bowel cancer.' He selected one of the manila folders and opened it. 'Anyway, I looked through the full report, including the transcripts of his examination. As you suspected there are a great deal of similarities between the recent victims and Ms Hope. Both had their lungs, intestines, liver and stomach removed and placed in containers around the body in a ritualistic way. Although at the time, the SIO thought the murderer had been disturbed in the middle of harvesting them.'

He leaned forward and handed Marshall a photograph of Hope's body in the derelict garage. The same image of her pale white corpse laid out on cardboard, the skin of her chest and abdomen peeled back like a fruit.

'There was one interesting thing, not of the murder itself, but in something Makepiece found in the removed intestine.'

The next image he handed her, showed a small white ruler placed next to a distended piece of grey tissue with a deflated white sac attached to one side.

Gates read directly from the notes. 'On closer examination of the victim, there was evidence of previous wounding from a major trauma. The kind one only usually associates with war zones, more specifically an Improvised Explosive Device or IED. There was severe scarring in the duodenum which would seem to indicate the shrapnel having been present in the body for some time.'

'What kind of shrapnel?' asked Novak, studying the image over Marshall's shoulder.

Gates shrugged. 'Hard to say, the body can internalise all manner of foreign objects as long as they're not affecting any vital systems — and they don't cause infection of course.'

'How long ago did this happen?' Marshall said, handing him back the photo.

The doctor sat back in his chair and took off his spectacles. 'By the look of the thickness of the scar tissue, I would hazard it at approximately fifteen years, but whoever eventually removed the shrapnel managed to do so without puncturing the inner wall of the intestine, a tricky operation.'

33

KRISTIANSEN

Battersea Park. Saturday 17th April. 13:00

Anubis stood in the shadows of the trees watching Martin Kristiansen as he sat patiently on a bench beside the Peace Pagoda.

Kristiansen's appearance was hardly flamboyant, certainly not that of a self-made billionaire — just an old man feeding the birds, the strands of his thinning white hair like wisps of flax teased out in the wind. He wore a thick Burberry coat, a pair of leather gloves and a scarf to stave off the cold.

Keeping his distance, Anubis studied the tourists and dog-walkers. Spotting two bodyguards a few yards away. Their body language would have fooled most, but not him. They were good, probably ex-Russian FSB, trained to melt into the background.

Kristiansen was expecting Al-Shammari to make the exchange in person after failing to show at the Museum.

Anubis had found his number in Shammari's burner phone and arranged the meeting, pretending to be the Saudi dealer.

The response had been short and direct.

Eight million dollars. Saturday, Pagoda, Battersea Park. 1300hrs.

The sum was far greater than Al-Shammari had told them the gems were worth.

Anubis cursed the *Nassaab, the swindler.*

His brother had met the dealer during the war and convinced him they could trust the man. In a cafe in Tikrit, Al-Shammari had explained that such rare stones would be hard to move, that only a specialist collector would be interested, but it had all been a lie.

The *swindler* had kept them in the dark about the deal with Kristiansen. Making them believe he was getting them a good deal. The Norwegian businessman was obsessed with the ancient past. According to the internet, the old man was richer than a Pharaoh, and a compulsive collector; his private library of ancient manuscripts, which included many priceless artefacts like the Dead Sea scrolls, and was second only to the Museum of Cairo.

But his most prized possessions was the necklace of Puabi, an ancient Queen of Sumeria. The British Museum's website told of how the jewels that once adorned the golden treasure had been lost for millennia. Now, thanks to Kristiansen, the half-restored necklace was the centrepiece of their latest exhibition.

Anubis had judged the *swindler*, weighing his heart and finding it wanting. Now Al-Shammari would be making his way to Ammit, the devourer of souls.

And he would take his place, like *Set* the shapeshifter, god of chaos.

He felt in his pocket for the stone, his fingers wrapping around the calf-skin pouch, still stained with the blood of the woman who carried the jewel for so long.

It took nearly three years to track down Naomi Fox, and the elusive fourth diamond nearly cost him his life. The army medic had fought bravely.

Eight million dollars. He reminded himself, walking across the grass towards the old man, wondering what his brother would say now. *Not so stupid now, am I Akhuya?*

34

DOBSON

C atherine Dobson lived alone in a small cottage in the Surrey Hills.

Most coppers retired after twenty-five to thirty years of service and moved away, usually to the coast, or in some cases Spain or Portugal. Warmer climates and generous final salary pensions made the Iberian Peninsula a popular destination amongst retiring officers — how long they enjoyed it was another matter.

Marshall was still nine years away from retirement, but she had no intention of waiting that long. She only needed to look at Donovan to know that those last few years could seriously shorten your life expectancy.

According to her file, Dobson served twenty-six years before the Hope case, and it was her last. After two years of failing to solve it, the DCI opted for early retirement and headed for the hills, quite literally.

Novak drove them through the winding country lanes, waxing lyrical about how she'd cycled the same route during the previous year's Ride London event. Marshall did her best to appear interested, but cycling was the sporting equivalent of watching paint dry to her and changed the subject once they passed Leatherhead.

'What's Stirling like?' Marshall asked as Novak turned the BMW X5 towards Dorking.

The DS shrugged, her hands slipping around the wheel. 'He's a good boss. Doesn't take any shit. '

Marshall was hoping for more.

'So, how did you end up on his team?'

The woman chuckled. 'Do you know about the Wingates?'

'No.'

'A rich family. Had this huge mansion out in Suffolk near Framlingham. Daddy is something in the city, or so the locals thought. Turns out he's an accountant for the Ukrainian Mafia, and the Albanians hired a hit man to take him out. Except that they don't just take out the father, they kill everybody: wife, three kids and the house-keeper. I was a DC at Ipswich CID, first to the scene, and I notice that the family car is missing. Anyway Stirling turns up with a couple of the specialists and I happen to mention to him that I can't find the Range Rover. Next thing you know they've put out an APB on them and boom. Case solved.'

'And you don't regret the move?'

'Have you ever been to Ipswich?'

Marshall shook her head. 'No.'

'You're not missing much.'

Dropping into a lower gear, she overtook a slow moving truck. Her driving was only marginally better than Biggs's and Marshall made a mental note to drive back.

Novak continued. 'So no need to ask how you got his

attention. The Alchemist was one seriously crazy bastard. Is it true he carved the password on your arm?'

Marshall pulled back the sleeve of her jacket to reveal the last four characters. It had quickly become part of the mythology surrounding the case, and it wasn't something she liked to show off, but there was something about Novak that made her want to prove herself. From the widening of the DS's eyes she could tell it had done the job.

'Fuck,' Novak said, her gaze flicking between the road ahead and Marshall's scars. 'Did it hurt?'

'Not at the time, I was pumped full of drugs.'

'And he killed himself?'

The image of Fabell falling into the raging storm waters flashed into her mind, the hilt of the dagger embedded in his chest.

'Sacrificed himself,' she corrected the DS. 'He believed he was giving his life for a greater cause.'

The satnav pinged, breaking the moment: 'Turn left in two hundred yards and you will have reached your destination.'

Dobson's home was an idyllic, thatched cottage at the end of a wooded lane. Her garden was fenced off from the forest with neatly trimmed holly hedges and clematis-covered trellises.

Dogs barked as they got out of the car. They sounded big and vicious, but reaching the gate, they turned out to be two very eager chocolate Labradors.

'Ben, Sam. Heel!' A woman's voice commanded and the two dogs moved to their owner's side without another word.

Catherine Dobson was dressed in green combat trousers and walking boots, her Lowe Alpine coat unzipped to reveal layers of fleece and a North Face t-shirt. She looked every bit the rambler, and nothing like the photo in her file. Her hair was long and white, and the stern, ice-maiden stare was gone. She was patting the dogs heads and feeding them treats as Marshall walked through the gate.

'You'll have to excuse them, they love strangers. We don't get a lot of company out here.'

One of the labs trotted over and began to lick Marshall's hand.

Marshall always wanted a dog, ever since she could remember, but no one seemed to want to take her seriously. Not her parents, not James and now there was no one at home to look after it even if she did.

'Would you like some tea?' asked Dobson, hanging up the dog leads on a hook by the door as she went in.

'Coffee?' Novak replied.

Dobson laughed. 'It's decaf I'm afraid, haven't drunk caffeine since I left the force. Slept like a baby ever since.'

They sat in her kitchen, which was straight out of Country Life magazine. An Aga sat squat and warm against one wall. Herbs hung from the oak beams, and jars of spices lined the shelves. There were silver-framed photos of children between the willow pattern plates on the Welsh dresser.

Dobson filled the kettle and placed it on the stove. 'So how can I help you DI Marshall?'

Marshall took the files from her bag. 'I wanted to ask you about your last case, Alexandra Hope.'

The woman sighed and picked up the report. 'Not my favourite case. One of the most random murders I've ever had to work on. No motive, no witnesses, no leads. I started with twenty detectives on it, two years later it was just me and a DC, and a pile of nothing.'

The kettle whistled and she put the notes down and picked it up off the Aga with a tea towel.

'Why did you think it might be organ-harvesting?' Novak asked while Dobson poured the boiling water into the teapot.

'Because there were a spate of abductions back in 2018. The victims were drugged and woke up a day later minus a kidney. We managed to trace it to a Ukrainian gang in East London. They were involved in all manner of human trafficking, mostly young women, until they realised that there was a more profitable market for organs.'

She brought the tray of cups over to the table.

'Not that we could ever pin Alexandra on them, but it was the best we could come up with at the time.'

'How did you identify her?'

Dobson paused for a moment, her eyes glazing over slightly as she poured the tea.

'There were metal plates in her legs from an accident, we were able to identify them from medical records.'

Marshall looked up from her notes. 'Do you know what kind of accident?'

The old DCI sat down in her chair and handed each of them a cup. 'She was a translator working for the British Embassy in Iraq, got caught in a bomb attack. Have you spoken to her parents?'

Marshall shook her head. 'They're next on my list.'

'Why all of the interest in this old case? Do you have a new lead?'

Novak tasted the coffee and grimaced. 'New information.'

The old woman's eyes widened slightly. 'There's been another murder?'

Old detectives never really retired, their keen instincts dulled a little perhaps, but Marshall could see there was still a hunger to solve this one. 'There have been two in the last week. Same MO as Alexandra.'

'Do you have the files?' Dobson asked eagerly, then tempered herself. 'Sorry, old habits. I know you can't discuss an active case.'

Novak glanced at Marshall, raising one pencil sharp eyebrow. Marshall nodded and the DS took them out of her bag and handed them to Dobson.

'Was there anything else unusual about the murder?'

Dobson was distracted by the crime scene photos, her eyes welling with tears as she studied the detail. 'Sorry,' she replied, wiping them away with her sleeve. 'It's ... it's just that I can't believe it's happening again.'

'It's not your fault,' Marshall tried to reassure her, it was obvious that she was still carrying the guilt.

'Yes, it is,' Dobson responded sharply, putting the photos down on the table. 'If I'd caught the bastard back then, these people would still be alive!'

'Is there anything else you can tell us? Something that wasn't in the notes?' asked Novak.

It was a good question, most SIOs formed instincts about their cases, something that could only be developed from thousands of hours of poring over the witness statements and reports.

Dobson went to one of her kitchen drawers and pulled out an old packet of cigarettes.

'Haven't touched these since I retired,' she said, lighting one and taking a long deep draw on it. 'We had a ton of theories. That's what happens when you have an absence of evidence, you chase down the tiniest lead. Give too much credence to the craziest ideas.'

'Did any of them make it onto the short list?' asked Marshall, while Novak gathered up the files and put them back in her bag.

'There was the drug that was used to sedate her.'

'Which was?'

'Midazolam. It's not your run-of-the-mill anaesthetic, and the dosing was spot on. For a while we thought the killer may have been a surgeon, or at least an anaesthesiologist.'

35

DUGGIE

Charing Cross Police Station. Monday, 19th April. 06:30

Marshall got in early.

Stepping through the doors, the station felt busier than usual. One of the patrols hung around the custody desk while the custody sergeant tried to process a very drunk and very smelly homeless man. Everyone was keeping him at arm's length.

'Fuck off!' the man shouted, waving his hands at them. 'I know my rights!' he slurred, swaying from one side to the other.

The arresting officers looked tired and bored. Marshall knew the feeling, there was nothing worse than a D&D just before you were due to clock off.

'If you would just give us your name sir,' the sergeant asked calmly for the third time.

The homeless man laughed, tucking one leg behind himself. 'Long John Silver.' Then proceeded to fall over.

Marshall recognised the laugh, it was a manic cackle that was rather unique.

'Duggie?' she said, walking up to the desk.

The man struggled back to his feet, his wild eyes trying hard to focus on her face and failing. 'What's that?'

She turned to the desk sergeant. 'This is Douglas Bentley, better known as Old Duggie. He usually sleeps in Steelyard Passage under Cannon Street Station.'

The sergeant looked relieved, as did the two officers flanking the homeless man.

'What are you doing over here Duggie?' she asked, raising her voice and speaking slowly as though to a deaf grandparent.

The old man grinned, his ruined teeth creating a broken line of yellow tombstones between his thin, papery lips. 'Got lucky.' The overpowering smell of vodka on his breath could have taken the paint off a door.

She knew that meant he scored enough cash to buy booze, but that didn't explain what he was doing out of the City.

'What brings you out this way?'

Duggie shrugged. 'Bad dreams.'

She stepped back, the smell of urine and booze making her feel sick. 'Take care of yourself Duggie.'

The reason Marshall arrived so early was not to impress DCI Stirling, but because Dobson's comment about the sedative triggered something deep in her brain and she'd woken up at four o'clock in the morning — her head buzzing with unanswered questions.

Knowing it was pointless trying to go back to sleep, she switched on the bedside lamp and opened up the case file. One of the many upsides to sleeping alone was it meant she could spread her notes over the bed and not worry about waking anybody up in the middle of the night.

Or be kept awake by his snoring.

Opening the pathology report on the museum victim, Marshall flicked past the gory details of his injuries, searching for the blood tests so she could compare them with those of Hope and Avery.

They all showed differing levels of Midazolam in their toxicology reports.

'Finally a fucking lead,' she whispered to the darkened room. This was an expert, someone who knew exactly how much to inject into his victim. In his usual fastidious way, Gates noted that the levels in the blood were carefully measured to match their body weight as per the BNF guidelines, ensuring that the victims would have been aware of what was happening to them, but feel no pain.

What a way to die.

Sitting at her desk, watching the team drift into the office over the next hour, Marshall began to realise what an eclectic bunch they were.

Their bios made for interesting reading. Every one of them had proved themselves in a high profile case, standing out from their peers in various ways. Most were in their late twenties or early thirties, picked from very diverse areas of the force. She could see how Stirling selected them for their specialisations: cybercrime sat next to vice, while drugs was getting a coffee with an ex member of the Flying Squad. She scrolled through their details, memorising their names, until finally, she came to Stirling's file. It was an unusual career: transferring in from the Military Police, he'd climbed the ranks quickly, working his way through the departments until they gave him a squad of his own.

They were all rockstars in their own fields.

Which begged the question: *what was she doing here?* The Alchemist had been an unusual case, but it wasn't what Special Projects were into. It was hard to ignore the nagging feeling of being an imposter; to forget the fact that Gresham was the one who discovered the link to Alexandra Hope, and remind herself that she'd found a possible link between the other victims.

'DI Marshall,' said Stirling, stopping at her desk. 'How was Dobson?'

He was wearing leathers and carrying a helmet as if he'd just got off a motorbike.

'Sir!' said Marshall, closing the laptop and hoping he hadn't seen that she was stalking him. 'She was good. I've got a potential lead.'

Stirling held up his gloved hand to stop her: 'Save it for the briefing.' And made his way to his office.

Ten minutes later, Novak arrived and sat down opposite Marshall holding two cups of coffee. 'Didn't know how you took it,' she said, pulling a fistful of sugar and milk pods from her jacket pocket.

'Thanks,' said Marshall.

'Any progress on the anaesthetic?'

Marshall nodded. 'Midazolam, it's a sedative, they use it in lethal injections. All of the victims had traces of it in their system.'

Novak whistled through her teeth. 'So it could be the same guy?'

'Yeah.'

'Okay team!' Stirling announced across the room, clapping his hands. 'Let's hear the updates! Marshall you're on first.'

The others rose from their seats and made their way to the briefing room.

Marshall grabbed her coffee and took a long drink.

'Nervous?' asked Novak, her mouth twisting into a quizzical smile.

'No,' sighed Marshall, putting on her jacket and picking up her computer. 'Okay, maybe a little.'

The briefing room was already packed by the time she arrived. She could feel every pair of eyes trained on her as she walked towards the large display. Alexandra Hope's face was staring innocently out from the screen as Stirling stepped aside to let her take control.

'Okay,' she began, opening up her laptop. 'So we spoke to the SIO on the Hope case yesterday and it turns out that Alexandra was drugged with the same type of anaesthetic as the latest victims, a benzodiazepine called Midazolam.'

'Don't they use that as part of the lethal injection cocktail?' asked one of the others.

Marshall nodded, impressed by how sharp this team were — she'd had to look it up. 'Exactly. Injected directly into the bloodstream it would knock someone out in under two minutes. The victim would be paralysed for hours.'

'So we're looking for someone with medical training?' asked Stirling.

'Potentially, yes.' Marshall plugging her PC into the screen. Hope's image was replaced by the toxicology reports for the other victims. 'As you can see, they all had differing levels of Midazolam in their bloodstream. The killer knew what they were doing, measured the dose to match their body weight.'

'Anaesthetist?'

Marshall shrugged. 'Potentially, but you can find the dosing guidelines on the internet. They were given enough to paralyse but not kill. There would have been no pain, but they would have known what was happening to them.'

'Sick fuck,' said one of the others.

Stirling stepped in. 'It's pretty clear they all have the same MO. What we don't know is what the killer has been up to for the last three years and why he's suddenly killed twice in the last week.'

Marshall closed her laptop and sat down.

'Is there any way to trace access to this drug?' he asked.

She shook her head. 'It's restricted, but there's no reason it couldn't be bought on the dark web.'

Stirling folded his arms, his expression hardening. 'Well, it's something. Run some checks on the hospitals, see if anyone's reported a missing supply lately.'

He turned towards the rest of the team. 'Bates do we have anything on the museum victim?'

The man who recognised Midazolam as a lethal injection drug stood up. 'No sir, although Doctor Gates is positive that he's of Middle Eastern origin, we're checking with Misper about anyone fitting the victims general description.'

'Nothing on DNA?'

'Nothing.'

Stirling nodded and swiped on the display. The image

changed to Michael Avery. 'Okay, so what do we have on the paramedic? Nicholls, give me some good news.'

Another officer stood up as Bates sat down. She was a woman with short blond hair and sharp, nordic features. 'He was fifty-two, married with three kids. I spoke to Avery's wife yesterday, he'd been a paramedic for the last ten years, before that he worked in aid relief in various disaster zones around the world: East Africa, Congo, Iraq. Quite the hero by all accounts. Although she said he never really spoke about it.'

'Has the other paramedic been able to give us any clues as to who attacked them?'

Nicholls jaw set hard, as though she were clenching her teeth. 'No boss, she's got no memory of the attack.'

'Did they check her bloods?' asked Marshall.

The blonde woman stared at her blankly.

'Midazolam can cause memory loss,' explained Marshall.

'What about the emergency call, do we have it?' asked Stirling.

Nicholls nodded and took out her phone.

'Ambulance service, is the patient breathing?' The recording played back through the phone's speaker.

'I think he's dying,' said a man's voice, filled with panic.

'Can you tell me where you are?' continued the female operator calmly.

'Hallfield Estate. Hurry he's tachycardic. I think he's having a heart attack.'

Stirling held up his hand and Nicholls paused the playback.

'Tachycardic isn't a term most people would use to

describe someone having a heart attack. So I think we can assume he's definitely had some form of medical training.'

'That fits with the drugs he's been using,' agreed Marshall.

Stirling turned to one of the younger men, the only member of the team in jeans. 'Jacobs, see what you can do with the sound, isolate the man's voice and try and get a fix on his accent.'

Jacobs nodded.

'Hamilton, how's the CCTV from the car park looking?'

A tall, bespectacled black man stood and tapped something into his laptop. Grainy video images appeared on the display behind Marshall. After a few seconds, an ambulance drove up to the barrier. The time read 00:35.

'Is that it?' Stirling asked as the vehicle drove out of shot.

Hamilton nodded. 'The ambulance was parked on a floor with only one working camera, so he'd done his homework. This one is used for number plate recognition, so we know what time he got there, but no one came out. The killer must have left on foot — there's no coverage in the south stairwell.'

'Nothing from the street?'

The officer shook his head. 'Still trying to get hold of it.'

Stirling looked frustrated. 'What about the footage from the Hallfield Estate?'

Once again, Hamilton keyed something into his computer and the car park footage was replaced by a row of sixties tenement blocks. They watched as the ambulance arrived on scene, the timestamp read 23:40. Two paramedics got out and walked towards one of the six-storey buildings.

'There are three cameras covering this area of the estate, this is the only one with a half decent view,' noted Hamilton.

He scrubbed through the footage until a dark figure

appeared from the shadows. They were running while carrying someone over their shoulder. The figure threw the body into the back of the ambulance and jumped into the cab.

'Did you manage to enhance it?' asked Stirling, squinting at the image.

Hamilton opened a second window, showing the grainy figure enlarged but with no significant detail.

Stirling titled his head. 'What's he like? Six-foot-two?'

'Analysis says six-one and a hundred and eighty pounds,' replied Hamilton.

'And can run with a man on his back — so he's fit,' added one of the others.

Stirling sighed. 'Okay, anything else I should know?'

There was a general shaking of heads.

'Marshall follow up on the drugs. Hamilton see if you can get anything from the surrounding streets at the NCP. Let's get this fucker before the press get wind of it.'

36

DONOVAN

Charing Cross Police Station. Monday, 19th April. 08:30

Marshall's phone started vibrating the second she walked out of the briefing room. There were three missed calls from Biggs which she hadn't noticed.

'Hey. Not a good time right now,' she answered in a hushed voice.

'I just thought you should know that Donovan's had a heart attack. He's been rushed into The Royal.'

The colour seemed to drain out of the world around her, and she felt an icy knot forming in her stomach. 'I'm on my way.'

The Royal was one of London's oldest hospitals, although you would never know it. The building had been transformed into a twenty-first century, seventeen-storey tower block, its blue-on-blue glass edifice dominating the skyline over Tower Hamlets.

Walking through Accident and Emergency, Marshall thought it seemed unusually quiet, but then it was Monday morning, nothing like the Friday nights she used to spend keeping the drunks under control when she was on the beat.

Flashing her warrant card, she asked the receptionist where Donovan was being treated, a nurse duly showed her into a side ward. One of the perks of being a copper was that you were well cared for by the NHS, *we're all on the same team.*

The DCI looked a hundred years old; his skin grey and pallid like a corpse, propped up in the bed surrounded by machines. There was something unnatural about seeing him without his usual shirt and tie, as if he'd lost his superpowers, the crumpled gown making him small and vulnerable.

His eyelids were closed and his breathing shallow. He looked peaceful and Marshall hesitated at the door, wondering if she should disturb him. The scene reminded her of her father less than four months earlier. Except, when he'd opened his eyes there was hardly any recognition, the stroke having robbed him of his memories.

'Marshall?' Donovan whispered, his eyes blinking open as she sat down bedside the bed.

'Guv,' she replied softly, taking his hand, her eyes stinging with tears. 'How are you?'

He squeezed her fingers. 'You're not going all soft on me now are you?' Muffled by the oxygen mask, his voice sounded hoarse.

She sniffed. 'No Guv. What happened?'

'I got old,' he said with a sigh, pulling the mask away

from his face. 'I keeled over in the middle of a briefing, can you believe it?'

She let go of his hand. 'Because of those pills?'

He shook his head. 'Because of Davidson. The man's bloody useless, he's brought a bunch of his goons in and achieved the square root of fuck all.'

One of the machines pinged, and Donovan gave it a sideways glance. 'Got to watch my blood pressure apparently.'

A nurse appeared at the door and he waved her away. 'I'm fine.'

'Don't you get him excited,' she said, wagging her finger at Marshall.

Donovan waited until she drew back the curtain. 'They're talking about a bypass. Apparently my veins are shot to shit.'

'Arteries,' she corrected him.

'Whatever. Chances are that's me out; too close to retirement to put me back, the union rep is coming around later to discuss my options. I was so close to thirty years, I doubt it will make much difference to the pension.'

They both new that the thought of retiring filled Donovan with dread, he lived for the job, the idea of him sitting around idly tending to his roses was his idea of hell. The boredom would kill him.

'So how's the new job?' he asked, changing the subject.

Marshall shrugged. 'Not bad, they've given me a DS whose like a female version of Biggs, but Polish, so a little more blunt.'

Donovan chuckled. 'The Boy Scout is missing you. Devlin is doing his best to keep him busy, but he's like a puppy waiting for its master to come home. Keeps glancing at the door.'

'Does he?' She'd tried not to think about what Biggs was up to, they had formed quite a bond over the last few years. Novak's abruptness didn't really compare to his boyish charm.

'You any closer to working out who it is?'

Marshall shook her head. 'No, I've got one decent lead, but nothing concrete.'

'You'll find him. You always do,' he reassured her.

'It's a weird case. I can't put my finger on it. The victims have nothing in common, apart from the way they were killed. Even the cold case.'

'Cold case?'

'Back in 2018, he killed a primary school teacher. The SIO at the time thought it was some kind of botched organ harvesting.'

Donovan grimaced, scratching at the cannula holding the drip in his arm. 'And what do you think?'

'I think it's someone with a medical background. They knew what they were doing with the drugs. Measured the doses out perfectly so they don't feel anything, but keeps them conscious while he carves them up.'

'Sounds like a sadistic bastard.'

'I think it's more than that. Gresham says he's recreating an ancient Egyptian ritual — one that they used as part of the mummification process.'

She paused, her eyes catching the displays on the monitors. His heart rate was increasing.

'And?'

'Why the gap? Why three years since the last one?'

He smiled. 'You're assuming he hasn't. There may be other bodies to find. Sounds like you have the means. Now all you need is a motive and an opportunity. Look into the victims lives, there'll be something they've got in common, you just can't see it yet. Do you have a copy of the files?'

Marshall took the case file out of her bag and his eyes lit up, as did the machine beside him.

'Just something for you to look through while you're stuck in here,' she said, with a smile.

37

HOPE'S PARENTS

Highbury New Park, Highbury, London. Tuesday, 20th April. 11:30

Alexandra's parents lived in a five-storey Victorian villa on the end of a terrace in Highbury.

DS Novak whistled as she climbed out of the car. 'Four million easy,' she added, admiring their large house.

Marshall checked the address and walked up the path to the front door.

'What does the father do?' asked Novak while Marshall rang the bell.

'Tax consultant, but the mother has the money. She owns a clothing company.'

Novak looked impressed. 'Good for her.'

A well-dressed older man in a suit opened the door slightly, the chain stopping it from going any further.

'Good morning,' he said, 'DI Marshall?'

They showed their warrant cards. 'This is DS Novak. May we come in?'

Mr Hope nodded, removing the chain and opening the door. He bowed slightly. 'Please.'

The house even smelled expensive. Fresh lilies were arranged in Japanese vases along the hallway as they followed him through to the kitchen.

His wife was sitting at the large oak table with a laptop and numerous pattern samples scattered across it.

'Darling, the police are here.'

She looked up with the same dark eyes that Marshall recognised from Alexandra's photograph, but there was a tightness around her mouth, and lines creased across her brow. *She doesn't trust us,* Marshall thought, *Dobson failed them and nothing was about to change that.*

'What can we do for you?' she asked, taking off her glasses and closing the laptop.

'We wanted to ask about your daughter's accident,' replied Marshall.

Mrs Hope's lip twisted into a snarl. 'Don't you mean her *murder*?'

Her husband winced at her tone, he obviously bore the brunt of his wife's temper. Marshall had seen it before, their shared grief was the only thing keeping them together.

'No, I'm sorry, her report mentioned that she'd suffered a previous injury.'

Alexandra's mother sighed and ran her hand through her long dark hair, there were signs of grey but she appeared to be a lot younger than her husband.

'Please sit down,' said Mr Hope as if suddenly remembering his manners. He waved at the chairs on the other side of the table. 'Would you like some tea?'

They both declined.

'My daughter was a brilliant linguist,' he explained proudly, taking a seat next to his wife. 'She worked for the Foreign Office and was stationed in Iraq in 2001, at the British Embassy.'

'Before the war?' asked Novak.

He nodded. 'Yes.'

'Until she was blown up,' added his wife.

'A car bomb near Tikrit,' explained Mr Hope. 'She was flown to a field hospital near Basra, but unfortunately the damage was too extensive, they were forced to remove her womb. She was our only child.' He took his wife's hand. 'She could never have children.'

Novak scribbled notes as Marshall continued. 'When exactly was this?'

'Twenty-fourth of June 2003,' he repeated instantly.

'What has this got to do with our daughter's murder?' Mrs Hope snapped, getting up from the table and going to the window.

Marshall could sense the tension between them, three years of waiting for some kind of justice had obviously put a massive strain on their relationship. Which made what she had to say even more difficult.

'We're currently investigating another incident.'

Mrs Hope turned towards them, her face flushing as she spoke through gritted teeth. 'He's killed again?'

Novak caught Marshall's eye, as if warning her to tread carefully.

Her husband took off his glasses and buried his face in his hands.

'We can't say at the moment, but there are definite similarities.'

Mrs Hope came back to the table. There was a hint of desperation in her voice when she spoke. 'But you have a new lead, yes? That imbecile Dobson was fucking useless!'

Marshall took out her business card and handed it to Alexandra's mother. 'As soon as I have something for you I'll be in touch.'

She took the card, staring directly into Marshall's eyes. 'You have to catch him, for Alex — she deserves that much at least.'

They both felt a sense of relief when they got back on the street. The tension in the house was palpable, like walking on thin ice.

'Didn't Nicholls say something at the briefing about Avery working in Iraq?' Marshall asked when they got back to the car.

'I think so.'

'Can you check?'

'Sure, do you think they're connected?'

Marshall took her keys out and started the engine. 'My old boss used to say: there's no such thing as a coincidence.'

38

TIKRIT

Charing Cross Police Station. Tuesday 20th April 16:00

Marshall left Novak to look into Avery's past. Strictly speaking it was Stirling's case and she didn't want to tread on any toes.

She wanted to find out more about the Tikrit bombing.

A quick Google search produced a list of articles on the event. They were mostly press reports, none of which named any of the victims, but described how a convoy of civilians and their military escort had been attacked on the road from Mosul to Baghdad.

A bus loaded with barrels of shrapnel was driven at the convoy by a member of the terrorist organisation Jama'at al-Tawhid wal-Jihad, whose leader, Abu Musab al-Zarqawi, claimed responsibility a few days later.

According to a Times article: twenty-two people died and forty-five were seriously wounded, including members of the British embassy and the soldiers who were protecting them.

Marshall made a note of the reporter's name, James Albright, and moved onto the next article.

Half an hour of digging and she'd learned little else. No one was naming any of the victims of the blast, but from the pictures it was clear there were at least a dozen civilians.

An email from Novak appeared in her inbox. The subject line was short and to the point.

Nicholls found this.

Avery's medical records were attached.

Opening the file, Marshall quickly scrolled to the relevant year.

2003 - Major internal injuries, Tikrit IED. Treated at 33 Field Hospital, Camp Coyote, Basra.

Marshall felt a cold chill run down her spine. Michael Avery had been injured in the same attack as Alexandra Hope. She could feel another piece of the puzzle sliding into place.

Opening the autopsy report on the museum victim, she could feel the excitement building as she searched for any mention of a previous injury, but there was nothing. *Catching criminals isn't supposed to be easy,* she heard her old sergeant say, *if it was we'd be out of a job.*

Novak was standing behind her, reading over her shoulder.

'Looks like you found our first solid lead,' she said, sounding mildly impressed.

Marshall arranged the desktop windows so that all three reports were side-by-side. 'Two victims from the same attack, but nothing on the third.'

'Still it's got to be more than a coincidence right? Gates's report says that the body in the museum was of Middle-Eastern descent. This could all be related to Iraq. Maybe it's some kind of terrorist attack?'

'Doesn't feel like a terrorist, feels more personal. What on earth could a forty-year-old primary school teacher have done that was so bad they disembowelled her?'

Novak shrugged. 'She wasn't a teacher back in 2003. Maybe "Translator" was another term for "Spy". I've heard the Taliban do a lot worse to their captives, especially women.'

Marshall didn't look convinced. 'I doubt the Taliban would wait fifteen years to finish her off. And what have they being doing since they killed her? Where's he been hiding for the last three years?'

'Maybe there are more,' suggested Novak.

Scrolling up to the top of Avery's medical records, Marshall made a note of his address in her notebook. 'I think we need to pay the wife a visit. Find out what Avery was doing over in Iraq.'

As she closed her laptop, DCI Stirling came storming in through the doors waving his phone.

'The fucking press have got hold of it!'

Everyone grabbed their phones and opened the news app. "Death at the Museum," was the top story on every feed, with accompanying crime scene photos.

'Who leaked it?' asked Novak.

Stirling glared at Marshall. 'That's the question I'm asking myself.'

'It wasn't me!' Marshall barked back at him.

His eyes narrowed. 'My office now.'

She followed him like a scolded schoolgirl, her face a stoic mask of shame and anger.

. . .

Stirling closed the office door.

'Did you share the case files with your old boss?'

The colour flushed in her cheeks. 'Yes, but he's one of us, he knows better.'

He walked around to the other side of his desk and threw his phone down. 'The press office traced it back to a member of cleaning staff at The Royal.'

'Fuck!'

The DCI looked extremely pissed off. There were only a few times in Marshall's life when she could remember screwing up this badly, this was going to go down as one of the worst. Donovan would blow hot for a few hours, then calm down and move on, but Stirling was notorious for not giving second chances.

Marshall considered telling him about the Iraq connection, but something in his expression stopped her, he wasn't about to listen to a half-baked theory.

'He was offering to help. He's a good copper.'

Stirling scoffed. 'He's a brilliant copper, but still doesn't mean you share intel. Especially with a man who's on a serious amount of medication. You need to decide whose team you're on Marshall, I don't take kindly to divided loyalties.'

'Sorry,' she said quietly. 'It won't happen again.'

'Damn right it won't.'

'You're taking me off the case.'

He nodded. 'I'm putting Nicholls on point. Novak can stay on the Hope case. You can help Hamilton with the CCTV. They've just got the footage back from Bishop's Bridge Road.'

'Okay, sorry boss.'

Better than getting kicked off the team, but only just, she thought walking back out of his office.

39

GRESHAM

King's College, London. Tuesday 20th, April. 18:00

Gresham was finishing a lecture when Marshall walked into the back of the theatre. The room was dark and a medieval illustration of a half-naked woman being roasted over a fire was projected onto the screen behind him.

His head was down, reading from his notes, and she slid onto one of the benches unnoticed.

'You'll find the depiction of witches changes dramatically during the middle-ages. The classic characterisation of Old Mother Shipton, the wizened old crone riding a broomstick, was developed as part of the Catholic Church's attempt to demonise the wise women of the village. One of the earliest examples of mass propaganda.'

Marshall closed her eyes and listened. Letting the deep and sonorous tones of his voice soothe her, wondering how his students managed to stay awake throughout the whole thing.

They hadn't spoken since last Thursday. He'd finally stopped trying to call her by Sunday, leaving a voicemail along the lines of: "Call me when you feel like talking".

She couldn't put her finger on what was so annoying about him. His wealth was obviously an issue, as was the arrogant sense of entitlement. And yet, he was the most intelligent guy she'd met in a long time, in many ways he reminded her of Will. She'd always been drawn to clever men, there was something deeply interesting about them, like abstract art, she liked their complexity, liked the layers.

Gresham was more closed-off than most. Something Marshall enjoyed at the beginning, not wanting to get into another serious relationship. After the split with James, she promised herself she would never go out with another copper, and there was something appealing about an uncomplicated, no-strings affair, especially one that stepped straight out of a millionaire romance novel.

Although now it was beginning to get complicated.

Stupid little things he did were beginning to annoy her, which meant she was starting to care about him. There were strings now, tiny lines of attachment between the two of them and it bothered her that she wanted them. *Why do I need any of it? Why can't I deal with this by myself?*

Over the last few days, the bed felt too empty without him in it. This angered her even more, she didn't want to *need* anybody, didn't want to feel like something was missing from her life.

Except she did, she felt lost.

The most important man in her life had cheated on her. Knowing that there was another child, a sister, that her father had hidden from them, left Marshall spinning like a rudderless boat in the middle of a storm.

Gresham had somehow become the nearest thing she had to a stable relationship and she'd pushed him away, when right now she needed someone to talk to — or rather rant at.

But he was too polite to get into a fight, certainly far more well-mannered than any copper she'd ever dated, and perhaps that was part of the problem; he didn't understand what it was like on the job — he was an outsider, a civilian.

Opening her eyes, Marshall blinked at the sudden brightness of the lights. The demonic slide had been replaced by a list of book titles, the students reading list for summer term.

She waited for everyone to leave before walking down to the front.

'Hello,' he said, his voice still amplified by the clip mic.

'Hi, want to go for a drink?'

Gresham looked genuinely surprised. 'Yes, of course.'

'My treat,' she added before he could suggest somewhere too fancy.

The pub was busy, but they managed to find a small nook at the back.

She bought two pints of IPA, not bothering to ask what he wanted, and before he could complain about the lack of decent wines on the list.

Gresham took the drink without a word and sipped it slowly.

'I'm sorry about the other day,' she began. 'I've had a lot on my mind lately.'

He nodded, his expression softening slightly.

She told him about the birthday card, about Martha Jones and her father's infidelity. He sat and listened without interrupting her. It felt good to share her feelings with someone else. Talking to Biggs had felt more like another case, she'd left all of the emotion out of the conversation. Now she could cry, not that she did, instead she felt the rage unravel like a coiled snake.

And he sat, and drank, and nodded.

'So, do you think I should contact her?' she asked, before taking a long drink of her beer.

He frowned, removing his spectacles as he always did when he thought deeply about something. It was a Clark Kent kind of move, as if he was hiding his superpowers behind his glasses.

'What do you expect her to say?'

She hadn't expected the question and it took her a moment to react.

'I don't know. Sorry, I guess.'

He put his glasses down and took her hand. 'Do you think she wasn't aware that he had another family?'

Marshall sighed. 'I don't know. She's like this ghost. I keep trying to imagine what happened back then, it's driving me crazy.'

'But he stayed with you,' he squeezed her hand. 'She's the one that grew up without a father.'

It was true, he had chosen to stay with them. Marshall hadn't thought about it that way, that no matter what he'd done, her dad made a choice.

'Whatever your father did in his past, perhaps even before you were born. The man had to live with it for the rest of his life, but from what you've told me, he never stopped loving you, never left you.' There was a hint of sadness in his voice, reminding Marshall what Gresham went through growing up.

'I'm being selfish,' she said, letting go of his hand and wiping her eyes.

'No, you're being human. It's a sad day when we finally realise our parents are fallible.'

That was the hardest lesson of all. The memory of her father had become like an ancestral shrine, she'd placed him on some kind of pedestal, perhaps it was part of the grieving process — to forget all of the faults and just hold onto the happy times.

'I think they used to fight a lot. When I was younger,' she said.

Gresham looked surprised. 'He used to hit her?'

'No, he would never, but they would argue like cat and dog.'

She could vaguely remember sitting at the top of the stairs, listening to the shouting. Shivering in her nightdress, burying her head in her teddy to stop them from hearing her sobbing. There was more than one night like that, but they were distant memories, faded and insubstantial.

'Do you know why?' he asked.

Marshall shook her head. 'No, and I can't ask Mum either. She won't have a bad word said about him.'

He nodded. 'De mortuis nil nisi bonum — Don't speak ill of the dead.'

'Exactly. Why do people say that?'

Gresham put his glasses back on. 'It's attributed to Chilon of Sparta, one of the Seven Sages of Greece. I think the general theory is that the dead cannot justify their actions, can't speak for themselves.'

She laughed.

'What?'

'I'm pouring my heart out and you still manage to give me a history lesson.'

He shrugged. 'It's all I know.'

40

CCTV

Her head was still fuzzy from the night before. After the pub, Gresham insisted on taking her for dinner at Rules in Covent Garden — one of the oldest restaurants in London. The food was traditional British fare, and the steak and kidney pie was incredible, as was the wine, and as always – the drunken sex.

Rubbing her temples, Marshall prayed the paracetamol would kick in soon. Fortunately, she could look forward to a gentle start to the day. Analysing CCTV meant sitting in front of a screen for hours, drinking coffee and scrubbing through footage of normal people looking for the one who wasn't.

It was a job that was usually assigned to a lowly DC, but she wasn't about to complain about the demotion. The fact that Stirling hadn't kicked her off the team was a minor miracle, especially after the leak made it onto the six-o-clock news.

It wasn't her favourite part of detective work. She'd always preferred to be out in the field rather than at her desk. The problem with CCTV was that killers generally didn't walk around with a sign around their neck. In fact, most were unlikely to stand out in a crowd at all. They were shy, introverted types who, for ninety-nine per cent of the time, were law-abiding citizens, except for that singular moment when they weren't.

Marshall had dealt with a few murderers in her time, some more dangerous than others. She didn't believe in good and evil, but there were a couple of cases where she'd come close to changing her mind.

Most people died at the hands of someone they know. The number of stranger killings was statistically low, but ironically they were the ones that haunted society, the ones that the media like to go to town on.

Fabell was a man who had wanted justice for his wife, but the press turned him into 'The Alchemist', like some evil super-villain from a movie. His methods were cruel and even sadistic, because he was certifiably insane, but they created a demonic monster haunting the streets of London.

And now she'd given them a new bad guy.

Overnight the story had exploded, the morning headlines were calling him another 'Ripper' and a crowd of reporters were waiting outside the station when she came in this morning.

DC Hamilton sat quietly beside her, studiously poring over the night footage of the streets around Paddington Station. She could tell he was trying his best to avoid mentioning what was going on outside.

'Want another?' he asked suddenly, picking up his coffee cup.

'Yeah thanks,' she replied, handing him her mug.

Caffeine was a necessary fuel for maintaining concentration, even without a hangover. Officers spent so much time in the CCTV suite that the powers-that-be installed a Nespresso filter machine to save them walking down two floors to the canteen.

'Novak said that you had a solid lead,' he said when he returned with two steaming cups.

As icebreakers go it wasn't a bad start, she thought, although she made a mental note to tell Novak to keep quiet about Iraq.

She paused the video and took her coffee. 'We do, but I want to do some more digging before I share it with the boss. I don't think he was going to listen to anything I said yesterday.'

Hamilton shrugged and sat down. 'He's not that bad. His bark is worse than his bite.'

'How long have you been here?' she asked, changing the subject.

'Two years. Before that I was SO15.'

Marshall hadn't expected that, Hamilton didn't look the type. 'Counter Terrorism? Did you ever work with Davidson?'

He shook his head. 'No, I was an analyst at JTAC. Never went out in the field.'

The Joint Terrorism Analysis Centre was based at Thames House on Millbank. It was a collaboration between Counter Terrorism Command, GCHQ and the various divisions of the Secret Service — it was commonly known as Spook Central.

'I bet you had better toys than this to play with,' she said, pointing at the screens.

He laughed. 'I could tell you, but then I'd have to kill you.'

The footage from the hight street was hardly any better than the car park. At midnight on a Tuesday, the foot traffic on Bishop's Bridge Road and Westbourne Terrace was sparse. It should have been simple to pick out a suspect leaving the car park.

But the only pedestrians for the hours after the ambulance entered the NCP were drunk businessmen from the Prince of Wales trying to find their Ubers. After that it was mainly homeless guys raiding bins.

'What if he left a car there earlier?' asked Marshall, opening a folder of NCP files. 'Did anyone drive out later?'

Hamilton turned away from his screen. 'No one came out I checked.'

Closing her eyes, Marshall felt the second dose of caffeine kicking in and her headache starting to clear. She ran through the timeline in her mind, visualising the various locations on a map. *The attack at the Hallfield Estate, the ten minute journey to the NCP, then how long to do that to a body? Twenty, thirty minutes? He couldn't have finished much before 12:45, then what? Where else can he go? Stay there until morning? Too dangerous, the longer you stay the more chance of leaving DNA. The victim was discovered at 05:00.*

She opened her eyes. 'Is there another way out? At the back?'

He shook his head. 'The main lines out of Paddington Station run right behind the building.'

'Are they covered by CCTV?'

'No idea, we'd have to speak to Network Rail. But it's all electrified, I doubt the killer would risk going out that way.'

Marshall turned towards him. 'He's chopped up a body, which means he's covered in blood and he didn't leave in a car. We know he scoped out the car park for blind spots. My guess is he's worked out an escape route that didn't involve too many cameras. How many trains leave Paddington Station after Midnight on a Tuesday?'

Hamilton keyed the search into his PC.

'The last train is 01:34 to Reading.'

'So he waits until that one leaves and makes his way across the tracks. Knowing GWR there were probably engineering works scheduled for that night, so all he needed to do was change into a hi-viz jacket, a hard hat and no one would have blinked an eye.'

She got up from her desk.

'Where are you going?'

'I like to see these places for myself, you can't get a feel for it from a video image. You want to come?'

He looked unsure for a moment. 'I don't normally—'

'Come on,' she insisted, putting on her jacket. 'Let's do some old-fashioned police work.'

41

PADDINGTON

Paddington NCP Car Park. Wednesday 21st, April. 10:30

They followed the NCP manager down to level three.
Walking into the dark, concrete bunker felt more like they were entering a tomb. Marshall shivered at the thought of what had occurred here. Murder scenes were strange places, filled with unanswered questions and echoes of terrible violence.

She spotted the bay where the ambulance would have been parked at the far end. The area was taped off and surrounded by yellow place markers and other detritus left behind by the SOCO team.

Marshall ignored the crime scene and moved further into the dingy space behind it.

'Is there an emergency exit?' she asked, her voice sounding incongruous in the cavernous space.

The manager looked uncomfortable, his eyes sliding away from the ambulance as if it wasn't really there. 'Further back, behind bay thirty.'

'Shouldn't the sign be illuminated?' Hamilton pointed out, walking past the crime scene and taking out a torch.

'For someone who doesn't do field work you came prepared,' observed Marshall.

He swept the torch across the piles of rubbish along the back wall, catching the swift movement of creatures scattering into the shadows. 'Guess I've watched too much CSI.'

Marshall stopped and took out her phone, using its LED to light up the area around her feet. 'What's with the lighting anyway?' she asked the manager.

'The rats,' he replied, keeping his distance. 'They keep eating through the wiring.'

She groaned, stepping over a pile of rubbish. 'Nothing I like better than rats.'

Hamilton found the fire door behind a stack of old cardboard boxes that stank of human faeces.

'You've had uninvited guests,' he added, placing his feet carefully between the bottles of what he assumed was urine.

The manager sighed. 'This isn't a manned facility. They get in from the tracks at night.'

Marshall turned her phone towards him and he raised his hand to stop the light from shining in his eyes. 'They come in from the railway? How?'

'Officially they don't,' he began, 'but off the record, there's an old access path under Westbourne Bridge.'

'Can you show us?' asked Marshall, pointing her torch towards the fire exit that Hamilton was barging open with his shoulder.

The manager grimaced.

'We won't mention the health and safety violations in our report,' she added.

.   .   .

The stairs at the back of the building were littered with empty food packaging and discarded rags. It was slow going as they stepped between the collected rubbish of years of homeless occupation.

'No chance of forensics on this,' she muttered to Hamilton. 'There's too much of everyone else's shit.'

At the top of the stairs was a set of double doors standing slightly ajar, an old shoe was wedged between them, stopping them from closing completely.

Stepping outside, they were immediately engulfed in a cloud of diesel fumes as a locomotive pulled out of the station, the deafening drone of its exhaust drowning out their voices.

Once the carriages had passed, Marshall surveyed the back fence of the property, finding the holes in the wire where the homeless must have cut through.

Hamilton was standing on a crate taking photographs of something with his phone through the barbed wire.

'What've you got?' she asked as he stepped back down.

He showed her the photo, zooming in on a bundle of bloody rags that had been thrown onto the tracks. They were already blackened by passing trains, but it was clear they had once been clothes.

Marshall took out her phone and called Novak.

'Hey, how's the CCTV going?' asked the DS.

'Yeah, okay. Look, can you get them to shut down Paddington Station?'

'Are you fucking kidding? Where are you?'

'At the NCP. We need to get out on the tracks and I don't feel like playing chicken with the trains.'

· · ·

It took an hour to get the confirmation that the power had been shut off.

The railway police turned up, assuming it was a jumper. Stirling arrived ten minutes behind with the forensics team, looking like a bulldog chewing a wasp.

'So, this is you taking a back seat is it?' he asked as they walked over the tracks towards the bundle.

'Well, the CCTV was inconclusive, so I took the initiative.'

The clothes were torn, ripped to shreds by foxes, but the blood soaked rags were clearly fresh and there was enough of the flesh exposed to know that it was a man's head.

While the SOCOs staked out the area and started taking photos, Marshall started walking along the tracks looking for exit points.

It was unusual to see London from this perspective, like a secret passage hidden between the buildings, one that most people hardly noticed on their way in and out of the station. A perfect escape route, especially at night.

Stirling left the SOCO team and came to join her.

'Good work, they've already confirmed it's Avery's head.'

'He probably went out under there,' she said, pointing towards Westbourne Bridge. 'Parked a car on the other side, leads straight out onto the Westway.' She held up her phone to show their location on Google maps.

The DCI nodded and shoved his hands into his pockets. 'I'll get Hamilton to check the CCTV. Traffic have a ton of cameras up there.'

He paused for a second, and then took out a packet of cigarettes and lit one. 'I gave up a few years back,' he said, in answer to her unspoken question. 'But this case put me straight back on them.'

He offered her the packet but Marshall refused.

'Novak tells me you might have a lead. Why didn't you mention it yesterday?'

She took a deep breath, suppressing the pang of anger at Novak. 'Because it doesn't quite fit, it doesn't explain the victim at the museum. I needed more time.'

And the fact that you looked as if you were about to rip my head off.

He took another drag on his cigarette and blew the smoke into the darkening sky. It would rain soon, and the SOCOs would lose precious evidence.

'So, it seems that leak might have actually worked in our favour.'

'How?' she asked, turning toward him, unable to hide the look of surprise.

He avoided her gaze, looking down the track towards the group of white suited men who were hastily trying to erect a tent over the scene. 'Someone's called in, says he knew both Hope and Avery.'

'Have you sent Nicholls to interview him?'

'I was hoping you might want to do it.' That was the nearest she was going to get to an apology.

Marshall nodded, trying not to look too pleased with herself.

42

RAMSVELD

Eight million pounds, Anubis repeated to himself, waiting for the jeweller to finish unlocking his front door. *More than all of the other stones combined.*

When his brother told him about Ramsveld it seemed like the perfect solution. A man who didn't ask too many questions and with the right connections to sell the rare stones without any provenance.

It was only later that he discovered there was a go-between, Al-Shammari — who, with the help of Ramsveld, had cheated him of millions.

Al-Shammari had already been judged, his heart weighed and found wanting.

The door opened and the fat-cheeked Ramsveld blinked in the daylight.

'Who are you? Where is Al-Shammari?' he snapped, looking past the visitor.

The door hit him in the shoulder as it was kicked, spinning him around and onto the floor

'I am Anubis,' he hissed at the floundering fat man, closing the door behind him and pulling out a long-curved dagger. 'I have come to weigh your heart.'

43

FOURTH STONE

Kensington, London. Thursday, 22nd April. 07:00

When Biggs pulled up to the apartment building, Doctor Gates was already packing his cases into the boot of his car.

'You took your time,' he said, pulling off his latex gloves.

The detective pulled out his mobile. 'Bloody phone died,' he explained, leaving out the part about how he'd woken up in some stranger's bed that morning and forgotten to charge it.

'How's the boss?'

Biggs shook his head. 'He's not great. They're talking about a bypass.'

The pathologist nodded, unzipping his Tyvek suit and taking out a crumpled packet of Marlboro reds. 'Ah yes, we're all destined to meet the coronary bypass at some point.'

Gates pulled out a cigarette with his teeth and lit it, blowing out a satisfying cloud of smoke.

'So is it Ramsveld?' asked Biggs, looking up at the apartment building.

'What's left of him.'

Biggs looked confused. 'How long has he been dead?'

'Less than twenty-four hours.'

'And he's already decomposing?'

The doctor coughed. 'Hardly. More like he's been deconstructed. Saw something very similar last week over at Paddington Station. One of Marshall's cases.'

'There's been another one?'

The medical examiner looked surprised. 'You know about the others?'

Biggs nodded. 'I was there when she got the call from the museum.'

Gates dropped the half-finished cigarette and ground it under the heel of his shoe. 'You should probably get in there sharpish. Stirling's lot will be claiming this one, you won't get a chance to see it once they get here.'

Ramsveld's apartment was on the ground floor, its front door standing ajar. Made from heavy oak with multiple locks, it showed no signs of forced entry. Biggs gave his details to the scene log officer and walked inside.

It was obvious that the jeweller lived alone. The flat had all the trappings of a rich bachelor: gilt-framed paintings hung next to shelves of rare artefacts — there were no photographs of family or children.

Treading carefully on the metal plates the forensic team left along the hallway. Biggs followed the smeared trail of blood into the kitchen.

Even through the mask Gates had given him, he could smell the corpse before he saw it.

Laid out on the large marbled-top island in the middle of the kitchen was the eviscerated body of the jeweller.

Four large china bowls were placed around him, two at his feet and one each side of his head. He was naked, his chest cracked opened from neck to crotch. There were flies everywhere, as was his blood. It covered every inch of the counter top and pooled on the floor, looking like some ancient ritual sacrifice.

Biggs stared into the gaping cavity of the dead man, trying to imagine what would drive somebody to such butchery. The incisions were neat and not frenzied, like an anatomy lesson, the remaining innards undamaged. From what he knew of the other murders it was always the same four organs and any means of identification.

Which, in this case, the killer had left in place. Ramsveld's head was twisted to one side, his eyes wild and staring, his mouth open as if caught in a scream.

Yellow plastic markers were placed around the kitchen indicating where the forensics team had found something of interest. Biggs ignored them, he could read about how the victim died in the report later, what was more interesting was why someone would want to kill Ramsveld.

He stepped carefully through the crime scene and towards the back of the apartment, searching for the man's office.

At the end of the hall was a small study filled with shelves of ledgers and box files. It looked more like an accountant's office than a jeweller's. There were a few framed photographs of Ramsveld with various officials at congresses and a large year planner with various Post-It notes stuck on key dates.

Biggs checked the last few days but they were blank.

In ten minutes the place would be off limits so he had to work fast.

Scattered across the desk were various receipts and bills. The mess looked out-of-place with the general order of the rest of the room. The killer had obviously been searching for something. Putting on a pair of latex gloves, he inspected the locks on the drawers. They were broken and most of their contents had been tipped out onto the desk.

In one drawer he found a diary, the last entry was on Wednesday 21st April.

Amongst a list of random numbers, which Biggs guessed were sales, there was a note: *Al-Shammari 7.30pm — Fourth Stone?*

Biggs took a photograph of the page with his phone and another of the wall planner.

The sounds of boots in the hallway signalled the end of his search. Voices echoed down the hall, one of which he recognised immediately — DI Marshall.

She looked surprised to see him when he walked out into the hallway.

'Hey,' she said, while Stirling examined the body.

'It's Ramsveld. The jeweller from Hatton Garden,' Biggs whispered.

'I know, I met him,' she replied. 'Did you find anything?'

He nodded. 'Someone's been through his things. There was an entry in his diary for yesterday about meeting Al-Shammari and a fourth stone.'

She glanced over to Stirling, but he was busy discussing something with Gates.

Marshall gestured to Biggs, and he followed her outside.

'It's the same guy,' she said when they were out of earshot.

Biggs scratched his chin, feeling the stubble where he hadn't had time to shave this morning.

'And the fourth stone?'

'Has to be the one that was stolen from Hatton Garden.'

'You think Al-Shammari killed Ramsveld?'

Marshall's eyes narrowed as she considered the idea. 'MI6 think he's linked to ISIS, which means he's potentially dangerous, or knows dangerous people. Has Davidson managed to track him down yet?'

Biggs shook his head. 'He's fallen off the grid. Gone dark.'

She laughed. 'You're spending too long with those twats in SO15, you're starting to sound like them.'

'Yeah.'

Marshall could tell from his expression that Biggs was uncomfortable discussing what was going on at City and changed the subject. 'How's the Guv?'

'He's okay, they've moved him to a surgical ward. They're going to operate tomorrow.'

She looked a little shocked. 'Operate?'

'Double heart bypass.'

Marshall grimaced at the thought of Donovan going through open heart surgery. 'He's not in great shape, it's too risky. Shouldn't they wait until he's better?'

Biggs looked down at his shoes. 'To be honest, I don't think he had that much longer. The doctor said his arteries are shot to shit.'

'Does he know?'

He shrugged. They both knew the man was in bad shape, and even if the medics did tell him, the DCI wasn't the kind of guy to take any notice of them.

'I'll try and pop in to see him tomorrow.'

'You should. He's still gutted about what happened with the press leak.'

'He may have done me a favour. We've got a witness that knew two of the victims. I'm going down to interview them this afternoon.'

44

CANVEY ISLAND

Canvey Island, Essex. Thursday, 22nd April. 14:30

Driving across the bridge on to Canvey Island felt as if they were leaving civilisation behind. Cut off from the mainland by East Haven Creek, the reclaimed land was only forty miles from London, languishing at the mouth of the Thames estuary, waiting for the day when the sea level rose and wiped it away.

Novak had turned up an hour later to Ramsveld's apartment, nursing an epic hangover, so Marshall drove.

By the time they passed beyond the M25 she'd learned all about how one of Novak's brothers had got engaged and the fact that most of her family could drink their body weight in vodka.

'Do you have any brothers or sisters?' Novak managed to ask, once the paracetamol Marshall gave her had kicked in.

Marshall didn't hesitate before answering: 'No.' Having thought of herself as a single child for most of her thirty-four years, it was an automatic response. But afterwards it felt like a lie. She consoled herself with the thought that until she actually met Martha Jones, it wouldn't be real.

'Ah, shame,' Novak continued. 'I've four brothers and two sisters. Mamma wanted more girls, but hey, you can't argue with nature.'

The sat-nav sent them down a long straight road across a flat marshland. The dark grey skies did nothing to improve the view.

'Bartoz is the eldest, but now he's getting hitched everyone will be looking at me. I'm next in line, although as his fiancé is already pregnant, it might buy me some time. Grandchildren are a great distraction.'

'What does he do?' Marshall

'Bartoz? He's a plumber,' she said proudly, 'like my father.'

'Anyone else in the force?'

Novak scoffed. 'They wouldn't make it through the first week. My brothers are not blessed with the brains. That stayed in the female side of the family.'

Marshall wondered what it would have been like to grow up in a house with six siblings, she couldn't imagine there was a great deal of privacy.

She couldn't deny that she'd always felt there was something missing from her childhood — being an only child was a lonely way to grow up. Although it prepared her in so many ways to be the independent and self-reliant woman she'd become, it meant she never experienced the closeness of a sibling.

Will was the nearest she ever came to a soulmate, and he'd died in her arms.

. . .

Queens Park Village was a retirement park on the east side of the island, a collection of static homes sheltering against the stormy winds rolling in off the North Sea.

'This is my idea of hell,' said Novak as Marshall parked the car in a visitor's space. 'Work all your life, only to find yourself in a caravan park next to an oil refinery.'

The land was so flat that the chimneys of the terminal could be seen from virtually any part of the island. Orange flames danced at the top of the stacks, battered by the winds.

'Mark Peters,' Marshall read aloud from her notebook. 'Cabin forty-five.'

Walking over to reception, it began to rain.

It was a cold, dirty rain, the kind that seeped into the back of your collar and chilled your bones. Marshall pulled up the hood on her coat and zipped up the front. It wasn't a good look, but it was better than getting soaked.

The office was closed. A badly written sign was taped to the window stating they would be back in twenty minutes. The weather was getting worse with every second. Novak took one of the less damaged umbrellas from the bucket outside the cabin and they made their way between the squat metal bungalows until they found forty-five.

Peters's caravan stood out amongst the row of pristine mobile homes: a large satellite dish was bolted to one side, with an array of aerials clustered on the roof above it. Around the outside, he'd built a wooden deck which was cluttered with old beer cans and engine parts. The cans were peppered with small holes as if they'd been used for target practice.

An old car chassis sat rusting under a flapping tarpaulin on the unkempt grass. Beside it, a pile of calor gas bottles lay stacked haphazardly, some blackened as if they'd caught on fire.

Marshall felt a little sorry for the neighbours, whose well tended window boxes and neatly trimmed lawns made his lot all the more shabby in comparison.

Novak knocked on the door.

'Fuck off!' came the response.

'It's the police Mr Peters,' Novak replied. 'You called us.'

There were the sounds of something heavy being dragged away from the door and it swung open to reveal a middle-aged man in a wheelchair. His blonde hair was long and greasy, and his beard looked as if it still had food caught in it.

'Can I see some ID?' he asked, in a voice rougher than sandpaper.

They showed their warrant cards, which he photographed with the camera on his phone and then pushed himself backwards to allow them to enter.

The caravan stank of dope, stale beer and sweat. Like the bedroom of a teenage boy.

Novak looked as if she were about to throw up, her face paled to a ghostly white.

'Excuse the mess. I don't get a lot of visitors,' Peters said, picking something off the coffee table and hiding it inside the pockets of his hoodie.

Marshall looked for somewhere to sit, but gave up and decided for Novak's sake to get through the interview as quickly as possible. She took out her notebook and flipped to an empty page. 'You said in your message that you knew both Avery and Hope?'

Peters pushed himself over to a desk stacked high with documents and picked up a folder from the top. Dropping it into his lap he opened a drawer and took out a bottle of whisky and a couple of dirty glasses, which he proceeded to wipe clean with a stained tea towel.

'You want one?' he asked, unscrewing the lid and pouring himself a large shot.

Novak looked as if she was going to throw up and went back outside.

'No, thank you,' replied Marshall.

He knocked the drink back in one go, wiping his mouth on his sleeve. Marshall could tell from his eyes that it wasn't the first one of the day.

'I was with Three Commando during Operation Telic in 2003. After we took down Abu Al-Khasib, we were ordered to help evacuate a bus full of civilians, embassy staff and contractors.'

Marshall made a note. 'And that's when you met them?'

He nodded, putting down the glass, he wheeled himself back and handed the file to her. 'They were being escorted to Mosul when the bomb went off. Big fucking truck, took out the lead vehicle and flipped our Humvee onto its roof. My legs were too badly crushed, had to take them below the knee.'

Marshall opened the file, it was filled with photographs of burned-out army vehicles and bodies scattered across a desert road.

'When I came round we were being air-lifted to the field hospital. Avery was on the same chopper, he was pretty badly shredded, the shrapnel opened up his gut,' he said, making a slicing motion with his hand across his stomach.

'And Alexandra Hope?'

His eyes glazed over a little. 'She came in later, on another medivac. They operated on her for twelve hours.'

'Who else was on that bus?'

Peters shrugged. 'Can't remember. I was pumped full of

morphine most of the time. There were at least four other civilians. I only recognised those two from the photos in the paper.'

Novak came back through the door, the colour returning to her cheeks. She shrugged apologetically.

'And the rest of your squad?' Marshall continued.

He sighed, pushing himself back to the bottle and poured himself another glass. 'All dead, except for Naomi Fox, she was our medic.'

'Do you know where she is now?'

Peters shrugged. 'Haven't seen her since 2012, at a regimental dinner, she was still on active duty then, not sure what she's doing now.'

'You're sure it was 2012?' said Novak, glancing at Marshall. The man didn't look like he could remember what happened last week.

He pulled up his shirt, revealing a long white scar over his ribs. 'Not going to forget that night in a hurry — someone tried to kill me.'

Novak took out her phone. 'Do you mind?'

Peters smiled. 'Knock yourself out.'

'What happened?' asked Marshall, while Novak took pictures.

'Not much. I left the dinner and was making my way back towards Piccadilly. Next thing I wake up in a hospital bed with thirty-five stitches in my chest. Police said they found me with a knife in my hand, so I guess I must have put up a good fight.'

He dropped his shirt and picked up the whisky glass once more. 'Used to be quite handy with a blade, back in the day.'

Marshall closed the file and went to hand it back to him.

'Keep it,' he said, waving his hand. 'I've got copies.'

'Why are you collecting all of this?' asked Novak, staring at the charts of battles in the Middle-East. Notes were pinned to maps that covered most of the back wall of what once had been his living room.

Peters's eyes lit up, clearly she had asked the right question. Pushing himself over to the wall he tapped on one of the maps. 'I'm researching Gulf War Syndrome. There are studies that show up to thirty-three thousand of us may have suffered chronic illness as a result of the meds they made us take before we went in. Some believe it's the depleted uranium in the armour-piercing shells, but I reckon the Iraqis were using nerve agents.' He moved further along, and Marshall realised it was a timeline of sorts. 'Same in 2003, they did something to us that no one can explain. I get these weird pains.' He pointed at his stomach. 'And my joints ache in the winter. Doc says it's just arthritis, but there are thousands of cases of veterans with similar complaints.'

'How would we find out who the other civilians were in Tikrit?' Marshall said, realising that the conversation was about to take an unnecessary diversion into his favourite conspiracy theory.

He pulled a half-finished joint out of the ashtray on the table and lit it. A glint of defiance in his eyes as he blew out the smoke.

'You'd need to talk to the Defence Inquest Unit, they'll have it all on file.'

45

DEFENCE INQUEST UNIT

Thursday 22nd April.

'The Defence Inquest Unit was created to help families of military personnel. They liaise with coroners to better understand the situations and environmental factors surrounding a fatality during a war,' Novak read aloud.

She scrolled down through the web page on her phone while Marshall drove them back into the city. She'd never been able to read while travelling. When she was a kid, the motion sickness stopped more than one family trip midway. Obviously whatever Novak had done outside Peters's caravan had cleared her hangover.

'Are there any contact details?'

Novak shook her head. 'Nope. Just usual MoD stuff.'

'Bollocks.'

They both knew how hard it was to get any information out of the Ministry of Defence. The paperwork involved would be painfully slow and probably involve the SIB, the Specialist Investigation Branch of the Military Police.

'Do you think he was telling the truth about the others?'

'About not knowing the victims? Why would he lie?'

Novak shrugged. 'I don't know, something about him wasn't right. He's hiding something.'

Marshall knew what the DS meant, after years of interviewing suspects you developed an intuition about lying. Something about the things they didn't say, patterns of speech that didn't match the norm.

Suddenly, a thought struck Marshall. 'Wasn't Stirling a red cap?'

Novak nodded, taking out her phone and putting the call through the car speakers so Marshall could hear.

'Hi Boss, the witness confirmed the connection between Hope and Avery.'

'Good work,' his deep voice booming out of the stereo.

'He says he was with them when they were attacked in Iraq in 2003.'

'Which regiment?'

Hearing the military tone in his voice, Marshall couldn't help but picture him in a uniform.

Novak continued. 'Not Army, they were civilians. Peters says he was escorting a group of civvies when their convoy got hit by a truck bomb outside of Tikrit.'

'Can he tell us who else was involved?'

'No Sir, we were hoping you might be able to talk to your contacts in SIB?'

'Send me the details. I'll see what I can do.'

He ended the call.

Novak glanced at Marshall, who shrugged. 'Man of few words.'

46

ANUBIS

The Ship & Shovell, Craven Passage, London. Friday 23rd April. 19:00

Biggs was slouched in a corner booth of the busy pub nursing a second pint, the first glass sitting empty beside it. He looked tired, there were dark shadows under his eyes and his usual cheeky greeting was missing when Marshall sat down.

'Sorry I'm late, just spent most of the day being bounced around the MoD.'

His eyes widened slightly. 'Military?'

She took off her coat and unwound her scarf. 'Yeah we've got a lead. Two of the victims were involved in the same incident outside of Tikrit in Iraq, 2003. It's a long shot but you know how I feel about coincidences.'

'There aren't any.'

'Exactly.'

'Do you want a drink?' Biggs asked, half-rising from the table.

Marshall took her purse out of her bag. 'I'll get them.'

.   .   .

By the time she returned, the DC had already finished his second pint. Which wasn't like him, Biggs was different to most coppers, she couldn't remember ever seeing him drink so quickly, let alone having more than one.

'Something bothering you?' she asked, putting down the drinks.

He frowned, picking up his glass. 'Apart from having SO15 turning the heist into a circus and a boss recovering from open-heart surgery?'

Shit, thought Marshall, Donovan's operation had slipped her mind.

'How is he?'

Biggs tilted his head from side-to-side. 'Well he's not dead — which is a start. Apparently the op lasted seven hours, they're keeping him in ICU at the moment. The ward's going to call me when he comes round — assuming he does.'

'Fuck off, he's a tough old bastard.'

Biggs put down his beer. 'He was asking after you.'

Marshall shook her head. 'I'll go and see him tomorrow. Turns out the witness who came forward has given us a solid lead.'

'The Army?'

She nodded.

He shrugged. 'That'll cheer him up no end. Make sure you do, you'll hate yourself if he pegs it before you get a chance to tell him that.'

That was true, she would, Biggs knew her too well.

She took a large sip of wine and changed the subject. 'So how's Davidson screwing it up?'

Biggs sighed. 'He's such a dick. He's convinced it's a

terrorist cell working inside the City. MI5 requisitioned all of the case files, including Gary Collins's phone.' He sat up straighter, a smug grin breaking across his face. 'Although not before Frazer managed to crack it.'

'What did he find out?'

'Most of it was just logistics: times and places, but Frazer managed to identify five contacts; all using codenames of course. The leader calls himself "Anubis". Apparently, he was the god of the dead, the one who ushered the souls into the afterlife.'

Biggs held up his phone and showed her the screen.

A jackal-headed idol stared out at her from the web page, *the Guardian of the Underworld*, the heading declared.

'I think you're right. We're looking for the same man.'

Marshall nodded, there was no doubt in her mind that the murder of Ramsveld brought the two cases together. The only problem now was trying to work out what the victims of an attack in Iraq had to do with a jeweller in Hatton Garden.

Biggs looked equally confused. 'But why steal a diamond and then go back and kill the guy you stole it from?'

'Maybe he was in on it,' she said, taking another sip of her wine and relaxing as the alcohol started to kick in. 'No, that doesn't make any sense. Why kill the others? We're still missing something. Have you managed to track down Al-Shammari?'

He laughed, shaking his head. 'No, the consulate finally declared him as a missing person. They're actually asking for our help now.'

'And does Davidson still think he's behind all this?'

Biggs nodded. 'He's convinced of it. And he's getting more support from MI6 now Al-Shammari's officially missing. They've already shared intel on some of the ISIS bank accounts he's been using. The fucking spooks knew he'd been funding the caliphate for years, mostly through illegal trades in gems and ancient artefacts. It was a very carefully planned operation.'

'So why butcher a paramedic in the back of his ambulance? Or a school teacher?'

'Or the guy in the museum,' Biggs added.

'Gates still not managed to identify him?'

'Nope.'

She finished the last of her wine. 'What if it's not Al-Shammari? What if we've been looking at this all wrong and there's some other pyscho running around carving up these people?'

'Like who?'

'Someone with a big fucking grudge. Someone who was in Iraq in 2003.'

47

THE ROYAL

Royal London Hospital, London. Saturday 24th April. 14:30

D onovan was asleep. His breathing calm, his heart beating in a steady rhythm across the monitor screen.

Marshall sat quietly beside his bed and watched him, wondering to herself what the old man might be dreaming about.

Her dreams were rarely ever good since the Alchemist, filled with terrifying moments in dark sewers, her face submerged in cold storm water. She would wake gasping for breath — it was one of the reasons she would never let Gresham stay the night — she didn't want him to know.

The Alchemist left her with more than just physical scars, his legacy would haunt her for years. Her old sergeant warned her about it on her first day: how every copper carried at least one horror story, a nightmare case that stayed with them. No matter how thick their skin grew, there was always at least one that got through — no one survived long in the force without picking up a few ghosts.

She remembered the case she'd worked with Donovan. He was hardly in better shape then, but there was a light burning in his eyes, one that she watched slowly fade away over the last five years.

The DCI was like something from another time, incorruptible and unwavering in his pursuit of justice. There were times, early on, when she doubted his motives, thinking he was too good to be true.

Until the night they broke the Kerrigan case.

Michael Kerrigan was a lawyer with a penchant for cocaine and prostitutes. He'd left more than one battered and bruised at the doors of A&E, yet none of them would ever testify.

Marshall volunteered to go undercover.

After a few nights hanging out with the working girls around the back of Liverpool Street Station, she saw his car. The Mercedes S Class pulled into the kerb beside her and she got in.

He was a handsome man, the kind of well-groomed rich guy from the cover of a billionaire romance novel.

They knew his usual M.O. was to take his victims to an Air BnB. Frazer managed to hack into all of the five fake accounts he'd created and Donovan deployed a team to watch the apartment he rented for that evening.

Marshall was wearing a wire, but the guy was clever, no mention of money, just charming banter.

When they pulled into the underground car park, she

knew it was the wrong place. Something had made him change his mind.

The radio crackled in her ear, losing signal.

It was then she noticed that he was wearing gloves.

The first punch knocked her against the passenger window, the second went into her ribs and winded her.

She must have blacked out for a few seconds because when she came around he was dragging her out of the passenger seat by her hair.

Marshall broke two of his fingers and kicked him hard in the ribs.

Kerrigan just laughed and smashed her head into the car bonnet, pinning her down as he pulled up her skirt.

'Wild cat,' he said through gritted teeth undoing his trousers with one hand.

She felt his other hand pulling at her underwear as he leaned on her back.

There was nothing she could do, her arms were pinned under her body and his entire body weight was holding her down.

She closed her eyes and screamed.

Donovan hit him with a fire extinguisher and he went down hard.

It turned out that the DCI hadn't been satisfied with simply waiting at the flat and tailed them from the pickup in his own car.

The Guv always did have great instincts.

Donovan sighed and opened his eyes, even beneath the mask she could tell he was smiling.

His hand reached out over the covers and took hers. 'Marshall,' he whispered, 'I'm sorry.'

'No need,' she said, squeezing his hand tightly. 'It doesn't matter.'

'Did you crack it?'

Marshall tilted her head slightly. 'No, but the leak gave us a solid lead. A witness came forward and identified two of the victims, Avery and Hope. Apparently they were involved in the same incident in Iraq during the war — a car bomb. We're waiting for Military Police to tell us who else survived.'

His eyes widened. 'You think there are more victims?'

She nodded. 'The witness said there were.'

Donovan chuckled. 'Good luck. The MoD don't tend to give much away.'

'Stirling's an ex-MP, he's got contacts.'

The old man pushed himself up in the bed, wincing at the pain of moving. 'Seems a bit of a long shot and it doesn't explain the murder in the museum.'

Marshall sighed. 'There's been another. They found Benjamin Ramsveld dead in his apartment two days ago. His organs were removed in the same way as the others.'

'The jeweller?'

She nodded.

Donovan took off his oxygen mask and scratched his chin, the stubble was turning into a white beard, which suited him. 'So the heist is connected to the murders. Has Biggs got any further on the stolen diamonds?'

'Frazer managed to crack Collins's phone. He got some GPS data and a bunch of dates and user names. Biggs is trying to reconstruct a timeline and match it with CCTV.'

The old man nodded, his eyelids drooping heavily. 'Sounds sensible.'

'You're tired, I should let you get some rest.'

He smiled weakly. 'Feels like an elephant sat on my chest.'

'Have they told you how long you're going to be in here for?'

'A couple of weeks at least. Depends on how well I heal. The fed rep says I could be shining my arse behind a desk by June.'

'They're going to let you come back?' she said, trying to hide the surprise in her voice.

He nodded, but she could see the doubt in his eyes. They both knew he was never going back to active duty, it would be something safe and very dull.

As she got up to leave, Donovan grabbed her hand. 'This one takes pleasure in the killing. This isn't some random terrorist, there'll be something in his past that drove him to this.'

48

SURVIVORS

Charing Cross Police Station. Monday 26th, April. 07:30

D CI Stirling stood with his arms folded across his chest while they filed into the briefing room.

It was a full house, everyone sat silently waiting for the meeting to begin, their faces showing signs of long nights, too much coffee and too little progress.

'Any update on the DNA from Paddington?' he asked Hamilton.

The detective shook his head. 'Nothing Boss, just Avery's blood.'

The DCI tried not to look too disappointed, but he had the kind of face that didn't hide how he felt.

'Nicholls, what do we have on Ramsveld?'

She stood up and opened her phone. 'Forty-four year old male with a heart condition. Lived alone. Partner in the Hatton Garden Diamond Exchange, which was recently raided to the tune of three-hundred and fifty-million pounds worth of jewels. Forensics haven't found anything conclusive in his flat, but Gates is convinced it's the same guy.'

'Nothing on the security cameras?'

She shook her head. 'Someone wiped them, even the offsite backups, but his diary said he was meeting a Saudi businessman named, Al-Shammari, about a fourth stone.'

Stirling's expression brightened. 'And who might he be?'

'A person of interest, according to MI6,' Marshall interrupted, feeling all eyes turning on her.

'MI6?'

'I was working on that diamond heist. We were investigating Al-Shammari when some chief spook showed up and told us to back off.'

'And did you?'

She shook her head. 'No, but he's gone missing, even his embassy doesn't know where he is.'

'Or aren't saying. Hamilton do some digging on Al-Shammari, preferably without alerting MI6.'

Hamilton nodded.

Stirling turned to Marshall. 'So, how did it go with Peters?'

'He recognised the two victims from the press article. Although he never knew their names until now. They were all involved in a bombing in Iraq in 2003. He's not the most reliable of witnesses; he's suffering from PTSD or Gulf War Syndrome. Believes the Army injected him with something that caused it.'

'Reliable or not, he was right.' Stirling tapped on the large display screen and an MoD report appeared showing a map and photographs of burned out vehicles. The DCI flicked through the images until he came to a list of names, some of which were redacted. 'I got in touch with some of my old team and they pulled the inquest report on the attack. Four vehicles were destroyed, eight soldiers and four civilians died and seven were severely injured,' he added, zooming in on the un-redacted names. 'Avery and Hope are there, plus these three: Welling, Dennison and Harrison. I've sent you their details.'

Their passport photos enlarged as he named each one. 'Marshall you take Welling. Nicholls on Dennison and I'll check Harrison. This is our first solid lead, albeit a cold one, the rest of you go back over the reports, see if there are any connections between the victims and the jeweller.'

Marshall went back to her desk and opened her email. Catherine Welling's face stared out from the screen, a forty-year old woman with hard eyes, standing in the middle of a war zone, she reminded her of Kate Adie.

In the notes, Stirling had included some links to her blog and the case link for her murder. She was discovered in a lockup garage in Glasgow in 2006, her major organs had been removed and placed in plastic bin bags. The crime scene images could have been those of Alexandra Hope, a pale body laid out on cardboard like a sacrificial offering.

Reading through the report, it was clear that the Scottish SIO had little in the way of leads and the investigation went nowhere. Their prime suspect, a mental patient from Gartnavel Royal Hospital, was arrested but committed suicide before he could come to trial. The case was marked as 'unproven' the following year.

Marshall clicked through to Welling's blog and read through some of her articles. She liked her writing style, it was gritty and powerful; pulling no punches when describing the horrors being inflicted, mostly on the women, of the regions she visited. Going back through the blog's archive, it seemed she'd travelled to virtually every war zone on the planet: from the Democratic Republic of the Congo to Sudan and Iraq, gathering a few battle scars of her own along the way.

All that time in some of the most dangerous places in the world and she dies in a dirty garage in a back-alley of Glasgow.

Marshall grabbed a pen and drew a timeline on her desk planner, marking the years from 2003 to 2021 and then adding the victims' names beneath the relevant dates. She drew a line between the three year gaps between the incidents.

Ripping the sheet from the pad, she walked over to Nicholls.

'Hey, when did Dennison die?'

Nicholls looked up from her laptop. '2009, why?'

Marshall showed her the timeline. 'I think there's a pattern.' She added Dennison's name below 2009. 'A three-year gap between each one.'

The blonde detective took the sheet and studied it carefully. 'So we're looking for two more victims?'

Stirling walked up behind them. 'You found something?'

Nicholls nodded. 'There's a three-year gap between them,' handing Marshall's sketch to the DCI.

Marshall wondered if Nicholls was going to take the credit.

'Marshall spotted it,' the woman added.

His eyes widened slightly as they scanned across the notes.

'If she's right, we're looking for two more victims around 2012 and 2015'

He shook his head. 'Not necessarily, but it's definitely a

pattern. Anyway, Simon Harrison is still very much alive when I spoke to him ten minutes ago.'

There was a moment of painful silence while their initial excitement drained out of the conversation.

Marshall snapped her fingers. 'Peters was attacked in 2012, someone cut him really badly, but he fought them off.'

Stirling considered the new information. 'Are there any other similarities about the dates or locations?'

'Not as far as I can see. Welling moved to Scotland two years before to look after her sick mother.'

'And I'm still checking on Dennison,' added Nicholls.

Stirling handed the timeline back to Marshall. 'It's a good start, but maybe the gap between 2012 and 2018 could be more important than the frequency.'

Marshall shrugged. 'Or there are more victims than just the civilians. Peters mentioned a medic called Naomi Fox.'

'I'll check with my contacts about Fox. You pull the records on Peters's attack, and see if you can get him to give you any more details.'

49

PETERS

Peters picked up on the tenth ring. He sounded rough, his voice raw and croaky as though he'd just woken up. It reminded Marshall of the way James used to sound on a Saturday morning after being out on a bender the night before.

'Hi, this is DI Marshall, I just wanted to ask you some more questions about the attack in 2012.'

'I'm tired. Can you call back later?'

'Can you remember what street you were on?'

He sighed. 'They found me in Mason's Yard. No idea how I got there, I was on my way back to Piccadilly.'

She keyed in the street name on Google maps. 'Where was the dinner?'

She could hear the sound of a cigarette being lit. 'The RAG. The Army and Navy club on St James's Square. Very posh.'

Mason's Yard was a small enclosed area off Duke Street, a perfect location to carry out a murder away from passers-by, and was less than three hundred yards away from the club.

'Did you get a crime report number?'

'Yeah, somewhere.'

The line went quiet for a while, and Marshall strained to hear the sound of drawers being opened in the background.

'4193/12'.

She made a note. 'Is there anything else you can remember about the attack?'

'The bastards kept my knife.'

'Who the police?'

Peters coughed. 'Yeah, I've had that since the Gulf. It's got sentimental value.'

'I'll see what I can do. It's probably sitting in an evidence locker.'

'Thanks.' His tone changed a little. 'I've been trying to get hold of Naomi. See if she could remember anything else, but she's not picking up.'

'Is that normal?'

'If she was on a mission, maybe. Her CO wouldn't take my call either.'

'Is there anyone else you can think of that we could speak to from the Tikrit attack? We need to try and find all of the survivors.'

The line went quiet again.

'There was a driver, he was a local. I've no idea what happened to him. Why don't you ask the SIB?'

'We've tried, they're not being very cooperative.'

'Try Captain Azir. He'll know.'

She scribbled down the name. 'Who's he?'

The line went dead.

. . .

Looking back through her notes, she ringed Naomi's name, making a mental note to follow her up with Stirling, and put a question mark next the word 'Driver'.

The local driver could explain one of the missing years, but even if he was another victim, tracking down the details of his murder in a country like Iraq would be virtually impossible, unless this Captain Azir was still in touch with the local police.

Marshall underlined the name of the captain.

Opening up a web browser, she typed his name into Google. All she got back was a random list of fan sites for a game called 'League of Legends'. Somehow Marshall didn't think that was what Peters was referring to.

More likely he was one of the redacted names on Stirling's list.

Staring at the timeline, Donovan's last words came back to her: 'There'll be something in his past that drove him to this.'

There was always a motive, however crazy, the old man used to say. The only trouble was Marshall couldn't see it. If the murderer was targeting anyone who survived the attack, the big question had to be why? Perhaps they weren't meant to survive. Did something happen out there that was so terrible that he spent the last eighteen years taking his revenge? It didn't make any sense, *but then murder never did,* until she could see it through the eyes of the killer, which was what she was missing right now. Marshall couldn't imagine what possible reason he would have for killing people who barely survived a horrific attack.

Unless he was one of the terrorists.

Suddenly, the pieces began to fall into place: the use of

gas at the heist, the ritual murders, the military grade encryption on the phones. If Al-Shammari was working for ISIS, then maybe he could have been involved back in 2003. There was no way to know without treading on MI6's toes, but why would they want to protect a killer?

Closing her laptop, she went over to Hamilton's desk.

'Hey,' she said. 'How's it going with Al-Shammari?'

Hamilton pointed at a series of open browser windows. There were various photographs of the man with members of the Saudi Royal family.

'Seems to be well connected.'

'Do you know where he was back in 2003?'

Hamilton frowned, looking back over his notes. 'I've not had a chance to go back that far and keeping away from official sources makes it trickier. Why do you want to know?'

Marshall shrugged. 'Just a hunch, let me know if you find anything.'

50

WORLD SERVICE

**BBC Broadcasting House, Langham Street, London.
Monday 26th, April. 16:30**

Catherine Welling worked at the BBC for over ten years before she was murdered, almost exclusively for the World Service, who were based in the iconic art deco building on the corner of Portland Place and Langham Street.

Novak followed Marshall into the reception, trying her best not to stare at the group of news presenters waiting with their camera crews for transport.

Welling had no family, but according to her bio she'd worked with the same producer for years. There were various photos of Philip Mayhew on her blog, celebrating birthdays and Christmases over the years. It was clear they were close friends.

Mayhew was now the Director of the World Service,

He was waiting on the other side of security, pacing in front of the lifts like an expectant grandfather.

'DI Marshall?' he asked, holding out a sweaty hand in greeting.

She nodded, shaking it. 'This is DS Novak. Can we go somewhere more private?'

'Of course,' he pressed the lift button. 'My office is on the fourth.'

The lift speakers were broadcasting the news as they stepped in.

'*Police are still refusing to comment on the Paddington Station murder...*'

'I assume you're here because of that,' he asked as the doors closed.

Mayhew had put on a lot of weight since Welling's death and the glass car felt claustrophobically small. 'We're part of the investigation,' replied Marshall, pressing herself against the wall.

He clapped his hands. 'Finally! After all these years.'

There were tears in his eyes as the doors opened and he waved them out. 'Please, my office is just down on the left.'

There were framed pictures of Welling taken in various locations on three sides of the room, the fourth was a large glass window looking out over London.

Mayhew went to his desk. 'When they told me how she died I told them it wasn't random.'

Marshall studied the closest photograph. Welling was standing in the middle of a bombed-out street holding a small child in her arms, another seemed to be attached to her leg.

'The Scottish Police were convinced it was Jeremy Bowen, but the man committed suicide before it could be proven,' he continued. 'The last time she called me, Kate was worried that her latest piece was going to put her in danger.'

'What was it about?' asked Novak, taking out her notebook.

He pulled a dossier out of a desk drawer and handed it to Marshall. 'She was injured in an attack outside of Tikrit in 2003, while she was investigating reports of artefacts being smuggled out of the country.'

'Artefacts?' Marshall repeated, opening the folder.

'Iraq was once known as Sumer, home of Babylon, Akkad and Assyria. There are hundreds if not thousands of tombs scattered over what was Mesopotamia. It was a treasure trove of antiquities, most of which were looted from the national archives during the war. While the coalition troops were guarding the oil, the entire cultural heritage of Iraq was being ransacked and sold off.'

Handwritten notes were filed between photographs of empty museums and men running through streets clutching armfuls of ancient artefacts.

'It was going to be her best work. There was talk of a book deal. Once she recovered from the operation they sent her home and she started on the manuscript.'

Marshall froze, her hand shaking as she held up one of the photographs.

'Do you know when these were taken?'

Mayhew took the picture from her, squinting as he placed a pair of spectacles on the end of his nose.

'She was near Assur, a world heritage site, a few days before the attack. I guess that was somewhere nearby. Why?'

Marshall took the photograph back and held it up for Novak to see. 'Who's that talking to the driver?'

'Peters.'

51

DENNISON

Charing Cross, Monday 26th, April. 18:00

Nicholls wasn't at her desk when Marshall and Novak got back to the office, in fact, most of the team were out. Stirling was on the phone in his office.

Marshall took off her jacket, sat down at her desk and opened Mayhew's file.

'So Peters knew Welling before the attack,' Novak said, sitting down opposite her. 'Doesn't really make him a suspect. Not with his disability.'

'Still makes him a liar. If she was investigating something that got her killed, he knew about it.'

'So why wait until now to get in touch?'

'Maybe the news of the other murders got him thinking.'

Marshall spread the pages out on her desk and began to read. Novak went to get coffee.

There were hundreds of notes, all with dates, but in no particular order. Some were typed up with comments annotated in red ink.

'Where were they going?' Marshall read one aloud. Her eyes drawn to a particular paragraph.

The Library of Baghdad was left burning after a second day of looting. Librarians and archivists tried in vain to hold back the locals, barring the doors while the staff tried to save the most precious manuscripts. Early copies of rare Islamic texts were wrapped in clothes and bundled into waiting taxis as the academics tried to save their national treasures.

Marshall skipped a few pages until she found a date closer to the attack.

Speaking to some of the British troops, it is clear that the military are aware of the desecration, but have orders to protect the oil fields. One contact told me that they'd spoken to a group at Assur who were stealing to order. Apparently Saudi and Russian oligarchs were willing to pay top dollar for the treasures.

Assur was a name she recognised. Gresham had said something about it. *But what the fuck was it?*

Stirling came out of his office and walked over to them.

'Nicholls spoke to Dennison's wife, apparently he was an air con engineer. Landed himself a lot of juicy military supply contracts before the Tikrit attack. He set up a property development business when he got back, but made a few enemies along the way. There was a dispute over a large contract for a Qatari hotel that his wife reckons was the reason he was killed.'

'He was killed in Qatar?' asked Novak, handing Marshall a steaming mug of coffee.

The DCI nodded. 'They found his body in the penthouse.'

'I don't suppose we'll get access to the autopsy reports?'

He shook his head. 'Nicholls is going to try, but it's

doubtful. The body was cremated before the British consulate had a chance to examine it.'

'Sounds like a cover up,' said Novak.

'So the killer isn't limiting himself to the UK. We should check on the flight manifests around the time he was murdered.'

Stirling folded his arms. 'Nicholls is already on it.'

Don't tell him how to do his job, thought Marshall.

'Did you serve in Iraq?' she asked, changing the subject.

Stirling's jaw stiffened, the veins in his neck standing out. 'I did, why?'

'You ever hear of treasure being smuggled out of the country?'

He relaxed a little. 'We had a few other things to worry about.'

'Welling was a reporter.' She held up one of the photographs, tapping on the image of a soldier. 'That's Peters behind her. Who I think was feeding her information about the looting that was going on. Apparently artefacts were being stolen to order.'

He took the photograph from her. 'You think Peters was involved?'

Marshall shrugged. 'I'm not sure. He was definitely holding stuff back when we interviewed him.'

'We had reports of widespread looting, but it was mostly local gangs, nothing that organised.'

'Her editor seems to think it was more serious. She told him she was scared.'

'Of who?'

Marshall looked down at the notes scattered across her desk. 'I don't know. I was going to ask Peters tomorrow. He mentioned a Captain Azir in his last interview. I don't suppose you knew him?'

Stirling's eyes went distant for a moment. 'With a name like that I would've thought he was from another force. There were over eight thousand troops deployed from twenty NATO countries. Do Welling's notes mention him?'

'I've only just started,' she said, waving her hand over the desk. 'This is going to take me a while to go through.

He handed her back the photo. 'I'll leave you to it.'

'Can you ask your contacts about Azir?'

'Sure.'

52

NIGHT VISION

Canvey Island, Essex. Tuesday, 27th April. 00:30

P eters woke at the sound of someone walking over the decking. The wood was old and warped, which he'd always planned to fix, until he realised it was the perfect early warning system.

He reached for his phone, bleary-eyed and still drunk, the numbers danced around, refusing to settle into anything he could recognise.

Laying back on the bed, he waited for the world to stop spinning. This wasn't the first time he'd caught the local kids screwing around, his caravan was like a magnet to the little fuckers.

He picked up one of his crutches and banged on the wall.

'Fuck off!'

There was no response.

The steps came back towards the door.

Peters felt under his pillow for the gun. The Browning Hi-Power was a memento from the war, one that allowed him to sleep at night. He felt the knurling of the grip against his palm and slipped his fingers around it.

Sitting upright he levelled the gun down the centre of the caravan.

If they were going to come, it would be now, he thought to himself. *All these years waiting for this moment.* In a strange way it was kind of a relief. To know he'd been right about the others, even though it would probably end him. There was some small victory in taking one of them down with him.

The door hinges complained as the door was wrenched open.

A thin line of red light lit up the kitchen.

Laserscope, night vision. It's what I would have done.

Peters flipped the lights on, hoping that the moment of blindness would buy him some time.

He felt the first bullet go through his right shoulder, knocking the gun out of his hand before he had a chance to fire it.

The second went through his forehead.

53

RIVERS

Thames Estuary, Tuesday, 27th April. 06:30

The body twisted away on the eddies swirling in the shallow lagoons, its passage going unnoticed by the lapwings and reed buntings that were nesting on the banks of Cliffe Creek. The sun was just rising, casting a low orange glow across the waters, slowly penetrating the early morning mists.

Sitting amongst the reeds, he whispered a silent prayer to Osiris.

Holding the stone up to the first rays of dawn, he marvelled at the inner beauty of its complex structure, facets cut by blades over three thousand years ago for a long dead queen.

The sounds of the water against his kayak reminded him of the times they would accompany their father. Before the troubles, before his childhood ended. Riding on his boat down from Luxor, cruising through the cool waters of the Nile like ancient Pharaohs on their way to the Temple at Edfu.

His father was a professor of Egyptology at Cairo University, and they spent every summer with him on research trips to the ancients sites, walking where tourists could only dream of going.

On their journey, he would tell them stories of the old world, of the long dead kings and their gods: Ra, Osiris, Horus and Anubis, pointing out their likeness on the walls of the temples they passed. They would spend the long summer days in the cool tombs of the Pharaohs: Thutmose III, Akhenaten and Ramesses II. Playing with his brother in the houses of the dead, making their own games amongst the ruins.

His brother had been a troubled child even then, obsessed by the inner workings of things. At home he would find his brother in the garden poring over the carcasses of local cats, birds and rats. He always had a morbid fascination for what went on below the skin, and their holidays in the world of the dead only fuelled his imagination.

In Saqqara, during the excavation of the ruins of Memphis, he found his brother with his hand inside the body cavity of a mummy. He could still see the look of glee on his face as he pulled a jewelled scarab beetle from the wrappings. Holding it up like a trophy.

He never told his father what Saadah did, it became their secret. He never got the chance, the war with Israel put an end to their adventures when his father was killed during an Israeli attack.

His father never got to see Saadah become one of the most gifted surgeons in Cairo.

. . .

Pushing away from the shore, he was careful not to disturb the birds, there would be people on the nature reserve soon, walking their dogs along the shoreline.

54

MURDER

Canvey Island, Essex. Wednesday, 28th April. 10:30

P eters's caravan was half-hidden behind a row of white
tents.

Working her way through the crowd of OAPs standing
behind the outer cordon, Marshall dodged around sharp
elbows as they held their phones high, trying to take
photographs of something morbid. Avoiding the walking
sticks and zimmer frames, she ducked under the blue tape.

The local force were following procedure, taping off the
area while a team of uniforms ran a grid search on the
grounds around his static home. Marshall spotted an older
detective as he stepped out of the tents and made her way
over to him.

'DI Marshall,' she announced to the man she assumed
was the SIO, flashing her warrant card.

'DCI Fellowes,' he replied, squinting at her ID until his
bushy eyebrows met over the bridge of his nose. 'City?
You're a little off the reservation?'

'I'm on secondment to the Met,' she replied, realising

that the warrant card still carried the insignia of her old unit. Once, not so long ago, she would have been proud of it, now she felt like she was apologising.

He shrugged. 'Still not sure how this involves your team. Unless of course there's something you're about to enlighten me on.'

She could tell that Fellowes was cast from the same mould as Donovan, he had the same look of a wily old fox with sharp eyes, although he was a lot taller, easily six-foot four.

'I was here last week, following up on a call Peters made to the station. He said he had information about a case.'

'Did he now?' The old man turned and barked at one of his younger officers who was about to enter the caravan. 'Matthews, put a suit on before you go in there.'

'What happened?' Marshall asked, watching Matthews struggling to pull a Tyvek suit over his clothes.

'One of the groundsman noticed Peters's door hanging off its hinges when he came to change the gas this morning.'

'Is he dead?'

Fellowes shrugged. 'Not sure. His neighbours said they heard fireworks the night before. Which were probably gunshots. SOCO says the blood splatter pattern is consistent with a headshot, but there's no sign of a corpse.'

Looking through a gap in the nearest tent, Marshall's eyes instinctively swept over the outside of the caravan, searching for signs of a struggle, of a body being dragged across the decking.

Following her gaze, Fellowes added: 'We're searching the area and there's CCTV at the main gate.'

'Can I have a look inside?' she asked.

He paused, considering her request, his lips forming a

thin straight line. Marshall knew the next question before he asked it.

'Is there anything I should know about your investigation that could be relevant to this case?'

She would have to give him something, after all they were all on the same team. Turning towards him, she opened her phone and showed him the front page of The Sun website. 'Peters recognised two of our victims from the news, says he knew them back in 2003.'

'From the Ripper murders?' Fellowes said, staring at the images of Hope and Avery.

The tabloids had gone to town on the gory details of the dissections, unhelpfully comparing them to the deaths of the prostitutes in 1880 and generating hundreds of calls a day from concerned curtain twitchers with nothing better to do.

Marshall put the phone away. 'Yeah, I needed to check something with him and he wasn't picking up his phone. Now I can see why.'

The last of the forensics team came out of the caravan carrying evidence bags, followed by Matthews who gestured to his boss.

'Looks like they've finished,' said Fellowes, gesturing towards the door. 'After you.'

Marshall stood on the decking, breathing shallowly, trying to ignore the smell of damp and sweat, allowing her mind to clear so she could read the scene.

The door to the static home hung from one hinge, its metal frame buckled by the force of a crowbar. She could imagine it would have made enough noise to wake the dead. But Peters was a drunk with an addiction to painkillers, so it may not have disturbed him. The killer came in the middle of the night, and yet all of the light switches were still in their off position. So either he used a torch or night vision — she was guessing on the latter.

The inside of the caravan was like an overexposed photograph — lit by bright LED lamps, Peters home had been ransacked. Metal stepping plates were placed carefully across the floor to avoid contaminating the blood stained linoleum.

Moving carefully through the kitchen and into the living room, Marshall found Peters's research scattered across the floor. Someone had emptied every drawer and folder. The photographs on the pinboard had been disturbed too, there were obvious gaps in his montage. She snapped a shot with her phone so she could compare it with the one that Novak took on their last visit.

His bedroom was a mess: crutches lay across the bed, as if Peters tried to use them to defend himself, and there was a large blood splatter across the back wall, leaving her in no doubt it was a head shot.

'They found a gun,' said Fellowes, ducking his head as he came through the bedroom door. 'A Browning — military issue.'

'Memento from his army days,' guessed Marshall. 'Did he manage to fire it?'

The DCI shook his head. 'Forensics think not. There were only two shots, from a high-powered weapon.' He pointed at one of the holes. 'Walls are so thin it went straight through. Not much chance of finding the bullets.'

Looking at the state of the bedsheets, Marshall could imagine the half-asleep Peters scrabbling for his gun, struggling to get upright with useless legs.

'Why did he bother to take the body?' wondered Fellowes.

It was the question that was bothering her too. Peters was hiding something that cost him his life. If he wasn't dead from the second shot, he would have lost too much blood to crawl to safety.

She went to the window and looked out over the marshes towards the Thames estuary. 'Did you check the creeks?'

'For a body?' Fellowes came over to join her. 'They're tidal, we're waiting for it to turn.'

'Or an escape route.'

He scoffed. 'You think the killer came in by boat?'

She turned back towards him. 'There's no CCTV on this side of the park.'

'You make it sound like a military operation.'

She shrugged. 'I'm beginning to think it was.'

55

HARRISON

Charing Cross Station, Wednesday, 28th April. 16:30

'Fuck!' Stirling swore, throwing the report across his desk.

Marshall and Novak instinctively stepped back in case he decided to throw something else.

'Essex forensics reckons there will be a delay in processing Peters's caravan. They're saying it could take a fucking week.'

It was the first time that Marshall witnessed Stirling get angry — or swear, now she thought about it, somehow it made him a little more human.

'Did they say anything about the search?'

The DCI glared at her, there were dark shadows beneath his eyes, reminding her that the man probably hadn't slept much in days. He picked up the report and turned to the second page.

'Ongoing. Nothing on the CCTV at the gate, no witnesses.'

So he came in from the river, Marshall thought, wondering

if Peters's body would be somewhere at the bottom of the Thames Estuary by now.

Stirling screwed the printout up and dropped it into the bin. 'The only decent fucking witness we've had.'

'Did you get anything back from SIB?' asked Marshall, changing the subject.

'Nothing on Naomi Fox,' he said, turning to his computer. Stirling opened an attachment from an email. 'Or Captain Azir, but there was another officer, a surgeon by the name of Saadah Azir — although he was a Major.'

'Maybe Peters got it wrong?'

The DCI shook his head. 'He would know the difference.'

Novak made a note of the name. 'Where is he now?'

'Bedlam.'

'The nut house?'

Grimacing at the term, Stirling sat down. 'He's a schizophrenic. Been a private patient at the Psychosis Unit since 2018. Apparently the Major was medically discharged from the Army.'

Marshall pulled out her notebook and flicked through it to check the dates.

'The murders started up again in 2018.'

'So it couldn't be him,' said Stirling, leaning back in his chair and folding his arms.

'Do you know who's paying for his treatment?' asked Marshall, not ready to give up so quickly.

The DCI shrugged. 'I assumed it was the MoD. As a veteran he would receive ongoing care. What are you thinking?'

Marshall didn't know exactly, it was more of a hunch, but something about the dates was bothering her. 'Not sure. Did he serve in Iraq?'

Stirling leaned forward and checked the email. 'Egyptian born, but joined the British Army in 1990, his last tour was with Operation Telic, 2003.'

'So he was in Iraq in 2003? Do you know where?'

He shook his head. 'Doesn't say. Are you thinking of paying him a visit?'

'Maybe.'

He looked at his watch. 'You're going to need a DP9 signed off by the Chief Super, but before you do that, I need you to come down and interview Harrison — he's coming in at three.'

According to his bio, Simon Harrison was an Associate Director at Deloitte. He specialised in Risk Advisory for clients in the Middle East — whatever that meant, it paid well.

He was wearing a very expensive suit, and a smile to match when they walked into the interview room. There was an equally well dressed lawyer sitting beside him.

Harrison was in his early forties, with a sharp, angular face and blonde hair. His skin was tanned and smooth, except for a fine white scar above his right eye.

'Mr Harrison,' said Stirling, taking a seat on the opposite side of the table. 'This is an informal interview, there was no need to bring legal counsel.'

The lawyer sneered. 'My client was given no explanation as to the purpose of the interview today.'

Stirling laughed. 'Your client was asked to attend as part of an ongoing investigation. If he was a suspect I would have been knocking at his door with a warrant.'

'It's fine,' Harrison assured his lawyer, then turning to Stirling. 'What would you like to know?'

Marshall sat down and opened a file.

'On the twenty-fourth of June 2003, were you involved in an incident in Iraq?'

Harrison unconsciously touched the scar over his eye. 'I was.'

'Would you mind telling us what happened?'

He took a deep breath. 'Not at all. I was a graduate on the Arab advancement programme for Deloitte when the invasion kicked off. Working out of the Mosul office. I was told to evacuate and they stuck me on this bus with a bunch of other civilians and shipped us off to Baghdad with an army escort. We were about halfway there when someone blew a van up right beside us. The escort took most of the damage, but it blew the windows out in the bus, glass sliced us open like knives. There were a lot of casualties.'

Marshall bit her tongue, letting Stirling continue the questioning while she made notes.

'Did you know any of the other passengers?' he continued.

Harrison shook his head and took a sip of water. Marshall noticed his hand was shaking slightly as he drank. 'Not then, but I got to know a few of them in the hospital.'

'Where was this?'

'Initially, we were flown to the field hospital at Basra. Camp Coyote. After they'd stitched us up we were moved to Turkey, until we were fit enough to fly home.'

Stirling placed pictures of the three victims on the table. 'Alexandra Hope, James Dennison and Catherine Welling. Did you meet any of these people?'

He looked at each of the images in turn. 'They were younger then, but yes,' he tapped on Welling and Hope, 'I saw those two. This one asked a lot of questions,' he added about Welling.

'She was a journalist,' explained Marshall.

He raised an eyebrow. 'Was she? I thought I recognised her.'

Marshall took out a picture of Peters. 'What about this man. Was he part of the escort?'

Harrison's eyes narrowed. 'He's changed a lot since then, but yes I remember him. He was in a lot of pain, they pumped him full of morphine. High as a kite most of the time. He used to accuse the staff of stealing his stuff.'

'What stuff?'

Harrison shrugged. 'Something precious. I assumed it was the drugs talking.'

'Do you remember anything about the medical staff that worked on you?' asked Stirling.

'I had a two-foot shard of glass embedded in my abdomen. It took nine hours to cut it out and stitch me up. The surgeon was an Egyptian guy, a major I think.'

'Major Azir?'

He nodded and rubbed his stomach. 'Not the finest needlework you've ever seen but the man saved my life. All of us owe him that.'

'He operated on all of you?'

'More than once.'

Marshall stopped writing. 'How many times?'

'I had three operations while I was there. Most of the others had at least two. All the good it's done me. He may have saved my life, but it still feels like I've got a lump of glass inside me.'

'You've had pain?'

'God yes, every day. I've had a couple of CT scans and an X-ray. All they can say is that there's a lot of scarring and possibly some shrapnel. They say I'm lucky I didn't end up with a colostomy bag.'

Marshall glanced over at Stirling. *Same as Avery.*

'Would you mind if one of our medics gave you an examination?'

The lawyer tensed up. 'I don't think — '

Harrison laughed. 'Feel free, I've had ever other bugger poke around in there.'

56

GENETICS

Westminster Morgue. Thursday 29th April. 11:30

Doctor Gates didn't appear to notice Marshall when she walked into the lab. He was poring over the contents of his lunch, picking out various ingredients with a pair of forceps and laying them out on a tray beside a body. The presence of the corpse seeming to have no effect on his appetite.

'Marshall can you explain to me what's the purpose of salad?' he said, without looking up.

She put his coffee down beside the array of carefully arranged green leaves. Noting how they were precisely ordered by size, an obvious reflection of his OCD tendencies.

'Do you want the truth?'

He grunted, putting down his lunch and picking up the coffee. 'No, I get enough of that from the wife.' Removing the cup lid he inhaled the steaming vapours. 'At least I can still enjoy the restorative powers of caffeine.'

Marshall inspected what was left of his meal. A grilled

breast of chicken on a bed of couscous. She tried to ignore the fact that it was sitting in one of his steel specimen bowls.

'She's got you on the diet again?'

'Happens every year, just before my birthday. You have to give her credit for trying.'

Marshall had never met Gates's wife. The fact that he had one at all was something of a shock. She couldn't imagine him as a young man, not one that a woman would ever find attractive. According to Anj, everyone had a soul-mate. One day she hoped to meet Mrs Gates, shake her by the hand and maybe present her with a medal.

'So, your message was a little cryptic?' Marshall said, taking out her phone and reading aloud. 'Who has the highest rates of genetic disorders in the world?'

He smiled smugly, put down his coffee and walked over to a shrouded body. 'I thought you'd like that one.'

Gates pulled the sheet away from the corpse with all the theatre of a Victorian magic act, revealing the body from the museum.

'This gentleman may not have much in the way of iden-tifiable body parts, but he does have a very distinctive blood type: AB negative, and a very rare form of genetic disorder: Bardet–Biedl syndrome.' He pointed into the chest cavity. 'There are some interesting facts about the Arabic states. They have the highest rates of genetic disorders in the world. Nine hundred and six pathologies to be exact. Mostly due to the inter-marrying of cousins within small sects. I've been in contact with the Centre for Arab Genomic Studies in Dubai. And as it happens they have a database of genetic analyses of the population across most of the Middle East.'

'They have his DNA?'

'As I said, his condition is a rare one. Passed down through the maternal line.'

'And?'

'This, my dear Marshall, is none other than Ahmed Hussain Al-Shammari.'

Marshall stared at the body, trying to imagine what Davidson was going to say when he found out his principal suspect was actually one of the victims.

She wished she could be there to see his face.

'Did he have any previous internal injuries? Like the others?'

Gates shook his head. 'No, there are clear signs of abnormalities from his condition, but otherwise no sign that the man was ever injured in battle.'

57

SHAMMARI

Charing Cross Station, Thursday 29th April. 13:15

Novak was waiting for her at the door.

'Got your message,' she said, 'they're all waiting in the briefing room.'

'Did you tell them?'

The DS shook her head. 'No, I thought I'd leave that to you.'

Stirling was showing the team images from Welling's report when she entered the room.

'Marshall, finally. So what's the big news?'

She walked to the screen and flicked back through the case photos until she found the right one. 'Gates has identified the victim from the museum. It's Al-Shammari.'

There was a collective intake of breath as everyone realised they'd just lost their prime suspect.

'Shammari?' said Stirling, unable to hide the disbelief in his voice. 'How can he be sure?'

'His DNA's on a database of rare genetic conditions.'

The DCI's eyes widened. 'What was he doing at the museum?'

'He trades in illegal artefacts, maybe he was trying to sell something to them,' suggested Hamilton.

Marshall flicked to the image of Ramsveld. 'He was a known associate of Benjamin Ramsveld, who was supposed to meet him about a fourth stone on the day he was killed. I think this has something to do with the rare diamond that was taken from the heist.'

'What's so important about this bloody diamond?' asked Stirling.

She turned away from the screen. 'Other than the fact it was worth eight million pounds?'

'Except it doesn't explain the other victims.'

Marshall shrugged. 'Not yet, but they're all connected to Tikrit, whatever happened out there, Al-Shammari knew about it and Simon Harrison is the only survivor, the only chance we have of finding out.'

Stirling nodded. 'Gates has Harrison booked in at St Thomas's tomorrow.'

The meeting ended and the team filed out of the room.

'A quick word,' Stirling said to Marshall as she turned to leave.

Leaning against the table, he crossed his arms and waited until the room was empty.

'Just conscious that we haven't really had time to talk, and I wanted to let you know I think you're doing a great job. I know starting with a new team is hard, and I dropped you into the deep end, everyone thinks you're fitting in really well.'

Marshall was a little taken aback, praise was not something she was used to, certainly not from Donovan. 'Thanks Boss.'

'I know this was supposed to be a secondment, but there's a permanent place for you here if you want it. No need to decide now, take your time and think about it.'

She could feel her cheeks warming and tried to ignore it. There weren't many times when she could remember feeling so relieved. It felt as though she'd been holding her breath for the last week, waiting for him to tell her to go, especially after the leak to the press.

'I will, thanks,' she replied, trying to hold his gaze but finding it too intense. 'Did you get anywhere with Captain Azir?' she asked, changing the subject to cover her embarrassment.

'Nothing, my guy thinks he must have been with another force, or he wasn't regular army.'

She frowned. 'What does that mean?'

'SAS. There were special forces on the ground during the early days of the war. Their officers use pseudonyms, codenames to hide their identities even amongst their own side. Azir was probably not his real name.'

58

SISTER

Institute of Neurology, Thursday 29th April. 17:15

S he hadn't felt this nervous since her first day on the beat. Pacing around the reception area, Marshall checked the time on her phone again. It was quarter past five and there was no sign of Martha.

She re-opened the message from Martha, it was short and to the point.

'UCL Queen Square, five o'clock.'

Marshall wondered how many times her half-sister rewrote the line. It couldn't be more than the versions of the email she'd written before sending.

Hi, I found the card you sent my dad. I think we should meet.

Gresham helped her to word it. Convincing her that, out of all the random rants, brevity was a wiser option over emotional outbursts.

'Assuming you actually want to meet her,' he said,

pouring himself another glass of wine, 'and not just punch her in the face.'

It was true, he knew she'd be worrying about how the meeting would play out. There were times when she'd come close to cancelling and forgetting the whole thing. Family wasn't really her thing, and after all this time, she didn't need a sibling, especially one that was clearly more successful than herself.

Pull it together, she told herself. *You have faced worse things than this.*

'Hi Philippa,' said a soft voice from behind her. 'Sorry I'm late.'

Marshall turned to find Martha standing a few feet away, her arms crossed over her chest. She was dressed in surgical scrubs.

'The op went on longer than expected,' she continued, 'do you want to grab a coffee?'

Marshall couldn't think of anything to say and simply nodded. The woman looked even more like her in the flesh, like her twin, and her brain was finding it hard to process.

She followed Martha into the Starbucks and tried to think of something to say while her sister ordered first.

'What do you want?'

'Double-shot latte,' she replied automatically, taking comfort in finding that she could still form words.

'So you're a detective inspector,' said Martha while they waited.

Small talk, thought Marshall, *good place to start.*

'And you're a brain surgeon,' she replied.

Her sister's mouth twisted into a smile. 'You've got his sense of humour.'

The direct reference to her father took Marshall by surprise, but she could tell it wasn't meant as a criticism. 'He used to tell the worst jokes,' she replied, remembering the Christmas dinners when he would get drunk with Uncle George.

'I'd like to hear about him,' Martha said, picking up the coffees and beckoning to an empty table. 'If you don't mind?'

Marshall realised how good it felt to talk about him. 'Sure, why not.'

They spent an hour talking. Martha would ask questions, obviously trying to fill the gaps in her memories of him. It transpired that her mother had worked at Bath University at the same time as her dad. They were friends, she was teaching English while he lectured in architecture. It was a few years before Marshall was born, before he married her mother.

'When I was younger, he used to come and see me once a month,' she said, hardly hiding the pain in her voice. 'Mum said he was my uncle. She didn't admit he was my father until a few years ago. Just before she died.'

'So you never knew?'

'I guessed. Mum married my stepfather when I was eight and the visits stopped.'

Marshall felt a little guilty. Like somehow she'd stolen something from her. It was totally irrational but also impossible not to imagine what it would have been like if their lives had been switched.

'How did he die?' Martha asked with the cool, detached tone of a doctor.

It wasn't the question Marshall had prepared herself for

and it took a moment for her to collect her thoughts. She took a long sip of the coffee to buy herself some time.

'He suffered with dementia for the last four years, and then a series of strokes took him just before Christmas.'

Martha nodded. 'And how is your mother?'

Again an unexpected question. 'She's moved back to Bath to be with her sister.'

There was a pained look in Martha's eyes, as if she genuinely cared about what had happened.

'I wish I could have seen him one more time. Just to say goodbye, you know?'

Marshall sighed, feeling the grief rising inside her. 'It wasn't easy at the end. He hardly knew who any of us were.' She took out the dragon key ring. 'He used to call this his lucky charm. I gave it to him on holiday when I was five.'

Martha's eyes lit up. 'I remember it. May I?' she asked, holding out her hand.

Marshall gave it to her.

There was something odd about the way she held it, as if it was a priceless treasure. Marshall felt a twinge of selfishness at the thought of sharing it. It was linked to so many memories, ones that she'd buried deep, too painful to revisit just yet.

But at least she had them, Martha had nothing.

'I think you should have it.'

Martha looked stunned, her eyes widening. 'Really?'

Marshall nodded. 'I have thirty-four years of memories. I think the least I can do is let you have one of them.'

'So what's it like? Being a detective?' Martha asked.

'Hard, brutal in fact, but very satisfying when it goes right.'

'When you catch the bad guy?'

Marshall nodded. 'My old boss used to say that solving a case was like finishing a puzzle, one with no instructions.'

Martha considered the idea for a moment. 'Much like neuroscience. We only know a small percentage of what the brain does.'

'I was going to go into medicine.'

She laughed. 'Weird, I nearly joined the police. Why didn't you?'

Marshall thought about lying, blaming her grades and then decided against it.

'Someone died, someone I cared a lot about, and it changed my perspective.'

Martha's smile dissolved away in an instant. 'They were murdered?'

'Yes, how did you know?'

'I majored in psychology. The trauma would have to be extreme to change your mind about your career, and joining the police would indicate a need to resolve injustice.'

Marshall was impressed. 'So why didn't you join the force?'

Martha shrugged. 'Didn't like the idea of working nights. So tell me, what case are you working on now?'

59

SCAN

St Thomas's Hospital, London. Friday 30th April. 09:30

Harrison lay calmly on the gurney while the doctor injected the sedative into his arm. He seemed unfazed by the large MRI scanner or the small hole he was about to be slid into, but the medical team insisted on a dose as a precaution. Some patients didn't realise quite how claustrophobic it could be until they were inside.

Watching from the observation room, Marshall couldn't think of anything worse. She'd never been good with confined spaces, and the thought of being stuck in that tiny tube was making her sweat.

Gates stood beside her, his eyes fixed on the array of screens as the technician prepared the system. 'Never get bored of watching this,' he muttered to himself. 'Nothing short of magic.'

Leaving Harrison, the consultant walked back into the control room.

'So, what are we focusing on today?' she asked Gates, sitting down beside the technician.

'I'm looking for a foreign object in the bowel. Probably near the Ileum.'

She nodded and her assistant hit a button on his keyboard. The lights dimmed and the hum of the machine changed as Harrison was slowly transported inside.

Images of his body began to appear on the screens, as the repetitive thudding of the scanner got underway. Greyscale pictures like obscure maps flickered across the displays as the technician tapped in a series of instructions into the console.

Marshall had no idea what she was looking at.

'There!' shouted Gates, pointing to a white spot on the screen.

'What is that?' asked the consultant, putting on her spectacles. 'Shrapnel?'

'Not its denser than bone but not metal,' said Gates, squinting at the screen.

'Diamond?' suggested Marshall.

'Why on earth would he have a diamond in his lower intestine?' asked the consultant, her eyebrow arching.

Gates looked at Marshall. 'Something you want to tell us Detective?'

Staring at the enlarged view of Harrison' s bowel, it suddenly all snapped into place.

'I think someone's been using the victims of the Tikrit attack to smuggle precious stones out of Iraq.'

60

MI6

Charing Cross Police Station, London. Friday 30th April. 13:30

Malcolm Reed was sitting in Stirling's office when Marshall got back.

She could tell from the DCI's dour expression that the conversation with the MI6 section chief wasn't going well. Al-Shammari's murder meant the case was now a diplomatic incident, which would involve a serious amount of admin and red tape.

The Saudi Embassy would be expecting all the details of the investigation, as well as the opportunity to interview every officer involved in the case.

Going back to her desk, Marshall logged onto her laptop and opened her inbox. There were twenty new messages, and scrolling through them she saw Gates had already filed an official report on Harrison and opened it.

It was short and to the point. Someone inserted a foreign body into Harrison's bowel during surgery, and the immune response cascade encapsulated the object in scar tissue. Based on the thickening of the collagen, Gates estimated that it had been in the body for over fifteen years. Apparently the previous consultants had thought the shrapnel was too close to the bowel to remove.

A surgical team were planning to remove the stone the following week, much to Harrison's relief. He looked like a different man when they told him what they'd found. She realised then that he was secretly worrying about whether it was bowel cancer.

'Marshall!' Stirling's voice snapped her out of her reverie. 'In here now.'

Closing the laptop, she took a deep breath, her eyes catching Novak's across the desk. The DS tilted her head slightly and winked, as if to say: 'You've got this.'

Walking towards his office, Marshall tried really hard to believe that she did.

Reed stood when she entered the room. There was something of an old-fashioned gentleman about him, the kind of mannerisms a spy would have had before the Second World War.

'DI Marshall,' said Stirling, not bothering to rise from his chair. 'Mr Reed has some new information for us.'

She tried to hide her surprise, but failed.

Reed smiled, showing an impressive array of white teeth as he held out his hand. 'I believe we've met before haven't we?'

Marshall gripped it firmly as she shook it. 'I was at City.'

The spook's eyes narrowed, his dark brown pupils turning black. They were scrutinising every inch of her face, making her feel like she was suddenly under interrogation. 'Yes, the robbery at Hatton Garden. I heard the owner was subsequently killed?'

She nodded. 'Murdered. Same MO as Al-Shammari.'

He let go of her hand. 'Do you have any suspects?'

Stirling laughed. 'We did until he turned out to be one of the victims.'

Reed ignored the interruption. His eyes hardly blinking. 'What do you think Detective Inspector?' he asked in a cool, collected tone.

Marshall hesitated, wondering how much to tell him. He was the one who refused to cooperate on the diamond heist, actively blocking an entire line of enquiry. She didn't see any reason why she should start trusting him now that Al-Shammari was dead. *Let's find out what he knows.*

'I think the murders and the heist are linked — that it goes back to an incident in Iraq. Most of the victims were part of a convoy that was attacked in 2003. I'm not sure how Al-Shammari was involved in that, but he was supposed to meet Ramsveld about a fourth stone on the day the jeweller was murdered. If Al-Shammari was already dead, then the killer must have gone in his place.'

Reed nodded as if agreeing with her. 'Let me tell you about Ahmed Hussain Al-Shammari.' He gestured for her to take a seat.

'He was born in Iraq, his father was a general in the Republican Guard and a good friend of Saddam Hussein. Ahmed, being the dutiful son, followed in his father's foot-steps, becoming a Captain in the guard himself. When the US invaded in 2003, he helped his family escape to Saudi

Arabia, taking a few of the more valuable national treasures with them.'

'He stole from Saddam?' Marshall asked.

Reed laughed. 'Everybody did. It was every man for himself back then. With his family safely ensconced in Riyadh, the ever-resourceful Al-Shammari set up a network to liberate more of Iraq's treasures, and that was when he began to trade with the likes of al-Qaeda and Abu Ali al-Anbari.'

'So Al-Shammari was a terrorist,' said Marshall.

The section chief shrugged. 'More of an opportunist, I don't think he had any allegiances, other than to money.'

'But you said he was funding an active cell here in the UK?'

'He was. We've been watching their activity since the robbery. The funds from the diamond heist have already passed through a series of offshore accounts, but the crew have stayed onshore, which means they're planning something else, something bigger perhaps.'

'Do you know who killed him?' asked Stirling.

Reed turned towards the DCI. 'We believe it was the leader of the cell. He goes by the codename "Anubis", but we have nothing on him — he's a ghost.'

Marshall bit her tongue, it was hard to believe that MI6 had nothing on Anubis. Although the information he'd given them so far was good, it wasn't going to help them find the killer. Her gut told her that Reed knew more than he was telling, so she tried a different tack.

'We think Al-Shammari may have been at the museum to meet a buyer.'

The section chief nodded. 'He was, Martin Kristiansen, a wealthy Norwegian collector of Mesopotamian artefacts — it was the opening night of his collection.'

She sighed. 'I was supposed to go to that.'

Stirling was thumbing through the report from the museum. 'So Anubis's team were stealing the diamond at the same time he was murdering the go-between?'

Reed nodded. 'It would appear they cut out the middle man, quite literally.'

'And Kristiansen still bought the jewel?' said Marshall.

'Yes, apparently it's one of seven that belongs in the necklace of a Sumerian queen. Once he has collected all of them it will be priceless.'

Marshall did a quick review of the timeline in her head: Welling, Hope, Dennison, Peters, Avery and Harrison — that made six, one was still missing.

'Sounds like we need to pay him a visit,' Stirling said, getting to his feet. 'I take it you have no objections to us pursuing this?'

Reed stood up and straightened his jacket. 'None at all, assuming you share your findings. I will take the lead on liaising with the Saudi Embassy.'

'Of course,' agreed Stirling, who seemed relieved that he wouldn't have to.

She watched the DCI show the section chief out of the office, trying to work out what it was about him that disturbed her. It was something about the way he looked at her with those dark eyes, like someone had just walked over her grave.

'How did it go with Harrison? Did Gates find anything?' Stirling asked, closing the door behind him. He'd guessed that she purposely not shared the information with Reed.

'He's got a diamond embedded in his bowel. Gates thinks it's been in there for at least fifteen years.'

Stirling sat down in his chair and folded his arms. 'So what's your theory?'

Marshall looked over to the whiteboard on the other side of the office. 'I think the victims of the Tikrit attack were used to smuggle precious stones out of Iraq.'

61

THE BUYER

The British Museum. Saturday 1st May. 10:00

The sun shone down on the museum courtyard. Marshall paused for a moment, feeling the warmth on her face, appreciating the cloudless blue sky stretching over the columned entrance.

Finally, it was beginning to feel like spring had arrived.

'Haven't been here since I was a kid,' said Novak, taking a photograph with her phone. 'School trip.'

'I used to make my dad bring me here every time we came to London,' said Marshall.

Dragging her father around the museums was one of her favourite memories, even though he complained the entire time, he never once refused.

Novak looked confused. 'You're not from London?'

Marshall shook her head, it was an easy mistake to make, she'd never had the strongest West Country accent. 'No, Bath. In Somerset.'

'Ah. The Roman city.'

'Georgian, but yeah, the Roman baths are still there.'

The steps of the museum were lined with tourists forming an orderly queue as they waited to pass through security. A well-dressed man appeared from between the columns and walked down the steps towards them. He looked well-built under the expensive suit, and carried himself like a soldier — *private security*, thought Marshall.

'DI Marshall?' he asked, his sharp eyes flicking between the two of them.

She nodded, pulling out her warrant card. 'This is DS Novak.'

He took out a radio and spoke quietly into it. 'The guests have arrived.'

Novak glanced at Marshall, raising one eyebrow ever so slightly.

'Follow me please,' he said, turning his broad shoulders and walking back towards the steps.

A bewildered museum security guard stood back as the man ignored the queues and bypassed the metal detectors. Marshall wondered exactly how much money Kristiansen would have to donate to allow him such liberties. The Norwegian billionaire was obviously very concerned about his own safety.

Beyond the ticket desk, the corridors were hung with banners promoting his collection; images of ancient treasures were superimposed onto pictures of the old man smiling nonchalantly like a benevolent grandfather.

The security guard stopped at a nondescript door and keyed in a nine-digit code into the lock. Pulling it open, he gestured for them to step inside, his head rotating on a thick neck as he checked in both directions.

Two more similarly dressed men were standing inside,

one was holding a metal detector which he waved over them without waiting for their consent.

Once he was satisfied, they were escorted through another door and into the main collection.

Kristiansen sat on a chair in the middle of the room, surrounded by glass cases, each one displaying a golden treasure or carved stone artefact.

Standing beside him, a woman was taking notes on an iPad while he dictated to her in what Marshall assumed was Norwegian.

She placed a gentle hand on his shoulder and he looked up through thick spectacles as they approached.

He looked much older than the promo photos outside. There were deep lines in his face and his skin had a sickly hue that spoke of liver problems.

Resting heavily on his cane, Kristiansen pushed himself to his feet and held out a slightly shaking hand.

'Martin Kristiansen,' the old gentleman said with a curt, Nordic accent.

Marshall shook it, his grip stronger than she'd expected. 'Detective Inspector Marshall, and this is Detective Sergeant Novak.'

He nodded. 'Please to meet you both,' he said with the same benevolent smile and letting go of her hand. 'I was told you have some questions for me?'

His assistant hovered behind him, watching them both like a bird of prey.

'Yes, we're investigating an individual by the name of Ahmed Hussain Al-Shammari.'

The man's face remained impassive. 'Yes.'

'Have you ever met him?'

The old man paused, turning to his assistant for a second. She nodded and he sighed. 'I have had some dealings with the man.'

He walked slowly towards one of the exhibits, beckoning them to follow.

Inside the case was a porcelain bust of a beautiful woman, around her neck hung a golden necklace studded with red jewels.

'This is the necklace of Queen Pu-abi. The archaeologist, Leonard Wooley, found it during an excavation of the Royal Tombs of Ur in 1922. The Sumerians believed that it was necessary to bring gifts for the gods when entering the after-life. Bribes to ensure they had a comfortable stay. This particular piece is over four and a half thousand years old.'

He took out a set of brass keys from his pocket and unlocked the cabinet door. 'I have spent many years trying to locate the missing stones,' he added, pointing to the empty settings in the golden plates. 'Ramsveld contacted me a few months ago to say that Al-Shammari had come into possession of one. It's been years since any have surfaced, and I was beginning to give up hope of ever restoring the piece. Al-Shammari was supposed to be here on the opening night, but he never showed. Then there was all that fuss over the murder.' He stared at the golden exhibit for a moment, lost in his thoughts. 'I met him a few days later and purchased it. He said he knew where the others were too.'

Marshall glanced at Novak, who produced a picture of Al-Shammari on her phone. 'You met this man?' she asked, holding it up for Kristainsen.

He squinted at the image, his glasses balancing on the end of his nose. 'No. Not him. This was a younger man.'

Novak put the phone away.

'And how did you pay him?'

'Bitcoin.'

'Could you give us a description of the man you met?'

Kristiansen shrugged. 'Tall, dark-skinned. I would say in his late forties. He was softly spoken and polite. He had a beard and walked with a limp.'

Novak took notes whilst he spoke, but Marshall knew it would be of little use. 'Where did you meet him?'

'Battersea Park, near the Peace Pagoda. Is there a problem detective?'

'Al-Shammari was the one who was murdered on the night your collection opened. I believe the man you bought the stone from was his killer.'

The old man's eyes widened. 'Am I in danger?'

'I don't think so, but you say there are three more stones to find?'

'Yes, he promised me all of them.'

62

GREENWICH

The British Museum. Saturday 1st May. 11:00

L eaving the museum, Marshall took out her phone and scrolled through her messages. There were three missed calls from Biggs in the last twenty minutes.

'Hey, what's up?' she asked when he answered on the second ring.

'Just thought you should know. MI6 has passed SO15 the location of the terrorist cell they believe was behind the heist.'

She stopped at the top of the steps. 'You're fucking kidding me! I knew he was holding something back.'

'What?' mouthed Novak.

Marshall held up her hand to quiet the DS.

'When?'

'Half an hour ago. Davidson's already left.'

'Where are they?'

'It's an industrial unit near Greenwich. I'll send you the address.'

Marshall ended the call, opening her messages as Biggs's text arrived.

'They've found the terrorists. SO15 is going in now,' she explained holding up the phone to show Novak the address.

'You're not thinking of going?'

'I can't let Davidson fuck this one up.'

Lighting up the blues and twos, Novak drove like a demon through the busy traffic on Chancery Lane and onto Black-friars Bridge.

Marshall put a call in to Stirling, who didn't answer, which was probably for the best. She left a voicemail, just to cover her arse in case it turned into a shit show later.

'Must be on his way over there,' Novak suggested, taking a sharp right turn onto Southwark Street at fifty miles an hour. 'You think they'll take them alive?'

'Not if Davidson has anything to do with it. He always shoots first. Especially as they've used gas before, too great a risk to try and go in soft.'

Novak took a hard left, mounting the kerb to avoid an oncoming bus.

'You sure you know where you're going?' asked Marshall, pushing herself away from the car door.

'I live in Greenwich. I know the quickest way to get there.'

Marshall suddenly realised she'd never known that. She'd been so focused on impressing Stirling that she'd not bothered to get to know her new partner at all. It wasn't like they'd had much time to talk about the small stuff, somehow his squad didn't seem to get into that.

The streets around the industrial estate were sealed off by the time they arrived. Police traffic vehicles were parked across the junctions and officers were stopping cars and pedestrians from entering Norman Road.

Novak parked up on the pavement and they jumped out with warrant cards in hand.

It seemed eerily quiet walking past the black SUVs lining both sides of the street. They were the unmarked BMWs that SO15 favoured for rapid response. An AFO in black combats and body armour stood guard beside one of them, his MP5 slung over one shoulder. He gestured to them, indicating a command unit parked down a side road.

Stirling stepped down out of the van as they approached.

'What the fuck are you doing here?' he said, not bothering to hide his displeasure.

Marshall ignored him. 'Hatton Garden was my case remember? Have they gone in yet?'

The DCI's expression mellowed slightly and he nodded towards the open door. 'Davidson's team is doing a threat assessment. He's just waiting for the area to be cleared of civilians.'

Marshall peered over his shoulder and into the command centre. The banks of monitors were showing feeds from the body cams of the CTSFO team. They were positioned between rows of rental trucks, keeping low, the barrels of their guns trained on a set of garage doors built into the railway arches.

One of the screens switched to thermal, the ghostly image of a group of men appeared through the solid wall.

'This is Kilo Five-Five, targets acquired,' they heard over the intercom.

'Roger that,' replied a voice from within. Marshall recognised Davidson instantly. 'Wait for my command.'

'Roger. Standing by.'

'I think you need to leave,' said Stirling, lowering his voice. 'Davidson is going to want strict hostile event safeguards in place when they go in.'

Marshall sneered, folding her arms over her chest. 'More like he wants to reduce the number of witnesses.'

Stirling frowned and moved them away from the open door. 'You have a better idea?'

'Put them under surveillance, study their movements, find out who else is involved. Giving them to Davidson is literally like signing their death warrant.'

He looked as if he was considering the idea when they heard the first crack of gunfire.

'Shit!' Davidson swore. 'Hold your fire!'

But it was too late. Marshall followed Stirling back to the command vehicle as the teams engaged. Shaky footage of the men storming into the garages flickered across every monitor. Flashes of white light obscuring the night vision images as they fired into the pale green darkness.

Everyone watched in silence while the operation played out. Marshall studied Davidson out of the corner of her eye, there was a look of complete helplessness on his face.

'Targets neutralised,' reported the team leader a few minutes later.

There was a general sigh of relief and Marshall realised she'd been holding her breath.

Davidson seemed to suddenly snap out of his daze. Leaning into the mic, he asked: 'Any sign of chemical agents?'

'Negative,' said the voice. 'Tox readings normal.'

Images of bodies spread over the screens. It was just as Marshall feared, no one left to answer for their actions. She knew better than to labour the point. The top brass would see this as a win, another terrorist plan thwarted, thanks to the valiant efforts of Counter Terrorism.

Stirling turned towards her. 'Wait outside.'

Novak and Marshall did as instructed. They walked back out on to Norman Street and watched the secondary teams in Hazmat suits make their way through the metal gates as the Firearms units left looking all too pleased with themselves. Davidson came out to meet them, slapping them on the back and shaking hands like a football manager whose team had just won the FA cup.

'Did they kill them all?' asked Novak.

Marshall nodded.

It started to rain, so they went back to Novak's car and spent the next hour watching the various specialists go back and forth from their unmarked vans.

Bored, Novak settled down in the passenger seat, taking the opportunity to catch up on some sleep.

Marshall kicked off her shoes and tried to make herself comfortable. She'd never really been any good at surveillance; the thought of sitting still for hours on end was her idea of torture. Her grandmother used to say she'd been born with wandering feet. Even as a child she found it nearly impossible to keep still. Later, the educational psychologists gave it a name, Attention Deficit Hyperactivity Disorder, ADHD, but by then she'd found her own ways to deal with it. Using her imagination to construct a mental playground was something that came in rather useful in her line of work.

Slowing her breathing, she closed her eyes and thought

about the opening night at the museum. Using what Kristiansen and Gresham had told her, she reconstructed the party in her mind: the old Norwegian standing amongst his guests in the Egyptian Sculpture Gallery, their faces were indistinct like something from a dream. Except for Gresham of course. She mentally dressed him in one of his black turtle necks and a dark grey jacket, and left him talking to a group of white-haired mentors from Oxford.

Somewhere in the crowd was Al-Shammari, she turned around in the scene, placing the rather overweight Saudi beside the necklace of Queen Pu-abi, imagining him admiring the gemstones.

Kristiansen said he was waiting to buy the stone from Al-Shammari that night — although the man's name wasn't on the official guest list. There would be instructions left with his security team, orders that were never shared with the police.

She pictured the catering staff moving amongst the guests in their ceremonial masks, each one based on a different Egyptian god. Marshall knew that the killer was one of them, moving unnoticed through them, a perfect disguise to hide his identity from the CCTV.

Somehow Anubis lured Al-Shammari away from the party, persuading him to take the west stairs up into the Egyptian rooms. All it would have taken was a simple request from Kristiansen to meet upstairs, away from prying eyes; Al-Shammari would have been expecting it.

She imagined the two of them taking the stairs up to the rooms filled with sarcophagi. There was no way they would have avoided every camera, even with the mask giving him a sense of bravado. So why hadn't Stirling's team recognised that it was Al-Shammari from the tapes?

Snapping out of her reverie, Marshall pulled out her

phone and typed an email to DC Hamilton. He'd studied the footage from that night, so she asked him if there was anything from the west stairs.

A few minutes later she got a response.

'No.'

Putting her phone away, she saw the first of the body bags. Three were carried out by masked officers and placed into the back of a private ambulance.

Waking Novak, who was gently snoring, Marshall got out of the car and made her way towards the unmistakeable form of Doctor Gates. His body wasn't meant for such a tight fitting hazmat suit. She knew it was him before he'd even taken off his gas mask.

'Davidson and his cowboys have gone. It's all yours Marshall,' he growled, 'though I doubt you'll find much in there.'

Nodding her thanks, she ducked under the tape and walked into the yard.

Behind the rows of rusting white vans, were a series of garages built into the old brick arches of the railway line above. Each one had a shuttered door with signs warning about hazardous chemicals or flammable materials screwed onto it.

One of the doors was hanging off its hinges, the frame buckled from the impact of the battering ram. Walking inside, she caught the slight taint of gunpowder still hanging in the air, mixed with body odour, blood and engine oil.

The dingy space was lit up by forensic LED lamps,

exposing the fact that the arches were interconnected, creating one long chamber. Its curving walls were lined with metal shelves stacked high with old car parts, and plastic containers. There were two upturned plastic barrels sitting on a bench, wires and other electrical components were scattered across the top.

Biggs was standing with his hands on his hips, surveying the components. A forensic photographer was taking shots of the body outlines on the floor beside him.

'Hey stranger,' she said, standing beside him.

'They were making a bomb.' He picked up the remnants of a mobile phone with a gloved hand.

Marshall read the label on the side of one of the barrels, it was a chemical fertiliser. There were more barrels laying on the floor.

'Looks like they were planning something big,' he continued, nodding to a wall covered in maps and images printed from Google Streetview.

Stepping carefully between the dark pools of blood, Marshall walked over to it.

She recognised several locations: Chelsea Football Stadium, Waterloo Station and the Houses of Parliament, but the one that sent shivers down Marshall's spine was the London Tube map and the photographs of Embankment.

Detonating a bomb on a tube train under the River Thames had always been the Met's greatest concern. During the active years of the IRA, MI5 analysts identified it as the worst possible scenario. The water would flood the tunnels in seconds, shorting out the power, trapping everyone inside. TFL installed flood defences at either ends of the most vulnerable tunnels, but they'd never been used. 7/7 was the closest anyone had come to even attempting it and that had failed.

If it happened during rush hour, thousands of people could be trapped inside the network. It would bring London to a standstill.

'Do you think they were going to hit the tube?'

Biggs shrugged, stepping aside to let the forensic photographer take a shot. 'Who knows.'

She knew how he felt, there was a sense of despair and relief, the curse of knowing what could have been.

'You any closer to working out who the killer is?' he asked, turning towards her.

Marshall shrugged. 'Yes and no, but I think I know why.'

Biggs's eyes widened. 'And?'

'All the victims connected to the Tikrit bombing were killed in a ritualistic way. Their organs removed and placed into jars.'

'Like they were going to be mummified,' Biggs added.

'It was just a diversion, to hide the fact that they all had something embedded in their bowel. Something that was placed in there after the attack in 2003.'

'Shrapnel?'

She shook her head. 'Diamonds. I think someone at the field hospital was using them as couriers to smuggle jewels back to the UK.'

'Why the fuck would they do that?'

Marshall had forgotten how much she missed his blunt approach. Sometimes it was the obvious questions that got overlooked.

'One of the victims was a reporter, she was investigating a story about national treasures being stolen to order by local gangs. The military were too busy guarding the oil to focus on the pillaging. There was a soldier, Peters, who was selling her information about the operation.'

'You think the Army knew what was going on?'

'Gates says the murders were carried out by someone with medical training. There was a medic — a surgeon called Major Azir.'

'Fuck. So he could be Anubis?'

'I think he was involved, but he's been in a secure psychiatric ward since 2018. So it can't be him.'

'Have you questioned him?'

'No,' Marshall said, turning back to the wall. 'I'm still waiting for the DP9.'

Biggs scratched his head, something he always did when he was thinking deeply. 'So how the hell is this linked to the terrorists?'

She folded her arms and studied the maps closely. 'That's what I keep asking myself. Al-Shammari was financing ISIS, so he would have been too valuable to kill. Anubis was making a statement — marking him as one of the victims — same with Ramsveld.'

'If they were the middlemen, maybe they got too greedy.'

Once again, Biggs's instincts were so close to her own. 'That's what I thought. All we know is that he's going to want to sell the rest of the gemstones and there's still a survivor. Stirling has put him under twenty-four hour surveillance.'

'Fuck.' Biggs rubbed his eyes, he looked dog-tired. 'Maybe we're over-thinking this, maybe he's just some insane jihadi with a mummy fetish.'

She smiled. 'Maybe.'

63

JEWELS

Incident Room, Charing Cross Police Station. Sunday 2nd May. 07:30

'So here's what we know,' said Stirling, rising slowly from his chair and walking to the large screen. 'The three bodies recovered from the raid were all Iraqi nationals. They arrived from Dubai four months ago on student visas.' Three passport photographs of the men appeared on the screen. 'Counter Terrorism is working with MI6 on known associates and their movements since they arrived. We're assuming that this wasn't the entire team and that Anubis is still at large.'

Hamilton raised his hand. 'I heard they were planning to hit the tube.'

Stirling tapped on the screen, a picture of the wall filled with plans slid over the images of the dead men. 'It's one of the possibilities. JTAC has raised the threat level to critical and deployed armed response teams around the city, but until we hear more from the security services we focus on finding the ringleader.'

The DCI turned towards Marshall. 'How did you get on with Kristiansen?'

'He thought he was buying the diamond from Al-Shammari. According to him, the Saudi was asking for eight million dollars.'

'Can we trace the payment?' asked Nicholls.

Marshall shook her head. 'He paid in Bitcoin.'

'Eight million for one?'

'I got the feeling he's willing to go even higher for the last two.'

Marshall went over to the glass wall that made up one side of the meeting room, photographs of all the victims were taped onto it.

'Kristiansen told me that the diamonds are part of a Sumerian necklace that was lost four thousand years ago. I think they were smuggled out of Iraq inside the bodies of victims from the attack in 2003,' she said, underlining the names of Hope, Welling, Avery and Dennison.

Stirling came over to join her. 'From what the SIB told me, they were all operated on by the same surgeon. A Major Saadah Azir.'

'I think he deliberately hid the stones in the victims,' continued Marshall. 'We'll know for sure later. The only living survivor, Simon Harrison, is having his removed today at UCLH.'

'And where is this Major Azir now?' asked Nicholls.

'He's been in a mental institution since 2018. I've been waiting for the Super to approve the interview.'

Nicholls looked confused. 'So if he's not Anubis, who is?'

'That is what I'm hoping the Major can tell me.'

64

BEDLAM

**Fitzmary House 2, Bethlem Royal Hospital, Beckenham.
Monday 3rd May**

The Psychosis Unit was housed in a two-storey Georgian building in the grounds of Bethlem Royal Hospital. Bethlem was one of the oldest mental institutions in London. Gresham had told her about its notorious history, which included stories of Victorian carnival-like freak shows and work-house conditions — it was also the origin of the term 'Bedlam.'

Marshall parked the car and checked her messages. Her phone had been buzzing the entire journey. Most of them were just Biggs giving her updates on his case. Apparently Gold Command had just deployed SO15 to arrest two more members of the group after identifying them from CCTV footage. Which was bad news: they would go to ground and be virtually impossible to find, or worse still, they would carry out the plan.

The only other message was from Novak who'd stayed behind to check on the CCTV with Hamilton.

It was a grainy shot of a man in a jackal mask, making his way back down the West Stairs of the museum. Underneath she'd added 'Anubis?'.

Walking into the Pysch Unit, Marshall wasn't quite sure what to expect. Hospitals were not her favourite places, even before her father died, and secure units generally felt more like prisons than healthcare facilities.

A middle-aged nurse sat behind the reception desk, her greying hair tied back in a tight pony tail making her expression even more severe. Reluctantly, she took down Marshall's details from the warrant card and asked her to wait while she called the consultant-in-charge.

The waiting room was pretty basic with plastic seats screwed into metal benches. Nothing that could be picked up and thrown — similar to the ones at Wood Street.

Ten minutes later a tall, dark-haired man, walked out through one of the secure doors and came over to greet her. His thick-framed glasses and three-day stubble reminded her of Gresham, as did the black jeans and the grey polo neck. She wasn't a big fan of psychologists, but this one was cuter than most.

'Detective Inspector Marshall?' he asked politely, holding out a hand.

Marshall got up from the seat and shook it. 'Doctor Willoughby?' She tried to hide the doubt from her voice, but he looked nothing like a doctor.

Willoughby smiled, releasing his grip. 'Yes, sorry, we don't wear white coats here. It tends to act as a trigger for some of our more sensitive patients.' His voice was calm and reassuring, in that tone that made you want to trust him instantly.

'Understood.'

He took an iPad from under his arm and began flicking through the records. 'Your email said you were interested in the Major?'

She nodded. 'Yes, I need to talk to him about an incident that occurred while he was serving in Iraq in 2003.'

The doctor grimaced, taking off his glasses and revealing a pair of dark brown eyes.

'I can't agree to that.'

'Why?'

'You know I can't disclose patient information.'

Marshall smiled and produced the paperwork, which Willoughby took and read carefully.

'Prevention of Terrorism?' he said, his eyes flicking up off the form to stare at her. They were full of questions.

She nodded. 'It's an ongoing investigation. I can't disclose more than that.'

He folded the paper and put it into his back pocket.

'Come with me,' he said, turning to the door and swiping his ID card through the reader.

Beyond the doors, everything changed. A long white corridor stretched out before them. The windows looking out onto the road were barred and strong doors lined the opposite wall, each with prison-like observation ports set into the panels.

'Are they dangerous?' asked Marshall, looking through one of the ports as they passed.

'Psychosis can take many forms, but most involve some form of mania, delusions or hallucinations. Some of my patients are unable to differentiate between reality and their demons. Such persecution complexes can lead to violent or threatening behaviour, while others may believe they're the president. The mind is a powerful weapon in the wrong hands.'

'And Major Azir?'

'The Major suffered a serious psychotic episode during his tour in Iraq. He was diagnosed with PTSD in 2015 and admitted for treatment — which he responded to very well, but three years later he was back again, this time with acute schizophrenia. So, I'm concerned that any questioning about his past could trigger another relapse.'

Marshall tried not to sound too patronising when she replied. 'I understand your concerns doctor, but there is a very real threat to the public, and we think he may have vital information pertaining to the case.'

'Such as?' he asked, raising an eyebrow.

She lowered her voice. 'We believe he has links to an active terrorist cell, ones that have carried out a series of murders. I know he was the duty surgeon who treated every one of the victims back in 2003.'

Willoughby looked surprised, which was her intention, but not shocked. Marshall wondered what other horrors he'd been exposed to in his line of work.

'What do you think he's done?'

'I think he implanted jewels in them during their surgery.'

'Jewels?' the doctor exclaimed, stopping at a door and waiting for her to join him.

'Rare diamonds, worth in excess of forty million pounds.'

He keyed in the security code and opened the door. 'That's interesting. The first time I met the Major he was convinced there was a bomb inside him — he told me that his brother put it there. I'd always assumed that was just part of his hypomania.'

Marshall wasn't really paying attention, she was staring at the man standing in the small cell. He looked directly at her, same beard, same dark eyes — only these ones were filled with pain.

'Detective?' the doctor asked. 'Are you okay?'

Realising she was holding her breath, she forced herself to speak.

'Tell me doctor, what was his brother's name?' she said, taking out her phone.

'He was an officer, too. They joined together.' He flicked through the file once more. 'His name is Captain Menes Azir. He's an identical twin. I've been trying to get him into an MRI, to compare the internal structures of their brain, but he won't have it. Still, he's been funding our research for the past three years.'

Marshall turned to leave.

'Don't you want to question him?' the doctor said as she strode down the corridor.

She dialled Stirling's number. 'No thank you, doc. I've just got the answer I needed.'

By the time she reached the door, his voicemail kicked in.

'Boss, don't trust Section Chief Reed. I'll explain when I get back.'

CAPTAIN AZIR

Vaults of the British Museum. Monday, 3rd May. 16:00

The necklace glistened in the lights of the display cabinet.

Anubis studied the diamonds set into the golden plates, remembering every victim in turn. One stone for each of them.

Their deaths weighed heavily on his heart. Witnessing the lives his brother, Saadah, had ruined with his sick game: hiding things inside them, just like he used to do when they were children. The doctors spent years trying to understand his obsession with the inner workings of the body and all they could say was that it was symptomatic of a deeper psychological issue.

An obsession that once proved so useful to his medical career, making him one of Egypt's brightest young surgeons, had twisted and become something terrible.

He blamed himself.

After they'd lost their father, his brother became dependent on him. Following him into the Army. Such a fragile mind, dragged into the worst kind of war, it had broken him. Turning his delicate, brilliant little brother into a monster.

And now he was no better.

The night they'd brought what was left of the convoy into the field hospital was still a vivid memory. Anubis was on special operations when he heard about the attack at Tikrit. He was part of the extraction team that went in to rescue the convoy. The IED killed most of the escort and half of the civilians they were guarding. Peters and the medic were the only ones left standing, and he'd lose his legs.

Peters and his damned jewels.

The man was an opportunist. During his more lucid moments he'd told Saadah about how his team found the bombed-out temple near Assur. How he was the first to go in, joking about Aladdin's cave, and how they all took the piss out of him.

Until an hour later when he reappeared with pockets stuffed full of gold and gems.

When Peters accused Saadah of stealing his gold, everyone thought he was just high on the morphine. It was only later that Anubis discovered that his brother was the one who took them. While Peters was under heavy sedation, his brother must have gone through his kit and found the stolen treasure. It would have triggered memories of their father and the times in the tombs.

'You have the stones?' asked Kristiansen, hobbling into the

vault with a cane, two bodyguards flanked him on either side.

Anubis took the pouch from his pocket and handed it to the old man.

'You know who I am? What I've done to get this?'

The old Norwegian shrugged, pulling the strings of the bag apart and tipping the stones into his palm. 'I don't care.'

'Then you're a fool.'

Kristiansen laughed, looking around the vault. 'You're standing in a building that houses a wealth of priceless historical artefacts, stolen by imperialist explorers in the name of knowledge. I doubt any of them asked permission. In fact, many saw it as their duty to rescue it from the natives.'

Anubis smiled, the old man sounded like their father.

When they would visit him at the Cairo Museum, he would remind them of how the white man, Howard Carter, had taken their most precious King and his treasures. Tutankhamun had since been returned to his tomb, but many of his artefacts were still touring the globe.

'How much?' asked Kristiansen, squinting through a loupe as he held the jewel up to the light.

'Same as before,' replied Anubis.

The old man nodded. 'Agreed.' He waved his hand to one of his guards who opened a tablet. Twenty seconds later, the notification appeared on Anubis's phone.

'What about the last one?' Kristiansen said greedily. 'When do I get that?'

'All in good time.'

Walking out of the vaults, he took the stairs to the Great Court. The covered area was full of tourists and students, milling around the central stone structure that held the famous reading room. Anubis kept his head down, making his way into the toilets beside the shop.

Behind the cistern panel in the last cubicle he took out the delivery driver's uniform he'd hidden there a few days before and quickly changed out of his clothes.

66

BOMB

Monday, 3rd May. 17:30

Traffic ground to a halt as Marshall neared Brixton. It was rush hour and like most people, the thought of being stuck in gridlocked traffic stressed her out. Feeling the anxiety beginning to build, she contemplated dumping her car at the local nick and getting the tube back into the city.

As a girl it had been her worst nightmare, sitting in the back of the family car trying not to think about wanting to pee. Which was ridiculous, because the minute you did, the urge would come.

'You're a big girl now,' her mother would say sternly. 'You should be able to control it.'

Not the best advice you could give a seven-year-old, and more than once it ended with her father pulling over so she could go in the bushes.

The sensation of pulling down your pants in the freezing cold air of a forest was something that you never forgot. She made her father keep watch for bears, which he duly did, because of course, bears were very fond of little girls.

.   .   .

Her phone buzzed, it was a message from Biggs: one of the suspects had been spotted near Westminster and the entire CT team were being deployed.

Marshall called him, the phone automatically connecting to the car's hands-free system.

'Where are you?' he asked.

'Brixton. What's going on?'

There was a pause and sounds of him walking out into a hallway. 'Vauxhall Cross picked up a positive ID on one of the cameras near Westminster Bridge. The suspect's wearing a bulky coat, Davidson's deployed all of SO15 to get him.'

'Just the one guy? I thought there were two.'

'He thinks they're targeting Parliament. They're not taking any chances. JTAC has initiated the MTA plan. London is being locked down.'

'Did MI6 have anything to do with this?' Marshall asked.

'Yes, Reed contacted Davidson over an hour ago. Why?'

'Shit!' she said, pulling the car into the kerb. 'Listen to me. Reed is not to be trusted. I think he's behind the murders. I don't have time to explain but you have to get Davidson to stand down.'

Biggs scoffed. 'No chance of that, I've never seen him so happy. It's like all of his Christmases have come at once.'

'It's a diversion. Something else is going down, and Reed has sent SO15 on a wild good chase.'

The line went dead.

Marshall looked at her phone — no signal. Then she remembered as part of the emergency response they would use the access overload control scheme, shutting down the mobile network to stop remote detonations.

She slammed her fist into the steering wheel. 'Fuck!'
Getting out of the car she made for the tube.

67

FINDING

British Museum. Monday, 3rd May. 18:00

Walking through the black iron gates and out onto Great Russell Street, Anubis waved at the traffic warden who was writing a ticket for the delivery van he'd parked in a disabled bay.

Ignoring the warden's attempts to give him the ticket, he jumped into the cab and started the engine. Pulling out into the traffic, he saw the warden taking a photo of the registration in his wing mirror. He wondered if it would become the most famous photograph, turning the woman into a minor celebrity, when she shared the last image of the terrorist who burned down the British Museum.

Pulling out onto Montague Street, Anubis headed towards the service entrance, a narrow gate set between two red telephone boxes.

The guard stepped reluctantly out of a small wooden hut and took the work order from him. The courtyard ahead was filled with trucks and construction vehicles, all part of the restoration work on the building.

'Bay six,' the old man said, handing him back the docket and waving to his left. 'Put it next to the Sprinter. I'll let them know you're here.' He waved him on, pulling out a walkie-talkie.

It would take the site manager a few minutes to realise there was no record of his delivery, by which time he would be gone.

Switching off the engine, Anubis unzipped his jacket and reversed it. The inside was green, the uniform of a paramedic.

Saadah would be proud, he thought, leaning behind the passenger seat and switching on the timer.

68

ARV

Green Park, London. Monday, 3rd May. 18:00

Marshall stepped out of Green Park station and headed down Piccadilly.

The road was gridlocked, and crowds of people weaved between the stationary cars, heading in the opposite direction. They looked terrified, like lost children, anxiously looking around them as they made their way towards the station. She could feel the hysteria building, even with the phone network down, it was obvious something bad had gone down.

This kind of news travelled fast, made worse by the not-so-distant sound of sirens.

Looking up, she spotted a tall column of black smoke winding into the air over the buildings to the East, the wrong direction for Parliament.

Fuck! Sometimes she hated being right.

It was going to take her twenty minutes to walk back to Charing Cross Station and she was wearing the wrong shoes for a run.

Walking past the Ritz, she spotted an unmarked BMW parked in Arlington Street. The driver was wearing body armour and a black balaclava, as were the passengers.

They were a specialist firearms team, an armed response for rapid deployment.

Marshall pulled out her warrant card and walked up to the passenger door and tapped on the window.

The tinted glass slid down and the man pulled up his mask, revealing a well-chiseled, handsome face. The sound of radio chatter filled the car.

'SFO Stevenson. You lost detective?'

'DI Marshall. I need to speak to the Incident Commander,' she replied, trying not to stare at the machine guns laying in their laps.

'Negative. We need to keep the line clear.'

'It's not Westminster?'

He shook his head. 'British Museum.'

She looked confused. 'How many?'

'Over two hundred casualties, multiple fatalities.'

It didn't make any sense, thought Marshall. *Why hit the museum?* And then it dawned on her.

'My phone's not cleared for access. Can I borrow yours?' she said, pointing at his mobile. 'I need to call my boss.'

'Sure,' Stevenson said, handing her the phone.

She dialled the station, only realising that it was the number for Wood Street when Baxter answered. *Force of habit.*

'Baxter, it's DI Marshall is Biggs still there?'

'Marshall how the devil are you? No, I'm afraid DC Biggs has left, they all have, it's just little old me here at the moment.'

She took a breath. 'I'm fine. Okay, listen, can you get a message to DCI Stirling at Charing Cross?'

'Yes, of course, let me get a pen.'

The line went quiet and Marshall bit her lip, counting backwards from ten as she pictured the man searching his desk.

'Got one. Now what would you like him to know?'

'Tell Stirling that Malcolm Reed is Anubis, that this is all a diversion. I think he's after Harrison.'

'Anubis? As in the Egyptian god?'

'Yes, he'll know what it means.'

'Very well.'

The line went dead.

She handed the phone back to Stevenson and looked back down Piccadilly.

'I don't suppose you guys can give me a lift?'

'Sorry no can do,' said the driver. 'We're under orders.'

'Listen, I know who's behind the attack. He's heading for UCLH, and I've got a feeling he's going to kill again. So, unless you want that to go on my report, I suggest we get moving.'

UCLH

University College London Hospital. Monday, 3rd May. 18:30

T he streets around UCLH were lined with ambulances, orderlies and walking wounded.

Marshall jumped out of the BMW, thanking the team as she slid the Glock 17 under her bulletproof vest.

The accident and emergency department was like something from a war zone: stressed-looking doctors attended to badly wounded patients on gurneys while ambulance crews and nurses did their best to triage the new arrivals.

Marshall made her way towards the main entrance on Euston Road.

The receptionists were busy organising a stream of dazed and confused patients who were walking in off the street. She flashed her warrant card at one of the women. 'I'm looking for a patient: Simon Harrison, he was due to have surgery today.'

'Surgery, second floor,' she said, waving her hand towards the back of the atrium. 'Lifts are that way.'

· · ·

The place was in chaos, Reed had created the perfect diversion, he could walk into the hospital and take Harrison out without anyone noticing.

Marshall ran through the atrium and into one of the empty lifts.

Hitting the button for the second floor, she took out her phone and checked the signal once more.

Four bars lit up, as did three voicemails and seven messages.

'Boss, it's me,' said Biggs, 'they've hit the British Museum.'

She deleted it and move on to the next.

'Marshall this is Stirling, I got the call from your old station regarding Reed. Call me back immediately.'

'This is your mother. I've just seen the news...'

Marshall ended the call and scrolled through her messages. Which were mostly from Biggs, giving her updates on what SO15 were doing at the museum.

She dialled Stirling.

'Marshall. Where the fuck are you?'

'Hi Boss. I'm at UCLH — I think Reed is going after Harrison.'

'Why do you think he's Anubis?'

'Because his twin brother's in a psych ward, and I mean identical twin. Reed is Captain Azir, the one that Peters told us about. It makes total sense. He's ex-military with connections in the Middle-East. The doctor said that he's been paying for research into his brother's condition.'

'And you think he's going after the final stone?'

'Does Harrison still have a protection detail?'

There was a pause that told her all she needed to know. 'They were required elsewhere.'

'Shit.'

'Marshall, there's something else, SIB got back to me about Naomi Fox, apparently she's been training medics in Iraq. They found what was left of her body near the base in Taji last month. It's the same MO as the others. Don't do anything stupid, wait for backup.'

She ended the call and put her phone away, pulling out the Glock as the elevator doors opened onto the second floor.

70

SURGERY

The operating theatre was quiet, no one spoke as the surgeon made the first incision into the man's pale skin.

This is known as the McBurney Incision, cut at a forty-five degree angle, below the belly button, through the subcutaneous fat, the memory of his brother's instructions echoed through his mind as he worked. *Down until you reach the transversus abdominis muscle.*

Anubis increased the pressure on the scalpel, feeling the flesh parting under the blade, exposing the fatty tissue beneath. Blood poured from the wound and the nurses began to swab at it while he worked.

Marshall stepped cautiously out of the lift, looking both ways along the corridor. The second floor was relatively quiet compared to the floors below. A doctor in blood-stained scrubs walked quickly past her and into another theatre and she caught a fleeting glimpse of an operation in progress as the doors swung shut behind him.

Taking a deep breath, she shoved the gun into the back of her trousers and made her way down the corridor.

No one stopped her, everyone was too busy. When she reached the nursing station she pulled out her warrant card.

'Where's Simon Harrison?'

The sister pointed to the white board behind her. 'He's in OR-2.'

His name was scrawled in red on a grid of numbered operating rooms.

'Who's operating on him?'

The nurse frowned as she consulted something on her screen. 'It was supposed to be Mr Koustasis, but he was sent to the incident, so it's a locum, Mr. Azir.'

He could still remember the night when his brother had told him about the stones.

Standing outside the field hospital under a starless sky, the smell of the burnt flesh in his nostrils, trying to make sense of the manic ravings of his twin.

'I've hidden them deep inside,' Saadah began, lighting a cigarette. 'They're never going to know.'

'Retractors?' suggested the nurse, snapping Anubis out of his reverie.

'Retractors,' he agreed, taking the steel instrument from her and placing it into the edge of the incision.

This was how his brother had originally planned to remove the stones when they returned to Britain. A routine surgical procedure, no one was supposed to die. But after the war, Saadah's psychoses worsened, the paranoia and manic episodes forcing him into years in treatment, and every time he was released it would only lead to yet another murder.

His brother had come to see them all as *Shabti*, nothing more than a servant of the dead.

Marshall walked through the maze of corridors until she found operating theatre two. The doors were locked, needing a security code to enter. She pushed the buzzer, but no one answered.

She pressed her ear to the door, straining to hear what was going on, but there was nothing. Taking out the gun, she took another deep breath and kicked it open.

Anubis could feel the jewel, it slipped between his gloved fingers, enclosed in fifteen years of scar tissue, it had become part of this man.

Take the forceps and carefully separate it from the bowel.

His brother had shown him on his last victim. The ritual had been his idea too, to honour the dead properly and hide the fact that they were removing one specific organ.

'Forceps,' he demanded, holding out his hand.

The nurse placed them into his palm and he isolated the small lump of gristle and cut around it with the scalpel, careful to avoid the delicate pink tissue beside it.

Suddenly, there was a noise from behind him. A crashing sound.

He ignored it, focusing on the gleaming jewel that appeared from inside the sack of pus. Looking at the eyes of the masked faces around him that something was happening.

'Captain Azir, please put down the knife and step away from the table,' said a woman's voice.

He took a moment to recognise the voice.

'DI Marshall, you should know better than to enter a sterile theatre.'

He heard a click, the subtle sound of the trigger safety on a Glock 17 being depressed.

'Put your hands where I can see them.'

Azir slowly raised his left hand, holding the dripping jewel in the light. 'Magnificent don't you agree? How the body can absorb a foreign object.'

With his other hand he sliced through one of the major arteries in the patient's leg.

There was a collective gasp as the nurses rushed to stem the bleeding.

Azir turned to face Marshall. Standing in his gown and mask he could have easily been mistaken for his brother.

'Don't make this difficult,' she said through gritted teeth.

In one swift movement he grabbed the nearest nurse by the throat and pulled her in front of him, putting the scalpel to her neck. 'Oh, I intend to make this very difficult for you.'

She kept the gun trained on his head, feeling the weight of it, she used her other hand to keep it steady.

The monitors around the theatre began to sound their alarms as Harrison bled out on the table.

'I know about your brother. What you've done for him.'

'You have no idea what I have done!' he snapped, adjusting his grip on the nurse's throat. Keeping her close to his body and shielding himself from Marshall, he edged towards the theatre doors.

Marshall arms were shaking now as she tracked his progress with the gun. 'I've told Stirling you were coming for Harrison. He'll be waiting for you downstairs.'

Azir chuckled. 'Thanks for the warning.'

Her finger closed around the trigger, the firearms training reminding her not to jerk but gently squeeze. He was close to the doors now. The nurse's eyes were wide with fear, her head shaking, begging Marshall not to shoot.

'Where are you going to go? You think Kristiansen will buy that from you now?'

'He doesn't care. His soul belongs to the devourer of the dead.'

She knew he was right, the Norwegian's obsession with the necklace overruled any sense of guilt over how the stones were acquired.

Azir pressed the scalpel into the nurse's neck until a thin red line flowed down over his gloves. 'Do you know how the gods would judge your heart inspector?'

Keep him talking, she thought, *a few more minutes and Stirling will be here.* Then remembering what Gresham told her, she said: 'They would weigh it against the feather of truth.'

For a moment, he looked genuinely impressed, and the pressure on the woman's neck relaxed a little.

'Indeed, in the hall of two truths, Anubis would judge how pure your heart on the scales of Ma'at and if it was found to be wanting — feed it to Ammit to die a second time. Only the righteous would be given passage into the afterlife — to immortality.'

'Is that what you want? To be immortal?' asked Marshall, knowing this was probably her only chance to learn more about his motives.

He laughed. 'I think I've already achieved that haven't I? No one is going to forget the destruction of the British Museum.'

Marshall realised that the terrorist activity was nothing more than a diversion, a sleight of hand to keep the security services occupied while he finished his brother's work. Being a section chief at MI6 gave Azir all the authority he needed to have them chasing shadows.

'And what about your brother? How will he be judged?' she asked, feeling her palms begin to sweat. She tightened her grip on the gun.

His expression hardened. 'The war may have broken his mind, but Saadah has a pure soul.'

'I've been to see him, in Bedlam. The doctor told me the treatments aren't working,' she lied, praying that his brother was his weakness. 'All that money and they're no nearer to fixing him.'

Anger flashed across his face. 'He's still my brother!'

'He thinks you planted a bomb inside him.'

He grimaced, relaxing his grip on the nurse slightly. Feeling the change in pressure, the woman rammed her elbow in his stomach and pushed herself away from him.

'She shall not be remembered among the spirits, and nevermore shall her name be mentioned on the earth, she will not be buried in the West! Since Thoth has condemned her,' he chanted, raising the scalpel and launching himself towards Marshall.

Reflexively, Marshall fired two rounds into his chest.

Azir stopped in his tracks, looking down at the two red flowers blooming through his scrubs.

Marshall fired again, this time aiming for his head and his body jerked back with the impact and fell through the doors.

71

THE CAVALRY

Walking out into the car park, Marshall spotted Stirling getting out of his car with two ARVs pulling in behind him.

'You okay?' he asked, his weapon drawn.

'He's dead,' she replied, sitting down on the kerb and handing him the gun. 'I had no choice.'

'Reed?'

'Reed, Azir, Anubis. Same guy.'

'And Harrison?'

She sighed, running her hands through her hair to hide the fact that they were shaking. 'Nearly bled out on the table, one of the theatre nurses too. They're working on them now.'

Stirling pocketed her gun and turned to the SO15 teams that were climbing out of their cars. 'Secure the scene.' Then, as if forgetting something, he turned back to Marshall. 'Where exactly is he?'

'Second floor, OR-2.'

'You heard her, get your arses up there now!'

· · ·

Novak and Biggs turned up a few minutes later. Both of them looking worried.

'You okay boss?' asked Novak.

Marshall unclipped the bulletproof vest, pulling it over her head and rubbing her ribs. 'I could do with a drink.'

Novak laughed and handed her a bottle of water. 'All I got sorry.'

Marshall took it gratefully and drank deeply.

'Did you find out why he did it?' asked Biggs.

'For the money,' suggested Novak.

Biggs looked confused. 'So he's not a terrorist?'

Marshall shrugged, wiping her mouth with her sleeve. 'He was using them as a diversion. Working for MI6 made it easy to set it up, but really it was just about trying to save his twin brother, Saadah. He was the surgeon that hid the diamonds inside the Tikrit victims back in Iraq in 2003. According to his shrink, he suffers from acute schizophrenia, the war caused a major psychotic episode. He's been in and out of Bedlam for the last fifteen years.'

Novak nodded. 'Explains the gaps in the murders.'

She held up the diamond, a red stone the size of her thumbnail. 'Azir's been selling the jewels to fund research into finding a cure. He's spent millions on it.'

Biggs took the gemstone and held it up to the light. 'Where did they come from?'

'Peters found them during a mission, but Saadah or his brother stole them while he was recuperating in the field hospital. The reporter, Welling, was researching the tomb raiding when she got injured.'

Marshall got to her feet and kneaded her fists into her lower back. 'Now you guys should disappear before the Post Incident Manager arrives.'

. . .

They left her alone, both knowing how to take a hint.

Marshall wandered around the car park, trying to get the image of the bullets hitting his body out of her head.

Replaying the scene back in her mind, she tried to figure out if there would have been another way. If she'd waited for backup, what if she'd waited until he came out of the theatre. These were all questions that she was going to be facing in the post incident procedure. None of those scenarios end well for the theatre team or their patient.

She knew the next forty-eight hours was going to be a circus: Lawyers, Fed Reps and a whole ton of paperwork. There was a strict procedure to follow when a police officer was involved in a fatal shooting.

And beyond all that was the fact that she had killed someone, actually ended someone's life.

It didn't feel real, but that was the shock, her brain was still full of adrenaline. The heart monitor on her watch looked as if she'd just run a half-marathon.

Do you know how the gods would judge your heart inspector?

She wondered if she would make it into the afterlife, not that Marshall was convinced there was one, but his death left a question etched into her psyche. *What have I become?*

'DI Marshall?' she heard an officer say, walking towards her, she nodded.

'Will you come with me please.'

She took a deep breath and followed the man to a car. *And so it begins.*

72

SISTER

British Museum, London. Sunday, 16th June. 11:30

M arshall stood at the large iron gates of the museum, remembering the first time she'd made her father take her there. She could still see the look of disapproval on his face as they walked into the entrance hall, it still made her smile, even now.

The damage to the museum was superficial. The vehicles around Azir's truck took most of the blast, shielding the building, but wounding construction workers and passers-by. The Health and Safety Executive closed it for two weeks while a full structural inspection was carried out and the museum was declared safe to reopen.

Which was less time than it took for Marshall to be cleared for active duty.

The investigation after a police shooting was overseen by the IPCC, Professional Standards and Police Federation. It took nearly a month for her to be reinstated. Which she mostly spent down in Bath with her mother, helping out with the house.

Once Professional Standards were satisfied that lethal force was necessary, things could get back to normal. Her secondment with Stirling's team was over. The relevant forms were signed and she would be returning to City in the next week. Part of her was looking forward to it, but there was no denying that Marshall would miss the challenges of a Murder Squad.

There was even talk of a commendation, the top brass at Scotland Yard were making noises about a gallantry medal.

Gresham was waiting for her at the top of the steps to the museum. He looked completely in his element, standing beneath the Grecian edifice in his tweed jacket.

Martha came out from between the columns and waved to her.

'So are you ready?' asked the professor, after Marshall kissed him.

Marshall grimaced and turned to her sister. 'Do you really want to spend the day looking at a bunch of old dead shit?'

Martha laughed. 'No, not really.'

Gresham tried to hide his disappointment. 'But what about the necklace of Queen Pu-abi?'

'I think I've seen enough Sumerian jewellery for one lifetime,' she said, taking her sister by the arm. 'Would you like to visit some of Dad's favourite places?'

Martha nodded and they walked down the steps together, leaving a confused Gresham trailing along behind.

Detective Marshall returns in Human Trials

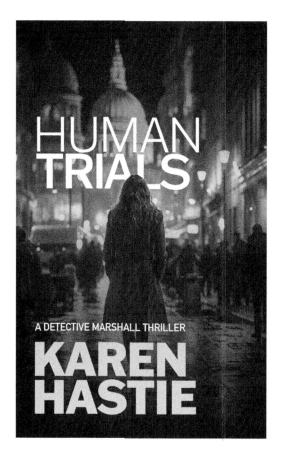

ALSO BY KAREN HASTIE

As Above, So Below

The Weighing of the Heart

Human Trials

ACKNOWLEDGMENTS

Thanks to everyone who has helped to make this book come to life. To my family for their advice, and friends for all their comments!

I hope you enjoyed it. Please don't forget to leave a review!

Thanks,
   Karen x

Printed in Great Britain
by Amazon

60057255R00211